Jewelweed Station

.

Also by Kim Antieau

Website
www.kimantieau.com

Jewelweed Station

For Deane,
Kris

Kim Antieau

with love,
Kim Antieau
7/6/12

Ruby Rose's Fairy Tale Emporium • 2012

Jewelweed Station
by Kim Antieau

Copyright © 2012 by Kim Antieau

ISBN-13: 978-1468057263
ISBN-10: 146805726X

Front cover photo © Raisa Kanareva | Dreamstime.com.
Back cover photo © Kim Antieau.
Book design by Mario Milosevic and Kim Antieau.
Special thanks to Nancy Milosevic and Ruth Ford Biersdorf.
Poem on page 175 copyright © by Mario Milosevic.

Electronic editions of this book
are available at most e-book stores.

A production of
Ruby Rose's Fairy Tale Emporium
Published by Green Snake Publishing
www.greensnakepublishing.com

www.kimantieau.com

For Mom

Prologue

Callie Carter stood near the east entrance of the Larmiteau ballroom while the orchestra played a Viennese waltz. She moved her handheld scarlet-colored iris-shaped mask to the side now and again to get a better look at women dressed in colorful silk gowns and men dressed in white ties and tails. They all wore masks to disguise themselves as some kind of exotic flora, but Callie was determined to discover the true identity of each and every person. Or at least, each and every person who interested her. She was equally determined to keep her identity a secret to everyone at the ballroom, except for Reby, of course.

Reby stood next to Callie dressed in a burgundy-colored satin dress. The long earrings Callie had lent her reflected the golden glow from the gas lamps. She kept turning her wrists so that the gold bracelets on her brown arms clinked together. Callie knew she was not accustomed to wearing jewelry. Reby's mask was shaped like the mythical black orchid.

"If I get caught," Reby said, "I am going to put all the blame on you."

"Of course," Callie said. "If I get caught, I will put all the blame on my poor upbringing. I'm an American and didn't know what I was doing." She fluttered her hand in front of her face.

Reby laughed.

Callie smiled. She liked being far from Virginia and the families who lived along the James River near Mount Joy, her father's plantation. For one thing, Reby was free here. They could walk the streets as sisters. Maybe no one bothered them because Reby was light-skinned for a slave and Callie was dark-skinned for a white Southerner, so no one knew what to make of them. Callie did not care about the reason. She only knew that here she was surrounded by culture, freedom, and handsome young men and women.

"Tonight I will be Contessa Iris Mountjoy," Callie said. "And you?"

"I will be Duchess Wilhemina Orchid," Reby said. "From Barbados. An *exotique!*"

"I think the Contessa will have two children and one husband," Callie said. "Or maybe she is a widow with three children."

"Last night the Baron Margrave actually believed you when you said you had three children. We are not yet eighteen. How could they think such a thing?"

"Mother says men know nothing about women," Callie said, "and we should take advantage of their ignorance because we have so few natural advantages out in the world."

"You have the advantage of being very good at pretending," Reby said. "This all makes me a little nervous."

"Father says it's the little liar in me," Callie said.

Callie heard someone say her name. She turned around. Their hostess Madam Larmiteau stood in front of Callie holding an opened telegram in her hand.

"Callie, dear, I'm afraid there has been some bad news," Madam said in French. "Will you come to the sitting room to hear it?"

Callie shook her head. "No, tell me here and now."

Madam Larmiteau held out the telegram to Callie and said, "I'm sorry to tell you but your parents have been in a terrible accident."

One

Callie Carter stood with her hand on the cold gray marble tombstone. She wanted to run her fingers inside the chisel marks that became her mother's and then her father's name: Emma Jean Ames Carter and Jacob William Carter. Beloved Mother and Father to Calantha Carter.

Her parents could not be dead. Not in some freak carriage accident. Callie had spent many wakeful nights during the winter she was forced to spend in France trying to figure out what had happened—and then even more hours trying not to picture the accident over and over in her mind's eye.

Now she stood quietly in the small family cemetery outside of the boxwood that surrounded the Georgian mansion that was her home. She couldn't see the mansion from here, at least not all of it. Pieces of the red brick became visible here and there through the bare branches of the willow and poplar trees.

She tried not to listen to Uncle Charles Ames drone on to Preacher Jones about the quality of the lettering on the tombstones. The day was too cold for March. Callie shuddered. It didn't feel as though spring was right around the corner. Everything looked dead. Felt dead.

Her old life was certainly dead. Seventeen years old and now her Uncle Charles, her mother's brother, was her guardian. Callie didn't like Uncle Charles. Something about his pale fat little fingers that didn't quite match his tall frame. Or the way he never looked anyone in the eyes even while he was smiling slyly. Or maybe it was because her mother had always tensed when he came into a room. Her true legal guardian was her godfather, Uncle James, who was on a botanical expedition to the Amazon.

No one had heard from him in over a year, so Uncle Charles convinced Judge Zebadiah that Uncle James might be lost for good and his "very young niece" must have adult supervision until such time as James's body was recovered, dead or alive.

Judge Zebadiah. Callie's father had never liked him much either. But he was a good friend of Uncle Charles's, so by the time Callie stepped off the ship in Norfolk, Aunt Elizabeth and Uncle Charles had moved into the main house. From there, Uncle Charles claimed, he could better oversee the plantation and Aunt Elizabeth could better oversee Callie.

Callie had not been in the house yet. Uncle Charles had whisked her immediately out to the cemetery, as though he was delaying her return to the house for as long as he could.

Callie wasn't sure why Preacher Jones was in the family cemetery with them.

She sighed. She was so tired she could barely breathe. Nothing in the world seemed right. Not a single thing.

A bird called out. She looked toward the sound. A crow hopped along the edge of the cemetery near the wrought iron fencing. It looked straight at Callie, then bounced up and flew away, quickly becoming a black speck on the overcast sky.

As Callie looked back at the gravesite, she glimpsed a bit of color. On the soggy ground near the tombstone, along the side of the grave marker, a single trumpet-shaped orange flower surrounded by egg-shaped green leaves grew up from the ground.

Callie smiled. *Jewelweed.* Usually it grew closer to the water and was surrounded by other jewelweed. It was one of her mother's favorite flowers. Her mother said people often didn't see jewelweed or ignored it altogether if they did see it even though it was a great healer. Get stung by nettle or touched by poison oak and the juice from jewelweed would soothe the inflammation away.

Her mother believed wildflowers could fix anything.

Uncle Charles cleared his throat. Callie dropped her hand from the cold marble and looked at him and Preacher Jones.

Mr. Jones smiled. "I wanted you to know, Callie, that your parents got a lovely service. Everyone in the community came out for it. They were well-loved and will be missed." Jones glanced at Uncle Charles, as if to see if he needed to say anything else.

"Your uncle spared no expense on these tombstones," he

said.

Callie glanced at the stone. Really? Then why was a crack running up the left hand side of the stone? And some of the chisel marks were ragged.

"I should like to pay for it myself," Callie said.

Jones looked at Uncle Charles again.

Charles said, "You mustn't worry your pretty self about such things now. The judge has put all that into my capable hands. Now say goodbye to Reverend Jones, and we'll get you something to eat. Unless you'd like to stay for dinner, Jones?"

Jones looked at Callie this time. She had not noticed before how small he was. Or how nervous. He kept smoothing his black hair over the ivory-white bald spot on the top of his head and then turning his hat in his hands. Callie's mother once said he had beady eyes.

"No, thank you," Jones said. "Let me know if you need anything, Callie."

Jones put his hat on his head and then walked back toward the mansion. Charles looked at Callie.

"Ready to go, dear?" he asked.

Callie tried not to scowl—or growl. She had to keep her own counsel for a time, at least until she figured out exactly what part Uncle Charles was to play in her life. Uncle Charles thought of her as a child. As a stupid child. She would let him. For now.

"We have got to keep this place looking better," Charles said. "Your mother always let every weed thrive. It's so untidy. I've hired an overseer. We'll get more work out of your father's worthless slaves yet and get this place cleaned up." He bent over. Before Callie could say anything, he pulled up the jewelweed and crushed it in his hand. Then he tossed it over the fence.

"Come, child," he said. "We have much to show you." He held out his arm for her. She gritted her teeth, then put her hand on his elbow, and they walked out of the graveyard, toward the boxwood and the mansion. Callie looked over her shoulder once to try and spot the ruined orange flower. But she saw only gray.

"Callie, I hope your time away was profitable for you," Uncle Charles said. "I know you disagreed with our decision to have you spend the winter in France. But we knew your parents would have wished you to continue your education, even though your aunt and I didn't quite understand why you were there."

Callie said nothing. She had gone to France to study art and improve her already remarkable drawing and painting skills—and to learn more about the world and get away from the sometimes claustrophobic community of people who lived around Mount Joy.

"It was difficult to be alone in a strange country mourning the deaths of my parents," Callie said.

Difficult was not the right word. It had been excruciating. After Callie got the news, everyone seemed a stranger, even those friends she had made during her time in France. She and Reby stayed inside the apartment together most of the time. Sometimes her tutors visited, and she drew a bit, painted even less. She had not been capable of coherent conversation. And she had no money. Her aunt and uncle cut off her funds so she could not get on a ship herself. Fortunately, she stayed with friends of her parents—Madam Larmiteau and her husband—so she was not thrown into the streets while she waited for permission to come home. Besides her mother's three brothers and their families, Callie had no other relatives. So she had waited until Uncle Charles released some funds. Then she and Reby headed home.

She shook herself and looked ahead as she and Uncle Charles neared the mansion.

It was a relief to see Henry standing just outside the door, so tall and straight, dressed in his black suit, his white-gloved hand on the door as he prepared to open it. He wore a black armband on his left arm—the black a little darker than his coat—in honor of her parents, no doubt. It was more than her uncle had done.

Callie let go of her uncle's arm and walked up to Henry.

"It is good to see you, Henry," she said. She smiled.

Henry bowed and said, "Welcome home, Miss Callie." He opened the door. Callie noticed his skin seemed a little ashy and maybe his hand trembled slightly. She would not ask him about it now. Instead, she strode through the open door into her home. Her parents were gone, but this was where she had grown up. This was where Henry, Pearl, Reby, Martha, and Joseph still lived—well, they lived nearby in the Little House near to this Big House.

As soon as Callie stepped over the threshold, she stopped so suddenly her uncle nearly ran into her. She heard Henry close the door behind them. She waited for her eyes to adjust.

Why was this room so dark?

They stood in a kind of foyer with gentle arches that led into the east parlor to her right and the dining room to her left. Beyond the parlor was the sun parlor, then the ballroom. Beyond the dining room was one of the pantries, the kitchen office, the kitchen, and another pantry. The stairs were straight ahead.

When Callie left for France a year ago, the walls had been cream-colored, and a vase of brightly colored flowers greeted guests and family all year round. Now a kind of dark gold urn stood on a tall black table and the walls were a hideous shade of brown.

Callie heard the rustle of satin. Aunt Elizabeth came out of the east parlor, dressed in blue satin. She smiled and held out her hands to Callie.

"Isn't this foyer lovely now?" Elizabeth said. "I can't imagine your mother actually liked that other color. It was so light! It gave me a headache. I hope you don't mind. We've made little changes here and there. We were certain your poor dear mother would have made the same changes had she lived."

Callie glanced at Henry. He practically blended into the walls. She reminded herself that she was going to hold her tongue until she understood the lay of this new land. She needed to get upstairs to see if Reby had found out anything yet.

Her aunt embraced her slightly, kissed the air on either side of Callie's face, and then stepped back to look at her.

"Oh my! Didn't they have parasols in France?" she asked.

"You're dark enough to be mistaken for a pickaninny! You're nearly as black as your dress."

"I hardly think that is true," Callie said.

Her aunt shrugged. "I have some powder if you want, before you see anyone."

"No, thank you," Callie said. "I'd like to go up to my room and change."

"Of course," Aunt Elizabeth said. "Dinner is at the usual hour. Heddie has made you a welcome home dinner."

"Who is Heddie?" Callie asked.

Aunt Elizabeth rolled her eyes. "How silly of me. You don't know anything about what's been happening, do you?" She looked over at her husband. "Have you told her nothing?"

"I leave it to you, wife," he said. "And now if you'll excuse me, I have some work to do." He bowed slightly. Then he slipped off his coat and handed it and his hat to Henry.

Callie watched her uncle walk down the corridor to her father's office, beneath the stairs. He unlocked the door, opened it, and went inside. Then he shut the door.

Callie closed her eyes. Uncle Charles was in her father's office! Her father would be appalled that Uncle Charles now knew all the intimate details of his business life.

"Heddie is the new cook," Elizabeth said. "Pearl was unbearable. I could not eat her food!"

"Pearl has been our cook since before I was born," Callie said.

"Yes, I know your mother brought her into her marriage," Elizabeth said. "But she is old and her food is bad. She's better off where she is now. She can be of more use there."

"Where is she?"

"She's out in the slave cabins by the fields. She can cook for the pickaninnies and field hands all day and night. They won't notice her tasteless food!"

Callie's stomach fluttered. Her heart started to race.

"Pearl has never lived with the field slaves," Callie said. "Mother promised she would come with me if she got too old to cook, to care for my children one day. She would have never put her outside."

"Dear, you're overtired and forget yourself," Elizabeth said. "She is a slave and goes where she is told."

"With the death of my mother," Callie said, "she becomes my responsibility."

"We are your guardians," Elizabeth said. "We could not, in good conscience, let you continue to eat that gruel Pearl cooked. Your mother wasn't able to send Pearl away. So I've done it for her."

"My mother would have never sent Pearl away!" Callie said.

So much for holding her tongue.

Elizabeth stepped back from Callie and arched an eyebrow.

"This household is now my responsibility," Elizabeth said, "and will be until you come of age. Pearl will go where I wish. Now, I noticed some of your dresses were a bit frayed. If that is how Rebecca takes care of your things, perhaps it is time to send her away, too. She's at a good age to breed."

Callie stared at her aunt. Was her aunt trying to intimidate her by threatening to take Reby away?

This was all so wrong.

How was she going to fix this situation? How was she going to get her home back? Her life? How could she get Pearl into the kitchen again? Panic rose in her throat.

How could her parents have left her so vulnerable to these people? Where was Uncle James?

This was not right. Not any of it.

She would write to Uncle Peter in Richmond again. Until then, she needed to keep things as peaceful as possible.

"I am very tired, dear aunt," Callie said. "I would like to go upstairs now."

"Of course," Elizabeth said.

Callie turned and started walking up the curving staircase.

"See if Reby can find you a dress that isn't torn or soiled at the hems," Elizabeth said. "And no more black. It depresses me."

"But, Aunt Elizabeth, I am in mourning for a year," Callie said. "It would be disrespectful."

"Nonsense," Aunt Elizabeth said. "Your mother was not that old-fashioned and neither am I. I am very proper, but not old-fashioned. With war so close at hand, we need to live every day to the fullest."

"Please, Aunt Elizabeth."

"I know you miss your parents," Elizabeth said, "and I certainly don't want to stop you from mourning in your own way. I'm giving you permission to take off the widow weeds. It is spring, after all."

Her tone was sugary and threatening. Callie felt nauseated.

She picked up the hem of her dress slightly as she walked up the stairs. She glanced at the portraits of her ancestors. Her four grandparents from both sides of the family. Her mother. Father.

She wished one of them could come to her rescue now.

"Oh dear," Elizabeth said. "I forgot to tell you that we've moved you to another room."

Callie stopped on the stairs and looked down. Elizabeth had her hand on the banister.

"Excuse me?" Callie said.

"It was time you had a grown-up room, away from your parents," she said. "So we put you in a room on the third floor. That way you have more privacy. Your room was so close to your parents' room. We're staying in your parents' room now."

"You are staying in my parents' room?" Callie asked.

Callie's fingers gripped her dress.

"Of course," Elizabeth said. "They were the best rooms in the house. This is an ordeal for us, you know, to be away from our home to care for you. We knew you would want us to be comfortable."

Callie chewed the inside of her cheek.

"Of course," she finally said.

She turned from her aunt and continued up the stairs.

Reby was sitting in a chair at the top of the stairs waiting for her.

"This way, Miss," Reby said formally.

Callie looked down the stairs. She couldn't see Elizabeth, but she sensed she was still there, listening, waiting.

Callie followed Reby up the second set of stairs and then down the hallway to the end of it. At least Elizabeth hadn't redecorated this floor. The wallpaper with pale red and pink roses brightened up the corridor still.

Reby opened the door to the last room. Callie went inside. She couldn't remember ever being in this room. Reby had already opened the windows. Good thing. It still smelled a bit stale.

Callie looked around the small room. She didn't see any other door besides the one they had just come through. A small window seat looked down at the garden, the row of poplars beyond, and the James River beyond them. A wardrobe, bed, dresser, dressing table, divan, and writing desk practically filled the room.

"Where's your room?" Callie asked. Reby had slept next to her nearly her entire life.

"Mrs. Elizabeth says I have to sleep in the Little House now with the others," Reby said. "She wants me to do more kitchen duty, help in the smoke house and with the sewing more. She says you don't need a maid full-time, and she doesn't have enough slaves to do all the work that needs to be done."

"There is truth that I don't need a full-time maid," Callie said, "but she doesn't need to know that."

Callie sat on the bed. Reby sat on the floor and leaned against the bed.

"Come up here and sit with me," Callie said.

Reby shook her head. "Mrs. Elizabeth catches us, we're done for."

Callie sighed. Everything had changed. Reby was acting and talking strangely. Like she was back on the farm.

Which she was. They both were.

"She was lookin' at your clothes," Reby said. "She said if I couldn't do a better job, she was gonna have Mr. Charles sell me."

"He can't do that," Callie said. "I know that for sure. According to the law, you are mine and I wouldn't consent to your sale."

"They've got Pearl down by the fields," Reby said. "I heard she's doing poorly."

"Aunt Elizabeth told me," Callie said.

"You ever been down there?" Reby asked.

"Once, when I was little," Callie said. "Father came close to whipping me when he found me." She had been sitting on the floor in the dirt, eating with the other children, when her father strode into the cabin.

"Mr. Carter," someone had said. Callie didn't remember now who it had been. "We was just comin' to git ya."

And then things got confusing. Her father yelled. The driver got out his whip.

Callie shook her head. She didn't want to remember that.

"It ain't fit fer man or beast," Reby said. "Not them places."

"Reby, quit talking like that," Callie said. "You sound like a field hand."

"We ain't in Paris any more," Reby said. "I've got to know my place and be in my place until this blows over or Mrs. Elizabeth is going to get rid of me. I talked to Martha. She says your aunt and uncle have come to stay, and they're going to run things wicked hard."

"My parents didn't raise a coward," Callie said. "I can fix this." She stood and began pacing the room. "I need to see a lawyer. Find out what my rights are. Uncle Charles showed me the papers the judge signed. And he signed. About them being my legal guardians for the time being. I tell you, I intend to spend no time being under their thumbs. I'll write a letter to Uncle Peter, too. But for a while, Reby, I will pretend to be on my aunt and uncle's side. They think I'm an ignorant child, so that's what I will be. But first I've got to dress for dinner."

Reby got off the floor. Callie turned around so her back was to her. Reby took off Callie's coat and put it in the wardrobe. Then she began unbuttoning Callie's dress. When the dress was loose enough, Reby helped Callie step out of it.

Callie walked to the wardrobe and opened it. She pulled out a blue satin dress. It was almost the same color as the one her aunt was wearing.

"It would be so gauche if I wore this tonight," Callie said. "Auntie might feel as though I was trying to outshine her." Callie nodded. "Perfect. She wanted me out of black. I will obey her."

She handed the dress to Reby. Reby took it. The two looked at each other for a moment. Callie turned away first. "I better hurry," she said. "Before she comes looking for me. You keep your head down, Reby. Let's not rock the boat until we're ready to sink it."

Two

Callie steeled herself to go down the stairs to join her aunt and uncle for dinner in her parents' dining room. She looked down at her dress and remembered she and her mother picking out the fabric. Her mother had said Callie would look good sitting next to the fire in it. Her blue eyes would look even bluer, and her black hair would look even blacker. Her mother had been so happy when Callie started wearing dresses. She thought Callie had outgrown her tomboy tendencies.

Callie had never had the heart to tell her mother she still preferred to wear men's clothes and actually did wear them sometimes when she was in Paris.

Callie heard a man's voice—not her uncle's—coming from the parlor. It sounded vaguely familiar.

"Who is that?" Callie asked Reby.

Callie heard her uncle say, "It has been extraordinarily cold for this time of year. Does that impact your business?"

"There are the normal number of colds and influenza for this time of year I should think," the man answered.

"Dr. Sawyer," Reby and Callie said at once.

The men came out of the parlor and walked across the central hall and into the dining room. Neither of them looked up to see Callie and Reby standing on the stairs. Callie felt a twinge of pleasure to see her old friend, Benjamin Sawyer, after all this time, only he looked all grown up now. She hadn't seen him since he had gone away for his medical training. In fact she had barely heard from him since then, even though she had written to him while he was in school.

"This is perfection," Callie whispered. "Reby, do you have a peppermint candy with you?" Reby reached into her pocket, pulled out a peppermint, and handed it to Callie.

"You do remember peppermint makes you ill," Reby said.

As if she could forget.

"I do indeed," Callie said.

Callie took the candy in her right hand and folded her fingers around it. She continued down the stairs, walked through the central hall, and then stood on the threshold of the dining room and looked around.

The light from the chandelier made the center of the room golden. Shadows still lingered in the corners. Callie's uncle sat at the head of the table. Callie wished peppermint calmed her stomach because she felt nauseated to see her uncle in her father's chair. Her aunt sat opposite her husband at the far end. Her mother never did that. The three of them had sat together at one end of the table, unless they had company. Tonight Dr.

Sawyer sat in the middle of the table, between her aunt and uncle. Callie's place setting was across from Dr. Sawyer.

"This is a nice surprise," Callie said as she walked into the room. She smiled brightly. She wanted them all to see how happy and healthy she was before dinner.

Her uncle and Dr. Sawyer stood.

"Welcome home, Callie," Dr. Sawyer said. He bowed slightly. Callie curtsied.

"Thank you, Dr. Sawyer," Callie said as she walked to her side of the table.

Sawyer smiled. "Callie, we've known each other since we were children. Please call me Ben."

Callie had left for France just as Benjamin had returned to work with Dr. Kelly. Unfortunately Dr. Kelly had died sometime during the time Callie was away, and the young doctor had been left on his own.

"She will do no such thing," Elizabeth said.

"We grew up together, Mrs. Ames," Sawyer said.

Henry stepped out of the shadows and pushed Callie's chair in as she sat down.

"Thank you, Henry," she said.

He stepped back into the shadows again. Normally Martha brought the family their food and then left the room.

Callie glanced around the room. It didn't look as though Aunt Elizabeth had changed anything in here. At least not yet.

Benjamin and Uncle Charles sat again.

"I am responsible for this household now and for Callie's upbringing, Dr. Sawyer," Elizabeth said. "My husband and I believe things have been a bit permissive and we're going to remedy that. Besides, you've worked hard for your title."

Benjamin glanced at Callie. She raised an eyebrow.

"It is good to be home," Callie said, "and to see a friendly face."

"I am so sorry about your parents," Benjamin said.

"Did you see them after the accident?" Callie asked.

"Callie!" Elizabeth said sharply. "That is not a proper subject for dinner conversation."

Benjamin started to answer Callie, but she shook her head to stop him.

"You there!" Elizabeth called, speaking to Henry. "Where is the first course? We're going to starve waiting for you."

Callie heard Henry leave the room.

"I will have him in the dog pen if he doesn't see to his job better," Elizabeth said.

"Henry has never served dinner," Callie said. "That was not part of his duties."

"Leave that to your aunt, Callie," Charles said, speaking for the first time.

A few moments later, Henry brought in soup and began serving it to them.

"Thank you, Henry," Callie said.

Elizabeth grimaced.

"Think of Elizabeth as your mother," Charles said. "You would never question your mother about the running of the household."

Callie said nothing. She dipped her spoon into the soup and began eating.

"We have brought our cook here," Elizabeth said to Benjamin. "We could not bear that swill Mrs. Carter's cook was serving us."

Callie sipped the bean soup. It wasn't bad. A bit salty.

"It looks as though you are making all kinds of changes in the household," Benjamin said.

"We wanted things to be nice for Callie when she got home," Elizabeth said. "We didn't want the place to remind her of her parents."

Callie could not keep quiet about this.

"I want to be reminded of my parents," Callie said. "I loved them, and they were wonderful people. I want to be reminded of them every day of my life."

She felt her throat close with emotion. She took another sip of soup. She did not want to cry around them. Her plan to act like the stupid adolescent was falling apart before it even began.

Callie breathed deeply.

"Dr. Sawyer," she said. "What brings you to Mount Joy this evening?"

"I heard you were home," he said. "I wanted to express my condolences in person. Since we had not heard from you in so long, my mother was anxious to see how you were doing and she was unable to call on you today because of a previous engagement."

"Thank Mrs. Sawyer," Callie said. "She was such a good friend to Mother."

"I know many people have written to you," Benjamin said. "Many people were at the funeral."

"So I understand," Callie said. Her uncle had made certain she saw the papers that codified her loss of freedom and gave it over to him and his wife, but he hadn't bothered to show her any correspondence she had received while she was away.

"Aunt, did you save the condolence letters for me?"

"Yes, yes," Elizabeth said. "I have them. After you have settled in again and are rested, I'll give them to you."

Callie swallowed the words she wanted to scream. "Get out of my home! Get off my land! Get out, get out, get out!"

This was all too difficult. She could not sit here and eat meal after meal with these people. She could not sit by while they changed her home and possibly destroyed it. She could not let Pearl waste away in some slave cabin.

She sighed, then breathed deeply. She could do it. She had to do it.

"I got very little mail while I was in France," Callie said. "I was surprised. I felt quite on my own, without family or friends after Mother and Father died, except for Reby, of course. I was so glad she was there. She reminded me of home."

Someone behind her reached for her half empty bowl. She looked up. It was Martha. Callie grinned. She pushed away from the table and flung her arms around Martha. For a moment, it felt like home again.

"I am so happy to see you," Callie said.

"It's good to see you, too, Miss Callie." Martha tried to pull away from her. Callie let go. Aunt Elizabeth was standing next to them. Martha hurried away. Elizabeth put her hand on Callie's back.

"Excuse us, gentlemen," Elizabeth said. "Ladies' business."

Elizabeth practically pushed Callie into the central hall.

"Callie," Elizabeth said. "You cannot treat servants like they are family! You can't be familiar with them like that. You put them and you put yourself in jeopardy."

"I have known them all my life," Callie said. "Martha raised me."

"She did not raise you," Elizabeth said. "She no more raised you than a cow that gave you milk raised you. Your mother and father raised you. And stop thanking them for doing what they are told to do."

"It is common courtesy," Callie said. "That is how I was raised."

Elizabeth looked at her. "You do not thank the chair you sit upon, and you will not thank the slaves that serve you as they should. It is unseemly. It's groveling."

"Thank you for that lesson in manners, Aunt Elizabeth," Callie said.

Her aunt glared at her. "Are you sassing me?" she asked quietly, her voice shaking.

"I am not," Callie said, trying to sound hurt. "I am truly thankful. I have been gone for some time, and I must have brought home some of the manners of foreigners. I apologize. May we return to dinner? I want more of that delicious soup."

Elizabeth nodded. They went back to the dining room. The men stood until the women were seated again. Henry brought in lamb with vegetables.

Callie dropped her napkin on the floor. She leaned down to

get it and popped the peppermint into her mouth. She sat up again and ate some of the vegetables.

Her stomach started to lurch as she sucked on the peppermint. Then she swallowed it whole. She knew she was going to vomit. She wondered briefly if she could aim it at her aunt or uncle. She put her hand on her stomach. Maybe this had not been such a good idea.

A second later, Callie Carter vomited her dinner, lunch, and anything left of her breakfast. Her aunt screamed. Benjamin ran to Callie's side. She felt a little dizzy. She decided to fall into Benjamin's arms in a faint. That would get her out of this room that now smelled like vomit and peppermint.

Henry and Benjamin helped Callie upstairs, one man on each side of her, lifting her. They laid her on her bed. She heard Reby come into the room.

"What happened?" Benjamin asked.

"Something I ate," Callie said weakly.

She could see her aunt and uncle standing just inside the room at the edge of the lamplight. They looked genuinely concerned. Probably because if she died, they'd lose access to the plantation and any income from it. She turned away from them.

"Most likely something you had on the ship," Elizabeth said. "We'll have Heddie make you some broth."

"No," Callie moaned.

"Please," Benjamin said. "I need to examine her. Would you all leave. Reby, you may stay."

Elizabeth, Charles, and Henry left the room. Callie looked over at the door. They had left it slightly open. Benjamin followed her gaze. He got up and closed the door.

"Can you sit up?" Benjamin asked.

Callie nodded and pushed herself up. Benjamin took a stethoscope out of his bag. He put one end against her chest, over her dress, and then leaned his ear into the other end. He moved it around here and there. Then he listened to her back. He felt her pulse. Had her stick out her tongue.

He sighed. "Callie, except for the vomiting, you seem fit as a fiddle."

"I'm sure it's the food, Dr. Sawyer," Callie said.

"Your tongue looks like you've been sucking on a peppermint," he said. "And you smell like peppermint. I seem to remember when we were kids you were allergic to peppermint. We're alone now. You can call me Benjamin again."

"Not allergic," Callie said. "It just nauseated me. But I'm sure there wasn't any peppermint in the soup, and I would be foolish to eat it on my own when I know how sick it makes me."

"Yes, indeed," he said. He glanced over at Reby.

"When I was a girl and got sick," Callie said, "Pearl made me the most amazing chicken soup. I'd be right as a trivet as soon as I ate some."

"Let's have Pearl make some up for you," he said. "Reby, can you ask Pearl to make the soup?"

Callie lay back against her pillows. She didn't remember the stomachache staying this long after she threw up the last time she had peppermint.

"Pearl doesn't work in the kitchen any more," Reby said. "They sent her packing and brought in their cook Heddie."

"She's a terrible cook," Callie said.

Reby said, "I think she cooks just fine."

Callie moaned.

"Reby, I need to talk with Miss Callie privately," Benjamin said.

Reby stepped back out of earshot.

Benjamin leaned forward. "Callie, what's going on?"

"We are no longer children, sir," she said. "I don't think it's proper for you to be this familiar with me."

"I am your doctor," he said.

"You are not my doctor. You are an old childhood friend who used to throw me in the pond in the hopes that the leeches would kill me off. I seem to remember you were friends with Barnaby. Anyone who could be friends with my toad of a cousin, the spawn of those two idiots outside the door—well, I don't know that you can be trusted."

Benjamin stared at her.

"I mean to say I am grateful for my aunt and uncle's care," she said, "but I would like them to vacate my home immediately. This conversation is strictly between patient and doctor, correct? Isn't there some kind of Hippocratic oath that prevents you from violating my confidence?"

"I thought I wasn't your doctor."

Callie growled and sat up.

"You were much better at hiding your feelings in the past," Benjamin said. "Such a great actor you were."

"I just lost my parents," Callie said, "and my home has been invaded. Did you know they have custody of me? As though I'm a piece of furniture they must watch over."

"That was why I came over," he whispered. "To see if you needed any help."

"I need a lawyer who isn't in my uncle's pocket," Callie said. "Or the other way around. My father once said that if you put an Ames man in a room full of rich men, by the end of the evening, no one would have any money."

"Did you make yourself ill so you could get Pearl back into the house?"

"Don't be absurd," Callie said. "Dinner made me ill. I don't think I shall ever eat again. Unless it's Pearl's soup. Or maybe her roast chicken."

Callie put her hand over her stomach. Right this minute she did not feel as though she could ever eat again.

Benjamin closed his black bag.

"Why didn't you write to me?" Callie asked. "I wish someone had. I was all alone, except for Reby, and I never heard from anyone. I wrote to you. Do you remember? You were homesick when you first left. I wrote you a letter every week for months."

"Of course I remember," he said. "I still have those letters. Every week you drew me a flower and wrote about where you'd found it and what you'd done that week. Those letters kept me steadfast in my studies. I wrote and thanked you."

"Once or twice," she said. "But that's not the point. Why didn't you write after my parents died?"

"I did," he said. "Your aunt insisted all correspondence come to her, and then she would send them on, since you were moving around and didn't have a permanent address."

"What?" she said. "I had the same address the entire time I

was there. I never got a single letter."

Benjamin shook his head. "I'm sorry, Callie. You must have felt very alone! Your aunt probably sent them as a package and it got lost in transit."

"Or she didn't send them at all."

Benjamin sighed. "You should have some sodium bicarbonate and then tepid water tonight and try to eat breakfast in the morning. I'll check on you tomorrow."

He stood and looked down at her.

"I'm sorry," he said again. "But I promise I wrote. And I know others did too."

Callie shrugged.

Benjamin left the room. Callie heard him in the hallway talking to her aunt and uncle.

"Go listen!" Callie said to Reby.

Reby went to the door and pressed her ear against the wood.

A moment later, she stepped away. "He said you had an upset stomach and recommended rest and sodium bicarbonate."

Reby came over to the bed and began unbuttoning Callie's dress.

"Ugh, I feel terrible," Callie said.

"And what did you accomplish by making yourself sick?" Reby asked.

Callie sat up and wiggled out of the dress. She went to the nightstand, dipped her hands into the basin of warm water, and splashed her face.

"I didn't accomplish anything tonight," she said. "But you'll see. It'll work out."

When Reby finally left for the night, Callie lay in bed, sleepless. Her stomach gurgled. And her bed was too soft. She kept tossing and turning in an attempt to find a comfortable spot. The noises were different in this room, too. She kept thinking she heard whispers—or movement—even though she knew her aunt and uncle were on another floor at the other end of the hall and the servants were all asleep in the Little House.

She closed her eyes.

"Is that you, Mother and Father?" she whispered. "I wish you hadn't left. I wish Uncle James would hurry home. I don't know what to do. How do I make things right?"

Silence vibrated in her ears.

After a while, she got out of bed, opened the door quietly, and went to the second floor. She tiptoed down the dark hall to her old bedroom. She turned the doorknob and slowly pushed the door in.

A whoosh of air rushed by her. She went into the room and quietly closed the door. She knew right where the bed was. Even in the dark. She hurried over to it, lifted the comforter, and got under it.

The sheets felt cool and familiar. She turned on her side and buried her face in the pillow. It smelled like her mother. A combination of lavender, cinnamon, and earth. Callie wondered if her mother had come into this room while she was gone and put her face in the pillow, like Callie was doing now, to get a whiff of her daughter's scent.

The thought brought tears to Callie's eyes. She started to cry.

She had barely cried since her parents died.

She wasn't sure why.

Now she cried. Silently. Burying her face in the pillow and then pulling the covers up around her when her sobs got louder.

After a time the sobs subsided, and Callie fell to sleep.

Callie awakened at daybreak. She got out of bed and walked over to the window seat, sat in it, and gazed out at the placid-looking James River. The golden light of dawn was beginning to sweep away the last remnants of night. Callie couldn't see the fields from here, but she knew the slaves were up and working. The blacksmith was probably at his forge. The kitchen slaves were making breakfast.

She wondered what Pearl was doing. Except for her time in France, Callie had seen Pearl nearly every day of her life. She had cooked for Callie nearly every day of her life. How could Callie let these strangers toss Pearl away like she was nothing?

Callie looked around her room. This was the last time she'd sleep here until she got rid of her aunt and uncle. She hoped that wouldn't be too far in the future.

Callie left her old room and hurried quietly back to her new room. She lay in the uncomfortable bed listening to the house wake up.

Soon enough, Reby knocked on the door and came in carrying a tray. She set the tray on the dresser and then came over to the bed. Callie sat up and Reby put a couple of pillows behind her.

"What's this?" Callie asked.

"Mrs. Ames said she didn't want a repeat of last night," Reby said, "so she wanted you to have your breakfast up here."

Reby went to the dresser, got the tray, and brought it to the bed. She set it over Callie, so that the legs rested on either side of her.

Porridge. Eggs, bacon, grits. Coffee.

"It smells heavenly," Callie said. "Who made it?"

Reby looked at her. "You need anything else?"

"Reby, who cooked this breakfast?"

"Heddie did," Reby said.

"Give me a peppermint," Callie said.

"No, you're going to make a mess everywhere," Reby said, "and I'm going to have to clean it up."

"Bring me a bucket," Callie said. "I will throw up in it."

Reby shook her head.

"You don't understand what you're doing," Reby said.

"Reby! Give me a peppermint!" Callie said. She held out her hand to Reby.

Reby made a noise and then drew a peppermint from her pocket and put it on Callie's palm.

"I won't swallow it this time," Callie said.

Callie ate a few bites of the porridge and eggs. She took a sip of the coffee. Then she popped the peppermint into her mouth.

"Here goes," she said.

Reby went to the wardrobe and took out a carpetbag and brought it over to the bed.

"How considerate," Callie said. "You better take the tray, too, or I might spill it all over."

She felt queasy. Reby picked up the tray and carried it over to the dresser.

Callie took the peppermint out of her mouth. "Here, throw it out the window. I don't want Dr. Sawyer suspecting it's peppermint again."

Reby took the peppermint and went to the window. Callie grabbed the carpetbag and threw up in it.

Then she looked at Reby. "Go get Aunt Elizabeth. Tell her I threw up right after I ate."

Reby didn't say anything. She just left the room.

"I don't know what's wrong with her," Callie mumbled to herself. "What I'm doing will get Pearl back. I know it."

She threw up again.

It had better work this time. She didn't think she could eat another peppermint.

Three

The door opened and Callie heard the swish of silk and satin. She didn't turn around to face her aunt.

"Put your hand on her forehead," Elizabeth demanded.

Callie felt Reby's cool hand on her face.

"Is she feverish?"

"No, ma'am," Reby said. "She's clammy."

Elizabeth made a noise.

Callie turned over and pushed herself up to a seated position.

"I'm sorry you're feeling so poorly," Elizabeth said. "I had no idea you were such a sickly child."

"I never have been," Callie said. "It must be the food."

"I think it's that awful European cuisine catching up with you," Elizabeth said. "Your system only needs to get used to our good country food."

"On the rare occasions I was ill as a child, Pearl could always cook me up something to make me right again," Callie said.

"Heddie can make you some broth," Elizabeth said.

"Whatever you say, Auntie," Callie said. "You know best." Callie slid back down under the covers and turned away from her aunt.

A moment later, a muttering Elizabeth left the room with Reby, and Callie was alone again. She was tired and her stomach was still upset; she shut her eyes and fell to sleep.

Reby brought Callie broth. Callie took a sip and said she felt nauseated. She pushed away the broth.

She lay in bed all day. Reby had opened the curtains and the windows in the morning, but Elizabeth instructed her to close up everything "nice and tight" later in the day.

"So Callie can heal in a timely manner without the impediments of cool air or any other distractions," her aunt said.

Callie didn't know her aunt very well, but she detected malice in her voice. She either did not believe Callie was ill, or else she liked punishing her for being ill.

Of course, Callie was not sick, truly, but that was not the point.

Callie refused lunch and dinner.

When it was night again, Callie tiptoed down to the second floor. This time she went to her aunt and uncle's room and listened at the door.

"The lawyer is coming tomorrow to have her sign some papers," Charles said. "Will she be better by then? He'll be reporting back to the judge."

"I know," Elizabeth said. "I'm doing my best."

"You should have let Dr. Sawyer see her today," Charles said. "If anything happens to her, they'll hold us responsible."

"I know that, dear," Elizabeth said. "I believe she is faking it all to get Pearl back in the kitchen. I can't give in to her tantrum."

"She was very convincing," Charles said. "She seemed quite ill to me."

"Yes, well, you are a bit gullible. That is why our son is able to constantly manipulate you to get whatever he wants. You always believe everything that comes out of his mouth. You still do. That's why we're near broke."

"If she wants Pearl back in the kitchen so much," Charles said, "let her have her. We've got more important things to worry about. The happier she is here, the happier we will be here."

"Do you want her running things or you running things?"

"Don't talk to me like that." Uncle Charles's voice suddenly sounded menacing. Callie heard the sound of a slap. She gasped and stepped away from the door. "I've broken more horses than you have. So watch your tone, wife. I know what we have to do."

Callie hurried back to her room. She went to her dresser, looked for a skeleton key, found it, and locked her door.

This night she felt alone and farther from home in her own house than she had in France after her parents died.

When the sun came up, Callie unlocked the door. She

opened the curtains and the window. The air smelled fresh and tangy. The James River ran swiftly by this morning.

Reby knocked on the door.

"Come," Callie said.

Reby opened the door and brought a tray of food into the room.

"Good morning, Miss Callie," Reby said. "I hope you're feeling better."

Callie got up from bed and closed the door behind her.

"What's wrong with you?" Callie asked. She picked up a piece of toast and bit into it. It tasted like ambrosia. She took another bite of the toast, then set it down on the plate.

Reby went to the wardrobe and pulled out a blue gingham dress.

"Reby, why are you giving me the cold shoulder?"

"I'm sorry," Reby said. "I meant no harm. Things are a little chaotic downstairs is all."

Callie considered Reby her friend, but she was a moody girl and Callie had long ago stopped trying to figure out why.

"You can take this food back," Callie said. "Tell Aunt Elizabeth the toast has made me ill."

"I made the toast," Reby said.

"Then never mind," Callie said. She picked up the half-eaten bread and finished it off. "Did you make the eggs as well?"

"No, Miss," Reby said. "Heddie made them."

Callie put a forkful of scrambled eggs in her mouth. They tasted delicious.

Callie pushed her plate away. "I will not eat again until I

can eat Pearl's food. I do believe all this food, except for your toast, has made me ill."

"Miss Callie, I don't think you understand what you're doing," Reby said.

Callie stood, went to the wardrobe, and took the dress from Reby.

"I must save Pearl," Callie said. "My parents would never have sent her out there to live."

"Other slaves live out there," Reby said. "What about them? They've lived there for years, decades."

"I can't do anything about them now," Callie said. "Besides, field slaves are different from you and Pearl and Martha. Henry."

"The difference is that you don't know them or see them," Reby said. She went to the bed and picked up the tray. "I will tell Mrs. Elizabeth what you said. But what you're doing is wrong. Pearl would be the first one to tell you."

"And she can tell me so," Callie said, "as soon as she's back in the kitchen where she belongs."

Reby left the room. Callie washed her face with the cold basin water and then put on her dress. She sat at the dressing table and brushed her hair. She did not understand why Reby was so upset, but it didn't matter. She knew better than Reby. That was a fact. It wasn't Reby's fault. She had a better education than Reby; therefore she had a better mind and could better determine the right course of action.

Someone knocked on the door.

"Come," Callie said.

The door opened, and Benjamin Sawyer stepped inside.

Elizabeth followed him into the room.

"Hello, Callie," Dr. Sawyer said. "How are you today?"

Callie looked at Elizabeth's face to see if there was any bruising from the slap she received from Charles. She appeared unharmed. Maybe Callie had been mistaken about what she heard.

"I am hungry, Dr. Sawyer," Callie said. "But every time I eat I get sick. Fortunately I was able to eat some toast this morning. I kept that down just fine. Good morning, Aunt Elizabeth. I hope you slept well."

"Dr. Sawyer, is she contagious?" Elizabeth asked. "Can you give her something? Does she need a hospital?"

Sawyer smiled at Callie. He held her wrist and took her pulse. Then he put the stethoscope on her chest and listened. She stuck out her tongue for him when asked. He looked in her eyes.

"Is your stomach still upset?" he asked.

"Only when I eat," she said.

"Mrs. Ames," he said. "Can you leave us alone, please?"

Elizabeth sighed audibly. Then she and Reby left the room and closed the door behind them. Callie sensed her aunt lingering close by.

She got up, went to the door, and kicked it with her heel. Her aunt squealed.

"Oh dear," Callie said loudly. "I thought it was a spider, but it was only a spot on the wall."

She went back and sat at the dressing table. Benjamin pulled the chair from her writing desk over to the table.

"Is there anything you want to tell me?" he asked quietly.

"Only that I would never kill a spider," she said. "It's bad luck. Especially for the spider." She smiled.

"Callie."

"Dr. Sawyer, I swear," she said. "I want to eat, and Pearl's food has always been so beneficial for me. I don't know about this new cook."

"We are friends," Benjamin said. "You can tell me anything."

"It's an entirely different world we're living in now," Callie said softly. "The court took away all my rights. I am a prisoner in my own home. I don't know who is and isn't my friend. I would have thought the courts would protect me. Instead they turned over everything I own and love to my uncle and aunt. So forgive me if I'm a little cautious about telling my friends anything about my life now. I am doing what I can to save those I love."

"I believe you did not think this through," Benjamin said. "You could cause great harm with this scheme. I hope you will be more thoughtful and less obvious in the future."

"The future is far away," Callie said. "I'm trying to get by now."

Benjamin nodded. He got up.

"By the way," Callie said, "I thought you were coming by yesterday."

"I did," Benjamin said. "Your aunt wouldn't let me see you. Said you were resting comfortably."

"I was sitting in the dark all day without food, sunlight, or air," Callie said. "Was that in my best interest?"

Sawyer went to the door and opened it. Elizabeth stood on

the threshold.

"Callie needs to eat," he said. "Her pulse is weakening. I suggest you have Pearl cook for her and see how that goes. If she feels better, it's probably best to keep Pearl here. I am obligated to report this to the court, since Judge Zebadiah wanted an update on her condition."

"Judge Zebadiah knows Callie is ill?" Elizabeth asked.

"She is a ward of the court, essentially," Sawyer said. "I saw the judge at dinner last night and when he asked about her, I told him."

Callie bit her lip so she wouldn't laugh. Her aunt looked like she was going to cry.

"I'll see to her meals at once," Elizabeth said. She turned around. "Well, what are you waiting for, girl! Go find Pearl!"

Benjamin glanced back at Callie. Then he went into the hall and closed the door behind him.

Callie waited in her room for the next couple of hours. She felt weak from hunger and buoyed by her success all at the same time. She wanted to run down to the kitchen and greet Pearl, but she felt dizzy every time she stood. Instead she sat on the window seat and thought how grand it was that she had sacrificed her health to save Pearl from a fate worse than death.

Then Reby brought a tray into Callie's room.

"Pearl made this especially for you," Reby said.

"Did she really?" Callie asked. "How does she look? Is she glad to be back?"

Reby put the tray on the writing table.

"You can go down and see her later yourself," Reby said.

"Do you need anything else?"

"No, thank you," Callie said.

She began spooning the soup into her mouth and barely noticed Reby leave.

"Now this is food," she murmured.

Elizabeth gave Callie leave to eat dinner in her room, since she was still recovering. After dinner, Callie went downstairs, tiptoed through the main hall past the parlor, then hurried through the dining room, down the service hall, and into the kitchen.

Reby, Henry, Martha, and Pearl sat at the long wooden table eating. They looked over at her as she came into the room. Pearl appeared gaunt and tired, but she smiled at Callie. Callie ran over to her and put her arms around her. The older woman embraced the younger woman. Then Pearl pulled away and looked at Callie.

"You've gained some weight," Pearl said. "You look good. I'm so sorry about your momma and daddy. It was a tragic thing."

"I'm sorry they sent you away," Callie said. "Are you happy you're back?"

The kitchen seemed quieter than Callie remembered. Henry, Martha, and Reby had all stopped eating.

"I am happy to be back," Pearl said. "These are frightening times. But, child, you must be more careful."

Callie sat on the bench next to Pearl.

"I would have fasted for weeks if that meant you'd be back home," Callie said.

"I'm glad you're well, Callie girl," Pearl said. "But Heddie is gone now. She was sent back to Miss Ames's plantation. Before she left, the driver came and whooped her for all of us to see and hear. Whooped her within an inch of her life."

"Driver Daniel?" Callie said. "He wouldn't. He is a kind and generous man."

Reby made a noise. Callie glanced at her.

"Why would they beat her?" Callie asked. "What did she do wrong?"

"She didn't do nothing wrong," Pearl said. "You said her food made you sick."

"I never thought anything would happen to her because of what I said."

"You have always been a thoughtless child," Pearl said. "It's not your fault. But now we are your responsibility. You have to understand better how things work. Unless you don't care what happens to us."

"Of course I care!" Callie said.

Martha said, "We are so happy you are home." She lowered her voice to a whisper Callie could barely hear. "But you have to be careful. Those running things now are cruel. They can't hurt you without someone noticing, but they sure can hurt us." Martha pulled up her sleeve. A deep purple bruise showed up on her brown skin. "Mrs. Ames pinched me hard after you hugged me at the dinner table the other night."

"They have no right to touch you!" Callie said. She stood. Pearl caught her hand.

"Callie," Pearl said. "You can't go tell them you know what she did to Martha. It would be worse for her. And all of us."

Pearl let go of her hand. Callie rubbed her face.

"I am sorry about Heddie," Callie said. "I am sorry about you, Martha. I will try to get help for us all."

"I told you not to do it," Reby said.

"Reby," Pearl said. "You can't talk to Miss Callie like that. What if Mrs. Ames heard?"

"I know," Reby said.

"France gave you both some bad habits," Pearl said. "You ain't in Paris any more. You best both remember that."

Henry got up from the table and took his plate to the sink.

"Excuse me, Miss," he said. "I got chores."

Henry solemnly left the room.

"Heddie is Henry's daughter," Pearl said. "It was the first time they'd been together since she was a girl. This has hit him hard."

"Oh my goodness," Callie said. "What have I done?"

The kitchen went silent again.

"You better leave us now," Pearl said. "We will do our jobs as best we can. For now, it's probably a good idea if you try not to do anything to help us. We'll all hope your uncle James comes back soon."

"You mean you don't want me to come to the kitchen any more?" Callie asked. Like she used to before she went to France. "You don't want me helping with chores?"

"They're only chores to you," Reby said. "But for us, it's our life. This is our life."

Tears filled Callie's eyes.

"I know this makes you feel like you're alone," Pearl said. "But you ain't. Your momma and daddy are looking out for you in heaven."

"A lot of good that's doing me," Callie said. "Or any of you." She wiped her tears. "I will do as you say, Pearl. I never meant any harm. I'll do my best to make it up to you all. Somehow. Tell Henry—tell Henry how sorry I am."

She glanced at Reby. Then she hurried out of the kitchen and into the hall. She felt as lost as she had when she first learned her parents had died.

This time she had no one to turn to, not even Reby. She had no one she could trust or confide in.

She had no idea what to do next.

Four

Callie ran by the parlor again, on tiptoe. She barely made a sound. Her aunt and uncle were both talking at the same time, so she doubted they would hear her anyway.

She picked up a candle from the entryway table, lit it off the lantern there, and then went up the stairs, a small halo of light traveling with her. Before her parents died, the house had always seemed light and merry and full of people and sound. Now it was quiet as a tomb, even though she could hear her aunt and uncle's voices. She wished someone were going upstairs with her.

She reached the third floor and walked down the long dark hallway to her new room. For the first time in her life, she felt uneasy in her own home. It felt filled with ghosts. Or filled with enemies. Empty of loved ones.

She went into her room, closed the door, and locked it. She left the skeleton key in the lock so no one else could use their key to get in.

She got undressed, put on a nightgown, and got under the covers. She had to figure out what to do next. She could get away from her aunt and uncle if Uncle James came home, but she had no idea where he was or even if he was alive. Maybe she could convince the court that she was old enough and capable enough to run the plantation herself. Then her aunt and uncle would miraculously disappear from her life.

She snuffed out the candle and turned to face the wall. It was too early for sleep, but she was going to try anyway. Perhaps her dreams would give her more ideas.

She heard a knock on the door. Reby, most likely, come to help her undress and dress for the night.

"Go away!" Callie said.

If Reby and the others could reject Callie, she could reject them. She was sorry for what had happened to Heddie. More than sorry. She was mortified. But she had not beaten Heddie. It was not her fault.

She buried her head in her pillow. Maybe it was a little her fault. But at the heart of it, at the core of it, her aunt and uncle were responsible. They were the ones who had moved in where they were not welcome. She had to get rid of them. She had to get her life back.

One way or another, she was going to see a lawyer tomorrow. Maybe she could get the law on her side.

Callie fell to sleep.

Someone was whispering.

Callie opened her eyes to darkness.

How long had she been asleep? An hour? Three hours? A minute?

She listened. Must have been dreaming.

Were those footsteps? In her room?

She froze. She held her breath and listened to the pulsating darkness.

No one else was breathing.

Yet she could swear she had heard something near the wardrobe.

She threw off her covers and slid out of bed. She got a long match from her writing table and struck it against flint. The match hissed. She lit the lantern. The light turned part of the darkness golden.

She carried the light over to the wardrobe. She knew it was impossible for anyone to be in the room, but she opened the door to the wardrobe gingerly and then quickly stepped back.

She saw nothing but her clothes. She moved closer and held the lantern inside the wardrobe.

Nothing and no one.

She went around to the back of the wardrobe. She hadn't noticed before that the wardrobe was about a foot from the wall.

But no one was hiding behind it.

Callie walked around her small room.

She was alone.

She got back into bed and went to sleep.

At breakfast the next morning, Callie told her aunt and uncle that she wanted to see the condolence letters.

"I'm afraid I haven't been able to find them," Elizabeth said. "I put them on your mother's desk and now they're gone."

Callie looked down at her plate. She hadn't gone to her father's study or to either of the parlors since she'd come home. She had hardly gone anywhere in the house. It was too painful. Most of it looked like her home, yet it didn't feel like home. She was afraid if she smelled her mother's scent or saw her father's handwriting she would fall to pieces. She had too much to do to fall apart now.

"I'd like to see them," Callie said. "Please do your best to find them."

"Perhaps if we whipped the servants," Elizabeth said, "they'd be less likely to lose things. Or perhaps they'd remember where they put the letters."

Callie glanced at her aunt. Had someone told her Callie was upset about what happened to Heddie?

Or maybe her aunt figured Callie was a decent human being and wouldn't want to see anyone whipped.

"You do not have my permission to put a hand on any of the slaves," Callie said.

Her uncle put down his fork.

"You do not have a say in that, child," Charles said. "It is my responsibility and your aunt's responsibility."

"All this belongs to me," Callie said. "You have been appointed caretaker to me, but you must do things that are in my best interest and in the best interest of this plantation. You cannot damage any of my property. That includes my slaves."

Callie looked at her uncle directly. She was not going to play the role of the stupid adolescent today. At least not about this.

Her uncle stared back at her. Something about his eyes was frightening. She recalled the conversation she had eavesdropped upon and his words to Elizabeth: "I've broken more horses than you have. So watch your tone, wife."

She remembered the sound of his hand hitting Elizabeth.

If that was what had happened.

Callie wondered if he wanted to hit her now.

He smiled. "Of course," Charles said, "we are doing everything with your welfare in mind. You want the letters. Your aunt believes she can find them if she disciplines the house staff. We'll look for the letters a little longer and spare the rod, for now. Is that acceptable to you, Elizabeth?"

Elizabeth took a sip of her coffee and raised her eyebrows in a shrug.

"I'm taking my horse out for a ride after breakfast," Callie said.

"The lawyer is coming soon," Charles said. "We have some papers for you to sign."

Callie dropped her napkin next to her empty plate. Then she pushed away from the table.

"I won't be signing anything," Callie said, "without the presence of my own attorney."

"But he is your attorney," Charles said.

"Is he the attorney my father employed?" Callie asked.

Charles hesitated. He seemed flummoxed by her resistance. Then he said, "I'm not certain, Callie. But he is your lawyer now. I have hired him to take care of any legal matters related to plantation business."

Callie smiled. "I'd prefer my own lawyer."

"The judge is your lawyer," Elizabeth said. "And he has decided we are looking after all your affairs. If your uncle wants you to sign something, you had better sign it!"

Callie looked at her aunt and then at her uncle. She continued to smile.

"Don't hold lunch for me," she said. "I don't know when I will be back."

"You cannot go running around the countryside by yourself," Elizabeth said.

Callie walked out of the dining room.

"Come back here, young lady!" her aunt called.

"Let her go," Charles said. "We can wait."

Her uncle's placating words frightened her more than her aunt's yelling did.

Callie hurried out of the house and headed to the stables. The sun was out, and Callie knew the crisp cool air would soon warm.

"Good morning, Miss Callie." Joseph came out of the stables to greet her.

"Good morning, Joseph," she said. "I'd like to take out Meager. Is he up for a ride?"

"Yes, Miss," he said. He turned to go back into the stables. Callie followed.

"I hope you have been well, Joseph."

"I have," he said.

She felt awkward. He probably blamed her for Heddie, too.

"We sure miss your momma and daddy," he said. "They were kind folk."

"I miss them, too."

Meager stuck his black head out of his stall and whinnied. Callie went up to him and stroked his soft muzzle.

"Hello, sir," Callie said.

"He's been missing your daddy," Joseph said. "He rode him nearly every day."

She heard another whinny. She looked up. Several horses had stuck their heads out and were looking her way, including Sergeant, one the horses who had been pulling the carriage when her parents died. The other horse had been injured in the crash and had to be put down.

Callie walked to Sergeant's stall. The horse nodded as she came near and whinnied very softly. Callie put her hand on the white stripe that went down his face.

"Hello, Sergeant." She peered into his dark eyes. She thought he looked sad. Could a horse look sad?

Sergeant moved closer and Callie pressed her face against his neck. He was the last living being who had seen her parents alive.

"All set, Miss," Joseph said.

Callie walked back toward Joseph. He put down a stool next to Meager. Callie stepped on it and then slid onto the horse. She hated riding side-saddle, but she didn't feel like going back inside and changing her clothes—and she was certain her aunt would throw a fit if she put on breeches.

"Was Sergeant hurt in the accident?" Callie asked Joseph as she adjusted her seat.

Joseph shook his head. "He had a burr or something that bloodied his back. That may have been why he bolted, if that's what happened. They were driving down Pike's Creek. Something happened as they came around the curve and the cart came undone from the horses, they think, and it kept going into the creek. And the creek was running strong."

"You mean my parents drowned?" Callie asked. No one had told her that.

Joseph looked up at her. "Yes, Miss. I thought you knew. I'm sorry."

Callie shook her head. "No, it's all right. I'm glad to know. It's not any worse than what I imagined happened."

"The cart turned over in the water," Joseph said. "And they was trapped."

Callie groaned. She didn't mean to. It just came out.

"You still want to go out?" he asked. "Maybe Reby should go with you."

"I'm fine," she said. "Thank you."

Joseph went to Meager's head and led him out of the stable and into the sunlight.

"Take care, now," Joseph said.

Callie nodded. She urged Meager forward. The two of them headed for the woods.

Callie barely glanced around as they went through the woods. She was intent on getting to the other side of it and onto the public road. It was all familiar to her—a place where she had spent much of her childhood. She didn't want to find out it was different, too, contaminated by her aunt and uncle.

Soon they were up on the road.

She hoped she didn't see anyone she knew. She didn't want to pretend all was well; she didn't want to hear condolences; she only wanted to find someone to help her.

She decided to go to the Sawyer house, where Benjamin lived with his sister Therese and widowed mother Maeve Sawyer.

Callie was almost to the drive when she saw a cart coming toward her from the other direction. She knew before the cart was close enough that her cousin Barnaby was the driver. He wore his bowler hat a little cockeyed. She was certain he did this because he imagined that was how the European gentlemen wore it. Someday she was going to take pleasure in telling him that she had never seen a single bowler on the head of any gentleman or any royalty. In her experience, only servants wore them.

Perhaps she would never tell him. Let him remain ignorant.

She urged Meager forward. Maybe she could turn down the drive before she'd have to meet Barnaby.

Too late.

Barnaby yanked his horse to a stop, right in front of the drive.

Callie stopped Meager next to the cart.

"Good morning, Callie," Barnaby said. He always sounded like he was sneering at her. He pushed the bowler back as he looked up to see her. He squinted slightly in the morning sun. His hair looked too blond and too short. His eyes were vacant.

"Hello, Barnaby," she said.

"How are Mommy and Daddy?" he asked.

"My mother and father are dead," Callie said. "Yours have taken over my house."

Barnaby laughed. "That's a shame, really."

"Have you run your father's plantation into the ground yet?" Callie asked.

"You've never known when to make a friend and when to make an enemy," Barnaby said. "You are in a precarious position, Callie. You might want to make nice with the boss."

"The boss?" Callie said.

"Come on," he said. "Do you think you're ever going to get your hands on Mount Joy again? My parents are there for good. Which is fine with me. I can oversee Riverfront and Mount Joy."

"You are going to be overseer?" Callie asked. She vaguely remembered her uncle talking about hiring a new overseer.

Barnaby grinned again. "You always thought you were better than me. Look at us now. Complete equals. Oh wait. I'm going to be running two plantations. And you? What are you going to be doing? Trying to survive until you're of age and the court lets you have your life back?"

Trying to survive? What was he implying?

"Maybe I'll get married and throw you all out!" Callie said.

She turned Meager to go down the drive before her cousin could respond. Barnaby had told her too much. He was stupid that way. Always said too much. Couldn't wait to gloat.

Meager began trotting down the road.

Not that she was much better. Threatening to get married. As if that was a threat. It was what they all expected her to do eventually.

Callie glanced behind her. Barnaby was following her to the Sawyer house. What was he thinking? They couldn't continue to argue like children in front of the Sawyers. That would be humiliating.

Meager and Callie trotted to the stables. A stable boy ran out and took Meager's reins. Callie slid off the horse and strode over to Barnaby's cart.

"Why are you following me?" she asked. "I have nothing left to say to you."

Barnaby laughed. He put on the brake and got out of the cart. "Don't let my horse get a chill, boy. I want her brushed down before I get back."

"Yessir!" the stable boy said.

"I thought you were following me," Barnaby said. "I have come to call on Therese Sawyer. She and I are engaged. Or soon will be."

"You and Therese Sawyer?" Callie said. "I don't believe it."

Barnaby pulled off his gloves and slapped them against his hand. "Why don't you believe it? She is an incredibly handsome woman and I am an incredibly successful business-man."

"Really? I heard you've gambled away what little fortune you had. Or was that your father?"

"If you repeat that slander, I will make life miserable for

you," he said. He hissed when he spoke. He had the same temperament as his father. How could she be related to these people?

They walked to the door together.

"Why are you here?" Barnaby asked.

Callie hesitated. Why *was* she here? If the Sawyers were in league with her cousin, they couldn't help her.

Now what was she going to do?

"I've forgotten why I've come," Callie said. "I was out for a ride. I won't bother them since they've already got their hands full with . . . you."

Callie hurried away from her cousin. She went into the stable and retrieved Meager before the stable boy could slip off the saddle. Callie got back on the horse and trotted down to the end of the drive.

She looked down the road in both directions. Where now? She didn't want to go back to the plantation. If she went to town alone to talk to a lawyer, people might think she was overstepping. Her situation was precarious enough without ending up in a lunatic asylum.

That was probably a slight exaggeration.

She hoped.

She heard someone calling her name. She looked around until she saw Benjamin coming down the Sawyer drive.

Damn. Now she'd have to talk to him. Pretend she hadn't come to ask for his help.

She turned Meager around and waited for Benjamin.

As she watched him run to catch up to her, she thought of her childhood, some of it spent running through the woods and down lanes like this drive with Benjamin. He had been very fast, but she had beaten him once or twice. He was taller and stronger, but he was cautious. Callie hadn't been afraid to fall and skin her knees. She hadn't been afraid, period.

That childish foolishness seemed so far away now.

"Barnaby said you were here and then left," Benjamin said. "Are you all right?"

"Of course I'm all right," she said. "Why would you assume I wouldn't be?"

"Because the last time I saw you, you were ill," he said.

Callie shook her head. "I keep forgetting you are a doctor!" she said. "And my doctor, no less. We must find a remedy for that. You cannot be my doctor. We're childhood chums. It's too strange. Anyway, I best be getting back home now."

She pressed the rein against Meager's neck to turn him.

"Wait, Callie," Benjamin said. "You must have come here for a reason."

"I wanted to see your mother," she said. "To visit."

"Come on back then."

Callie shook her head. "Not with Barnaby there. I didn't know he was courting your sister. You didn't tell me they were engaged."

"They aren't engaged!" Benjamin said. "I hope it doesn't come to that."

"So you aren't great friends again?"

"We were never great friends," Benjamin said. "Callie, I'm getting a crick in my neck from looking up at you. Tell me what's going on?"

"I need to see a lawyer," she said. "I thought maybe you

could come into town with me. I haven't access to any funds, so I can't pay anyone right now, but with you by my side, perhaps someone will actually listen to me."

"John Bowen is an honest and effective attorney," Benjamin said. "I'll take you in to see him. Did you want to go now?"

"Yes, please," she said. "But Barnaby can't know."

"We'll go straight to the stables and get a cart, and I'll have a message sent to my mother."

Five

A few minutes later, Callie sat in a cart next to Benjamin as the horse trotted toward St. Charles.

"Do you want to talk about what's been happening?" Benjamin asked after they had sat in silence for several minutes.

Callie looked around as they moved forward. Each stretch of land, every house, each plantation held a memory for her. Places where she had gone with her parents. Places where she had played as a child.

Callie looked over at her old friend. She could not see the child in him any longer. He was now a man, and she was still a girl.

Or so everyone believed. At least that was how they treated her. Her mother had been married by the time she was seventeen years old. She had suffered miscarriage after miscarriage until finally Callie had been born. A welcome relief, her mother always said. "Like a colorful wildflower coming up in a barren field."

"You cannot repeat anything I tell you," Callie said to Benjamin now. "You can't decide later that I'm a child and you're telling someone for my own good."

"Of course," Benjamin said.

"It's all been so peculiar since I returned home," Callie said. "My aunt and uncle are using the servants to keep me in line. I wanted to read my condolence letters, but Elizabeth says she can't find them. I asked her to look harder and she said she'd try to beat it out of the servants. She knew I wouldn't press her about it after she threatened to beat my slaves. My parents did not like Charles or Elizabeth much. My father said that Uncle Charles was a gambler. Mother didn't like her own brother. I'm perplexed why the court let them be my guardians. One, I don't need guardians. Two, why not Uncle Peter? Or wait until Uncle James comes home."

"Your uncle Peter was not willing to relocate, as I understand it," Benjamin said. "And the plantation needs someone to look after it."

"See! You know more than I do! Why didn't someone tell me this?"

"I don't know," Benjamin said. "But I don't think it's because of any Machiavellian scheme on your uncle's part. I'm sure they want what's best for you."

"Then why did Barnaby say my aunt and uncle were never going to leave?" Callie said. "He practically threatened my life."

"Practically?"

"He said something about me 'trying to survive' until I'm of age," Callie said. "And there was malice in his voice."

"There's always malice in his voice," Benjamin said. "He's trying to puff himself up, to sound like he knows more than he does."

"He says Uncle Charles has hired him as overseer," Callie said. "We don't need an overseer. And Barnaby has a mean streak."

"Barnaby won't last a month as overseer," Benjamin said, "not if it means being out of doors all day. He's soft as a dough ball. You have nothing to fear from him."

"Mount Joy is my home," Callie said. "It belongs to me. I am responsible for everyone who lives there now. I am responsible for the land. I want it back in my hands. I don't understand why I have to wait. If I were a male, I could fight a war at my age. Is the difference because I'm female? It certainly can't be that boys mature sooner than females because we all know that isn't so!"

"I can't argue with you about that."

"You shouldn't argue with me about anything," Callie said, "because I am always right."

"Were you right about faking food poisoning to get Pearl back in the kitchen?" he asked.

"She is back in the kitchen," Callie said. "But I didn't quite foresee all the consequences of that particular scheme."

"So you are not always right," Benjamin said.

"A gentleman does not argue with a lady," Callie said. "Let us sit in silence and enjoy the view."

Benjamin laughed. "Whatever you say, Miss Carter."

Before long, Callie and Benjamin arrived in St. Charles and were soon sitting in John Bowen's office. Bowen's secretary brought in a tray and poured tea for them.

After the secretary left and shut the door behind him, Mr. Bowen said, "I am so sorry about your mother and father, Callie. I hope you got my condolence letter."

"Thank you," Callie said, "but I did not get your letter. I didn't get any letters. My aunt has lost them. Or so she says. This is why I've come to you. I want you to get the judge to rescind my aunt and uncle's guardianship of me and Mount Joy. I am perfectly capable of handling my own affairs. I know how to run the house, and I could learn how to run the plantation. I could hire a manager until I knew more. Currently I have no money, no autonomy, they're changing my home without my permission, and they are cruel to my servants. What can you do to help me?"

Bowen glanced at Benjamin and then looked back at Callie.

"I was your father's attorney," Bowen said.

Callie hadn't known that.

"I am the executor of his will," Bowen said. "I tried to get the court to wait until you returned, but I didn't succeed. You were the sole heir to the estate, so essentially my duties were over once you inherited. Your uncle stepped in and asked to be your guardian, until you come of age. There was nothing I could do about it."

"That all sounds rather shady, doesn't it?" Callie asked.

Bowen looked away from her for a moment, and then he said, "It is the way things happen in our county. Your uncle wanted to be your guardian so he is your guardian."

"Could we get it changed so that he was only my guardian until I turn eighteen?" Callie asked. "That's only a few months away. I could manage until then. Perhaps."

"I could petition the court on your behalf," he said. "If I were your lawyer."

"Can't you be my lawyer?" she asked.

"Your uncle is supposed to make those decisions for you," he said. "However, under the law, you can retain me and I can do work on your behalf."

"Well?" Callie said. "How do I retain you?"

"He needs money," Benjamin said. "That makes it official."

"I have no money," Callie said. "My aunt and uncle have not given me any funds, and I spent my last coin on the ship home."

Benjamin pulled a coin from his pocket and held it out to Callie.

"A gift," he said.

Callie took the coin between her gloved fingers. Then she handed it to Mr. Bowen.

"Will this do?" Callie asked.

"It will," he said.

"I can't have my parents back," Callie said, "but I can have my home back. I know Judge Zebadiah is friends with my uncle, but he's a judge. Won't he see that this is not fair?"

"Perhaps," Bowen said. "In the meanwhile, you might

want to write your uncle Peter."

"And what about Uncle James?" Callie asked. "What can I do about finding him? Can I hire someone to look for him? Except I have no funds. Perhaps you can persuade the judge that I do need my own funds?"

"I will see what I can do," Bowen said.

"Isn't the law on my side?" Callie asked. "Doesn't it matter that the plantation is mine and that I am old enough to be on my own?"

"You understand that if you got married," Bowen said, "the guardianship would be immediately dissolved."

"Why would I exchange one prison for another?" Callie asked.

Bowen chuckled. "I don't know if I ever want you and my wife to meet," he said.

Callie left Mr. Bowen's office feeling buoyed. She could do this. She could outfox or out-lawyer her aunt and uncle. She looked up and down the sunny main street and breathed deeply for the first time in a long while.

"May I take you to lunch?" Benjamin asked.

Callie looked at him and smiled. He was a handsome young man. A kind man. She was glad she had trusted him.

"Don't you have patients?" she asked.

"Not until after lunch," he said.

He held out his right arm to her and Callie took it. Together they walked down the street.

"Would you prefer the Heritage Inn or Rooster's?" Benjamin asked.

"Where do you think Judge Zebadiah eats?" she asked.

"Probably at home," he said. "He only lives a few blocks away."

Callie looked in the direction Benjamin indicated. Should she go pound on his door and demand justice? No, that would make her seem immature. He had to see how responsible she was. How ready she was to take charge of her life.

"I'm guessing he sometimes eats at the Heritage," Callie said. "Let's go there. Don't worry. I won't cause a scene."

"I wouldn't care," Benjamin said. "It has been a little dull around here lately."

Callie laughed.

She and Benjamin went to the dining room of the Heritage Inn. It was overflowing with diners, inside and out. Several groups had taken chairs outside to sit and eat in the sun. The owner, Mr. Emerick, greeted Callie and Benjamin.

"I'm so sorry about your parents," he said as he took her hands in his. "Did you get my note?"

"Thank you, Mr. Emerick," she said. "I have not seen any notes yet. Apparently my aunt has lost them. Everyone must think me so rude."

"Not at all, dear," he said. "Not at all. Have you come to lunch?"

"Yes," Callie said. "But first, is Judge Zebadiah here?"

"He's right over there." Mr. Emerick tilted his head to indicate a table near the window. Callie spotted the judge right away.

"May we sit near him?" she asked.

"Certainly," he said.

Callie and Benjamin followed Mr. Emerick across the

room. He held a chair out for her to sit in at a small table just past the judge, but she stopped at the judge's table.

"Excuse me," Callie said. "Judge Zebadiah, I'm Callie Carter."

The judge stood. He took her gloved hands into his own bare hands.

"Of course you are," he said. "I'm happy to see you. I'm so sorry about your parents."

"I am glad to see you," she said. She hoped she sounded very adult. Very grown-up. "I wonder if I might come talk with you later about my situation."

"I'll talk with you any time, my dear," he said. "You must be relieved that all the legal matters are being taken care of by your uncle."

Callie glanced at the other people at the judge's table. Two women and one man. She did not recognize any of them.

She smiled. "I appreciate what you've tried to do for me, but my parents would have wanted my uncle James to administer the estate, and if he couldn't be found, then I'm sure they would have trusted me to do it."

Judge Zebadiah patted her hands and then let them go.

"Do you know anything about accounting, or bookkeeping?" he asked. "Do you know how to order feed for the stock or food for the slaves? Do you know how many lashes it takes to get a buck going again when he's being obstinate? Would you know whether a merchant was cheating you?"

"My parents taught me many things," Callie said. "Not the least of them was how to tell whether I could trust a person or not. I could hire someone to oversee the estate."

"But you see, I've done that for you," he said. "And it's a relative. How wonderful is that?"

Callie bit her lip. She wanted to shout, "But he's a gambler and probably a crook!"

Instead she asked, "Has anyone tried to find my uncle James?"

"Hasn't your uncle explained this to you?" he asked. He smiled again. "I'm sure he has and you forgot. My office sent many messages to James. We never heard back."

"I'd like to hire someone to go look for him," Callie said, "but I have no money."

"And isn't that a good thing?" the judge said. "Otherwise you might spend it foolishly sending someone on a wild-goose chase. Your uncle is an adventurer and—" He looked at the people at his table. They looked away. "Your uncle James is an adventurer. He will either turn up or he won't. In the meanwhile, Charles Ames is a much better choice to govern you."

"But he was not the choice my parents made," Callie said. "And that's what counts. And I definitely do not need governing!"

Callie glanced at Benjamin. This was not going as she had wished. The judge smiled grimly.

"Perhaps you do need governing if you think it is acceptable to interrupt my lunch to talk about these private matters in public," he said.

Callie grimaced.

She had rushed in too soon. She was never going to get him on her side now.

"I'm sorry," Callie said. "The deaths of my parents came

as such a shock, and now my house has been taken over by strangers who threaten me."

She began to cry. She was embarrassed, but tears streamed down her cheeks. Her knees felt wobbly. Benjamin put his arm around her waist. Or maybe it was the judge. Callie wasn't sure.

They led her out of the dining room and into some kind of anteroom. She sat in a hardback chair. Someone handed her a glass of water. Her hand shook as she raised the glass to her lips.

Then she looked up. Judge Zebadiah, Benjamin, and Mr. Emerick looked down at her. Now they would all think of her as a poor orphan who couldn't even control her own emotions. How could she run a plantation?

"Are you feeling better?" the judge asked.

Callie nodded. "I don't know what happened. I guess it just hit me. My parents."

"I wish you could trust me that I'm doing what's in your best interest," the judge said.

"I do," Callie said. "I really do." She didn't. She didn't trust him at all. But what did she know? Truly?

"Could you at least get me an allowance?" she asked. "And could you stop them from doing anything with the slaves without my permission?"

"I can talk to your uncle about an allowance," he said. "But what about the slaves?"

"They were talking about selling some of them," Callie said. Benjamin held out a kerchief to her. She took it and wiped her eyes. "I don't think that's right. I ran the household with my mother. And I don't think it's right they can sell our slaves without my permission."

She hadn't actually run the house with her mother, but the judge didn't need to know that.

"They cannot sell any of your property," the judge said. "At least not without my permission. I will speak with your uncle and make certain he understands his responsibilities."

"Must they live with me?" Callie knew she was pushing it, but she couldn't stop herself.

"You want to live there all by yourself?" he asked. "It wouldn't be fair to ask your uncle to have to come so far to manage things."

"Now he's got his son as overseer," Callie said. She couldn't help herself: She shuddered. Everything she felt and thought seemed too close to the surface now.

The judge didn't say anything for a moment. Then he said, "You shouldn't worry yourself about such things." Her uncle had told her the same thing.

"These 'things' are my life," Callie said. "It's my home. All that I have left of my parents. My cousin is a gambler. I suspect my uncle is, too. Their own plantation is practically ruined and now they're going to do the same to Mount Joy."

She knew she had said too much. The judge straightened and looked around. Benjamin cleared his throat.

"You cannot say these things," the judge said. "It's slanderous."

"Isn't it only slander if it's false?"

The judge shook his head.

Benjamin said, "Judge, I've known Callie all my life.

She is quite capable of managing her own affairs. I've never known her to prevaricate."

"I will get you an allowance," the judge repeated. "I will talk with your uncle about selling the slaves. But this conversation has convinced me that you do need a guardian. You must learn to be more circumspect in what you say in public. Benjamin, give my regards to your mother. Callie, I will see you soon."

The judge nodded and left the room.

Callie rubbed her face.

Then she looked at Benjamin.

"That could not have gone worse," Callie said. "I don't know what happened. Now he thinks I'm crazy and my aunt and uncle are the sane ones. I keep making one mistake after another. I was not prepared for any of this, Benjamin."

He held out his hand to her. She took it and got up from the chair. She brushed her hands down her green satin dress.

"You'll figure it out," he said. "Take it slowly. And if you don't figure it out, you'll be eighteen in no time, and the judge will reconsider your guardianship. Do you still want to stay and eat?"

Callie shook her head. "No, I want to go home." She started to leave the room, but then she stopped and pressed her lips together. "I don't have a home any more, do I?"

"I'll have Mr. Emerick make us up a picnic basket," he said. "We'll take it with us. It's going to be all right, Callie. It takes time to get used to your new life."

"I don't want to get used to this new life," Callie said. "And I won't. I will figure something out. I know my last couple of ideas haven't been exactly successful, but I will figure out something. I am not going to live like this. One way or another, there's going to be a change."

Six

Benjamin and Callie took their picnic back to Mount Joy, to the shade of a big old black willow near the river.

The tree was just beginning to leaf out, so its huge trunk was plainly visible. It looked as though twelve dryads had come together for some kind of spring dance and now they were all stuck together, forever dancing, forever reaching for the stars, and no one saw them as individuals any longer: just one huge old tree.

Callie had spent many afternoons under this tree.

Benjamin took off his coat and lay it on the ground near the tree.

"If you put that down for me, you've dirtied your jacket for nothing," Callie said. "I will plop right down here on the grass. Or I'll climb around the tree."

"And then what will you tell your aunt about the grass stains on your dress?" Benjamin said. "I seem to remember that was a source of contention between you and your mother when you were a girl."

"My mother was only trying to look out for me," Callie said. "It's none of Aunt Elizabeth's business what happens to my dresses."

She remembered Elizabeth had threatened to sell Reby because she didn't think Reby was taking good enough care of Callie's clothes.

"Although I suppose if I dirty them," Callie said, "she'll blame Reby and punish her."

Callie sat on Benjamin's coat. She rearranged the fabric of her dress as best she could so that her legs were covered. Benjamin sat near her and opened the picnic basket. He took out a steak sandwich and handed it to Callie. Then he took out one for himself.

They ate in silence for a few minutes. Callie listened to a woodpecker somewhere in the willow, searching for bugs. Tap, tap, tap. Pause. Tap. Pause. She peered up through the branches and didn't see any woodpecker.

"Do you remember coming here when we were children?" Benjamin asked.

"Of course I do," Callie said. "This is where I had my first kiss. My first and only kiss." Callie smiled at Benjamin. "You were older so you should have known better."

"You asked me for a kiss," Benjamin said. "So I obliged."

"I thought it was quite grand," Callie said.

"It was like kissing a fish," Benjamin said. "You'd been

swimming and you were all wet. You couldn't have been much older than five. I was twice your age, at least. It was a platonic kiss on the cheek. Lasted only an instant."

Callie laughed. "I suppose it wasn't that impressive for me either, since I haven't had another kiss since then."

Benjamin smiled. "We could always try again."

Callie smiled and smoothed her hands across her dress. Then she said, "Benjamin, what would you do about my aunt and uncle if you were me?"

"I'd give them a chance," he said.

"Even if they'd shunted someone you love off to some hellish place?" Callie said. "Even if you thought they might destroy your home?"

"I would," he said. "But that's me. I tend to take a wait and see approach. That has never been something you've been able to do. You might try using honey instead of vinegar with them. You know that old adage."

"You get more flies with honey," Callie said. "Yes, I know. I tried that in the beginning, for a while, but I was so out-raged I couldn't continue. Besides, I don't want any flies in my honey."

"What have they done that is so awful?" Benjamin asked.

"I told you," she said. "They sent Pearl to live in the slave houses. She hadn't lived there for decades."

"Why is it all right for some of your slaves to live in those places but not others?"

"What are you talking about?"

"You didn't want her living in some 'hellish place,'" he said. "But other people live in those places. Why is that acceptable?"

"Because they aren't my friends," Callie said. "Pearl is."

"You are old enough to know that sounds ridiculous," he said.

Callie finished her sandwich and then dusted the crumbs off her hands.

"I suppose so," she said. "I just figured it wouldn't seem hellish to those who were used to it. People get used to their lives, don't they?"

"Like you're getting used to your new life?"

"You're right, of course," she said. "Poor logic on my part. Are you saying I should make certain all my slaves live well? They are my responsibility. Is that what you do with your slaves?"

Benjamin laughed. "Callie, we don't have any slaves."

"But the stable boy," Callie said. "I saw him today."

"He is free," Benjamin said. "Everyone who works for my mother is free."

Callie's eyes widened. "Truly? I never knew."

"It isn't something we shout from street corners," he said. "Mother is a Quaker."

Callie gasped.

"When my father died, she freed all the slaves," he said. "Those who wanted to stay, she pays."

"I'm surprised you weren't debarred from practicing medicine all up and down the James River," Callie said.

"They were my mother's slaves," he said. "Not mine."

"So you don't agree with what she did?" Callie asked.

Benjamin looked at Callie. "Does it matter what I think?"

Callie shrugged. "It was so different in France," she said. "We didn't have to think about such things. We didn't hear about abolitionists or civil war. Blacks and whites were at parties together. It made no difference. Or if it did, I couldn't tell. Reby was my friend in France. We were equals. Or close to it. I liked it. Now we're back here and she's not my friend, and everyone is angry with me because of Pearl and Heddie. I would like to go back to France. I bet my aunt and uncle would like that too. Then they could do anything they wanted with Mount Joy. Are you going to answer my question?"

"Yes, I was glad my mother freed her slaves," Benjamin said. "I am glad I don't have to think about owning a slave. I am only a poor doctor, so no one expects it of me. Of course if you tell anyone this, I will be an even poorer doctor."

"Your secret is safe with me," Callie said. "If my slaves were free, I wouldn't have to worry about Auntie and Uncle hurting them. They'd be safe. Do you think the judge would let me free them?"

Benjamin laughed. "You can't be serious. He might let you sell them but not free them. Once you come of age, though, you'll be able to do whatever you want."

Callie shook her head.

"If this war comes, none of us will be able to do what we want. Benjamin, when I was a child my mother told me that blacks needed caring for. She said they weren't as smart as us, so we needed to take care of them. You're a doctor. Do you think my mother was right?"

"You aren't a child any more," Benjamin said. "What do you think?"

"But you're a man of science," she said. "I value your opinion."

"Or do you believe I am smarter than you are because I am a man?"

"*That* is nonsense!" Callie said. "I am far smarter than most of the men I've met."

"You've known a lot of black people, too," Benjamin said.

"Yes, but we weren't equals socially," Callie said, "so it was hard to tell. I suppose if I think about it I haven't truly noticed any difference in intelligence between those with black skin and those with white."

"Then why would you believe they need looking after, as though they're children?"

Something rustled in the tall grass near the river. Benjamin and Callie both looked toward the sound. Callie didn't see anything except grass and cattails in the near distance. Maybe a beaver or heron was making its way through the grass.

Suddenly a young black man wearing dark slacks and waistcoat emerged. He stumbled forward, swearing, then straightened up and bowed slightly.

Benjamin stood.

"I'm sorry," the man said.

"Do you need assistance?" Benjamin asked. He stood between Callie and the man. Callie pushed on Benjamin's leg to move him out of the way so she could see. He didn't move.

"I got lost," the man said. "Was coming over from—"

Callie sighed. If Benjamin wasn't going to get out of her way, she'd have to get up—and trying to stand on her own in this dress was going to be next to impossible. She figured the stranger couldn't see her and Benjamin couldn't see her, so she rocked forward and pushed herself up. She teetered a bit, so she grabbed a hold of Benjamin's arm. He turned around and helped her up.

She stood next to Benjamin.

"I've come over from the Randolph plantation," the man said. "I was given leave to see my sister." He didn't look at them.

Callie could see he was a strong man, and his clothes were well-kept, except for the mud stains on his pants.

"All by yourself?" Callie asked. "It's not Sunday is it? I do lose track of time! I do." She smiled and fanned her hand in front of her face as though she was hot. "Where you headed? We can give you directions."

"Mount Joy," he said.

"You're here then," Callie said. "The house is over yonder." She pointed. "You need to see someone here?"

"Reby is my sister," he said.

Callie looked at him. "I've known Reby all my life, and I don't remember a brother. Reby works for me. I'm Callie Carter."

"I remember you, Miss Carter," the man said. "I was here for a time when I was a child."

Callie stared at the man. Seemed like she would remember him, especially given he was Reby's brother.

"You're not Blackie are you?" She vaguely recalled a boy named Blackie who used to work in the stables for a time.

"I was called that," he said. He was looking right at her

now. It made her uncomfortable. She was not accustomed to a slave staring at her.

Now she remembered. He had run away several times until finally her father sold him to someone else. She hadn't known he was Reby's brother.

"You were called that but it wasn't your name?" Callie asked. "Then, pray tell, what is your name?"

"My sister calls me Walker," he said.

Her eyes narrowed. She did not like the way he was speaking to her.

"You should probably run along now," Benjamin said.

The man nodded. "I'd appreciate it if you didn't tell Reby you saw me. I want it to be a surprise."

"I think you'll get there before me," Callie said, "so I wouldn't worry about that. But yes, I will keep your secret."

In the next moment the man was gone, through the woods and around the bend.

"What a strange man he was," Callie said. "I bet you anything he is a runaway."

"If you thought that was the case," Benjamin said, "why were you engaging him in conversation?"

"I don't know," Callie said. "I thought it was kind of funny him sneaking around my plantation."

"I'm sure it was not funny for him if he was running for his life," Benjamin said. "And not funny for us if he was dangerous."

"What danger could he be?" Callie asked.

"When a man is running for his life, he could be all kinds of dangerous. We better get going."

"You're not afraid, are you?" Callie asked. "You're not going to report him? Especially if he is really Reby's brother. I can't do that to her."

"I'm not going to tell anyone anything," Benjamin said. He closed the picnic basket, lifted it, and handed it to Callie. Then he picked up his coat and shook it. "I have to get back to work." He smiled at Callie, but the smile was more of a grimace.

What was wrong with him? She shrugged and walked to the cart and got in.

Not long after, Benjamin dropped Callie off at the house. He offered to come in, but she assured him it wasn't necessary. He promised to send Meager back to Mount Joy before the end of the day.

Callie went up the steps to her house and through the front door.

Henry greeted her, as he always did, politely, with a slight bow. She wondered if he hated her for getting his daughter beaten. Beaten and sent away.

"Henry," Callie started to say. "I am so—"

"Excuse me, Miss," Henry said. "Mrs. Ames wanted to see you in the drawing room as soon as you came in."

"She can wait," Callie said. "I need to—" She stopped and looked at Henry. Then she glanced over at the entrance to the east parlor. If she didn't go in, Henry would get the worst of it.

"Thank you," Callie said. "I am sorry about Heddie. I had no idea she was your daughter."

"Don't think nothin' about it, Miss," he said.

He didn't look at her. He said all the right words.

Because he had to. It was dangerous if he didn't.

She didn't know what else to say.

"Is that you, Callie?" her aunt called from the dining room.

Callie smiled at Henry. Or grimaced. She wasn't quite sure which.

She walked down the hall and went into the parlor. A fire burned in the fireplace even though it was warm outdoors and it was not evening yet.

Uncle Charles stood near the fire, with his arm on the mantel, dressed in riding breeches and waistcoat. He looked like he was posing for a portrait. Elizabeth sat on the stiff-backed couch with her sewing in her lap. Callie felt a pang as she stepped into the room. Elizabeth sat where her mother had sat most every evening. Callie had sat next to her, or sometimes on the floor, unless she and her father played whist if they had company. Her mother was not a card player.

"Sit down, Callie," Elizabeth said.

"I'd like to go upstairs and change for dinner," Callie said.

"First we'd like to speak with you," Charles said.

"Of course," Callie said, agreeably. She sat on the other end of the couch from her aunt.

"Did you have a nice time in town?" Charles asked.

"It was fine," Callie said. How did they know where she had been?

"We were worried," Elizabeth said. "You were gone so long. Next time you leave the plantation, we'd like you to tell us where you're going. What if something had happened to you? Everyone would blame us because we didn't know where you were."

Callie laughed. "I grew up here. I know every inch of this county. I've never had to get permission to come and go."

"I don't believe that," Elizabeth said. "Your mother would not have been so foolish."

Callie didn't say anything. Of course, she had always told her mother and father where she was going, out of politeness rather than out of obligation—because they were a family and cared about each other's comings and goings.

"Judge Zebadiah's clerk came out to the plantation," Charles said. "With a letter from the judge. He was concerned about you. He said you seemed a little . . . distraught."

"He said 'distraught,'" Elizabeth said, "but he meant you acted inappropriately. I'm certain he blames us now." Elizabeth kept sticking the needle into her sewing and then quickly pulling the thread through. Deliberately, almost violently.

"We are going to give you an allowance," Charles said. "We didn't know you needed money. We're sorry you didn't feel as though you could come to us about this matter. Instead you bothered the judge in the middle of his lunch. Said all kinds of things about us, apparently."

Callie stared at the fire.

"He's also expressed concerns about Barnaby running the plantation," Charles said.

"Yes, Callie," Elizabeth said. "Now because of you, Barnaby won't be overseer of this plantation. You have stymied his career."

"Let him run your plantation," Callie said. "I don't think he's qualified to experiment on my plantation."

The room went silent. The fire popped and crackled. The wood must be green. It hissed a bit, too.

"You need to get yourself right about a couple of things," Elizabeth said. "This plantation is not yours. By right, it belongs to the Ames family. We are your mother's relatives."

"This is my father's plantation," Callie said. "He got it from his father and his father got it from his father. That is the way it works. Some of the slaves belong to my mother, but that is it. You have no more claim on this estate than a beggar man in New York City."

Elizabeth gasped.

"But your father has no living relatives," Charles said evenly.

"I am his heir. I am my mother's heir."

"Maybe," Elizabeth said. "Maybe not."

"What are you talking about?" Callie asked.

"You were always a dark baby," Elizabeth said. "Your momma did everything she could to keep you out of the sun. But you ran around in it. You got darker than some of those pickaninnies. And we think we know why. We think your momma's real baby died. And they substituted you, the offspring of one of your father's concubines."

This time Callie gasped. She stood. Her heart raced.

"What are you talking about?" Callie asked again. "You can't believe what you're saying."

Elizabeth shrugged. "Your momma is dead. She can't help you. I was in the house at your mother's bedside when she gave birth."

"You weren't!" Callie said. "Pearl was there and Martha. But that was all. Momma would have told me."

Elizabeth put down her sewing. "Who do you think the courts are going to believe? Two ignorant slaves or an upstanding white woman?"

"None of this is true," Callie said, "but even if it were, I am my father's child. He left the plantation to me."

"If your mother was a slave," Elizabeth said, "you're a slave. You are property. You can't inherit property. That would be like this couch inheriting that chair." She laughed.

Callie looked over at her uncle.

"You can't be serious about this," she said. "She was your sister, Uncle Charles. How could you do this to me?"

"We aren't doing anything, dear," Charles said. "We're merely pointing out how harmful slander can be."

She felt her face turn red. How could the judge have told her aunt and uncle the details of their conversation? She sat on the couch again, too wobbly to stand.

"Of course, you are my sister's child," Charles said. He came and stood near her and looked down at her. "We only want what's best for you. We want you to enjoy this time of your life. We'll take care of the plantation. You can have parties and be with your friends. This place can be gay again."

"To that end," Elizabeth said, "we thought we'd have a ball in your honor. You need to meet young people your own age."

"But I am in mourning," Callie said.

Elizabeth put her sewing to the side. "Nonsense," she said.

"That is old-fashioned. We want to show Judge Zebadiah that you are well and happy, so that we don't have to think about any of this other stuff."

Callie looked at her aunt. The woman smiled at her. Smiled as she threatened her.

"That would be fine," Callie said.

"It'll be small," she said, "this first ball. You've got that beautiful ballroom. We might as well put it to use."

"Yes, ma'am," Callie said. "May I go upstairs now? I'm feeling tired. I'd like to have my dinner upstairs, if that would be all right."

"No," Elizabeth said. "You may go up now, but you've spent too much time hiding in that room. We expect you down to dinner at the usual time."

Callie stood. Charles squeezed her shoulder. She wanted to jerk away from him, but she didn't.

"You'll see," Charles said. "You'll get to know us and understand we only want what's best for you."

Callie nodded and excused herself. Then she stepped into the hall and walked to the stairs.

If they actually wanted what was best for her, they'd pack up and go back home.

Callie hurried up the stairs. At least now she understood how bad her aunt and uncle were. She needed to come up with a plan. One that worked this time.

Seven

Callie opened the door to her room. Reby was standing at her wardrobe, looking at her dresses.

"Which one would you like for dinner, Miss?" Reby asked.

"I don't care," Callie said.

Reby stayed at the wardrobe. Callie walked to her desk, sat at it, pulled out a piece of stationery, dipped the pen in the inkwell several times, then began writing to her uncle Peter.

"Dear Uncle Peter," she wrote. She looked up at Reby. Would she and Reby ever be friends again?

Perhaps they had never been friends. Reby pretended to like Callie to survive. Callie made a noise. It wasn't her fault Reby was a slave. It was the luck of the draw. Or fate. Or whatever.

"I am home now from my time in Europe," she continued writing. "I am sorry to say I have received no letters from anyone and I feel quite at sea in my own home. Uncle James is my guardian, but no one can find him. I wonder if I could prevail upon you to look for him. Could you come for a visit? I'm worried about the finances and the plantation. I am concerned about my slaves, too. There is much I'd like to discuss with you. Your devoted niece, Calantha Carter."

Callie folded the sheet and slipped it into an envelope. She closed the envelope and wrote her uncle's address on it. Then she heated red wax and let it drip on the flap. She pressed her Mount Joy seal into the wax.

"Reby," Callie said.

"Yes, Miss Callie," Reby said. She held a maroon-colored silk dress in her arms.

"I know that you're angry with me," Callie said, "but I need to know if I can trust you."

"Of course," Reby said.

Callie tried to look into her eyes, but Reby avoided her gaze. Everything in the world had changed since she had come home from France, including Reby. It must be very strange for Reby, to have lived in freedom for a year only to come home to this, to worry about being sold and sent away from the only home she had ever known.

Callie sighed. She hadn't thought much about these things before. In France it had all seemed so abstract, and the plantation had seemed so far away.

"I need to get this to post without my aunt and uncle seeing it," Callie said. "If they see it, I'm fairly certain they'll take it, and it'll never be sent. Dr. Sawyer will be sending Meager back today. If you could get this to Joseph, he could give it to Dr. Sawyer's man to post."

"I could do that," Reby said, "but Henry takes out the post every day. No one ever checks to see what's in it."

"All right," Callie said. "That's a bit less complicated than my plan. But all right."

Callie looked at Reby. Reby tried to suppress a smile. She couldn't do it. They both started laughing.

"I'm so sorry for what happened to Heddie," Callie said. "It never occurred to me that she could be hurt by what I did."

"Your aunt and uncle can't physically hurt you," Reby said. "But they can hurt your possessions. They can kick the furniture."

"I wish people would stop comparing slaves to furniture," Callie said. "Besides, Heddie wasn't mine. They damaged their own damn property."

"In the eyes of the law, we are furniture," Reby said. "Plain and simple."

"Would you like to be free, Reby? We've never talked about this. Do you think you could get on in the world by yourself?"

"Do you think you could get on in the world by yourself?" Reby asked.

"If I didn't have my aunt and uncle blocking my way," Callie said. "I am relatively well-educated. I have funds at my disposal—or would have. I have this place. Yes, I could get on. Without it, I don't know. I'd probably end up in a ditch dead someplace. Or in a brothel."

"Callie!"

Callie laughed. "You asked. I have no idea what I'd do."

"Would you want to try?" Reby asked. "If you could be free of your aunt and uncle, but you couldn't have your money or your land, would you want it anyway?"

"But that wouldn't be right," Callie said. "I couldn't let them take everything."

"We're talking pretend here," Reby said.

Callie thought of her aunt telling her that she might really be a slave baby. The idea had terrified her—mostly because she couldn't imagine her life as a slave, without family or any money.

"I don't really know," she finally said. But she did know. For now, she had decided to be quiet, to play the little mouse, while she planned her escape from this situation.

"I know what I'd do if I had the choice," Reby said.

"You'd take your freedom," Callie said.

Reby nodded. She took the letter from Callie and put it in the pocket of her shift.

"You're braver than I am," Callie said.

Reby shook her head. "No, I have less to lose. Now let me help you get out of that dress. I hear you had lunch with Dr. Sawyer? Are you two courting?"

Reby began unbuttoning Callie's dress in the back.

Callie laughed. "Heavens, no. You know we were childhood friends. But I think he is someone I can rely on. At least I hope so. We have tough times ahead and I could use all the allies I can get."

Dinner with her aunt and uncle seemed interminable, but Callie got through it. She tried to amicably answer any questions they had. She ate quickly but not too quickly. Soon enough it was over, and she was allowed to return to her room when she told them she had a headache.

After Reby helped her undress and then dress for bed, Callie read for a time. Then she fell to sleep.

Sometime later, she once again awakened to whispers in her room.

"Reby?" Callie called.

She didn't get an answer. She quickly got out of bed, lit the lantern, and walked around the room. The light chased away all the shadows. She was alone in the room. She heard a distant noise that seemed to come from the direction of the wardrobe. She walked to the back of it. She held the lamp in the space between the wall and the wardrobe. She noticed for the first time a crease in the wall, or a line. She pressed her free hand on the wall.

When her hand reached the other side of the crease, the wall gave a bit. She pushed harder. She heard a click and a piece of the wall opened.

A secret door?

Callie held the lantern into the dark gap the open door created. She couldn't see anything.

She thought she heard whispers again. She opened the secret door a little wider and squeezed herself through the opening a little ways, enough to hold up the lantern to see where she was. It looked like a very narrow passageway.

Leading where?

Callie went all the way through into the secret room.

The floor felt solid beneath her. She stepped carefully forward. The air was musty, the walls close.

She thought she heard footsteps.

She hurried forward. Suddenly she was at the top of the rickety stairs. She looked down. Thought she saw a light. She stepped on the stairs and walked down, slowly, quietly. Following the light.

She went down one flight. At the landing was a kind of anteroom. She stood in the space for a moment, breathed deeply, then stepped on the narrow steps again and went down.

The light below her went out.

She came to the end of the stairs. She heard voices on the other side of the wall.

"Walker!" Reby's voice. "When did you come?"

"Earlier," he said. "I snuck in when everyone was away. I went up to the third floor but something was in the way."

"Miss Callie sleeps there now," Reby said. She whispered. They both whispered. Callie pressed her ear against the wall. "They banished her."

"You look good," Walker said. "You liked Paris."

"I did," Reby said. "We had a good time. Walker, you can't stay here. It's gotten very bad."

"I heard," he said. "But my work is more important than ever. As war nears, things will continue to get worse. Sellis was captured."

"I didn't know," Reby said.

"They're keeping it quiet," he said. "They don't want it getting out that a mere slave was able to get so many other slaves up north. They'll kill him after a time, I'm sure."

Sellis? Who was Sellis, Callie wondered. She didn't recognize the name. Of course, she didn't know the names of many slaves, especially if they weren't her own.

"Shh," Reby said.

Callie held her breath.

"I thought I heard someone coming," she said. "Not that Mr. Charles or Mrs. Elizabeth would ever come into the kitchen."

Ah, so they were in the kitchen.

"Callie already knows I'm here," he said. "I thought she would have told you. I saw her earlier, but she didn't recognize me."

"She didn't tell me," Reby said. "It has been strange since we got home. She wanted to get Pearl back to the house so she pretended Heddie was poisoning her. Almost got Heddie killed."

"I asked Callie not to tell you," Walker said. "I didn't think she'd do as I asked. I don't remember her ever doing anything anyone ever asked. She was a wild child."

The two of them laughed quietly. Callie thought about pushing open the door and surprising them. They could talk about their childhoods together and her trip with Reby to France. Like they were old friends.

Only they weren't old friends. Callie was their mistress. They were her slaves. At least one of them was. She wasn't sure what her relationship was with Walker. Hadn't her father sold him?

"Can Sellis tell them anything?" Reby said. "About the

others? Will they torture him to find out?"

"He can't tell them anything," Walker said. "I think it'll be all right."

"Why are you here?"

"Since I knew the area, Momma Gospel wanted me to come down and help."

"They catch you," Reby said, "and they will beat you down and sell you as a slave again. Your papers won't mean nothing here."

"We are all slaves until we are all free," he said. "Whether I'm working in the fields or up in Boston working for that lawyer, I can hear the cries of all people still in shackles."

They were silent for a moment.

"This is not the life our momma wanted for us," Reby said.

Callie suddenly realized she didn't know who Reby's mother was. Or her father. She knew very little about her. Because she hadn't cared. Callie had only thought of her in the context of her own life, her own world.

Just as she hadn't realized Henry was Heddie's father. She hadn't known because she hadn't taken an interest in their lives.

Callie felt sick to her stomach.

Because she viewed them as furniture, just like Reby said.

"No, this isn't the life she wanted for us," Walker said. "But our parents are dead. We're orphans."

Orphans? So their mother and father were dead.

"You all right here with the master and mistress gone?" Walker asked.

"I'm fine so far," she said. "That Barnaby has been sniffing around. I don't like the way he looks at me."

Callie's stomach lurched.

"I stay away from him the best that I can," she said. "Hopefully his daddy doesn't have designs that way either. I don't sleep near Miss Callie any more, so I am in harm's way."

Callie put her hand over her mouth to stifle a groan.

This couldn't be true, could it? Her cousin and uncle weren't nice, but they couldn't be evil.

"Momma told me to be prepared," Reby said. "It happened to her. Could happen to me."

Callie felt sick.

"I could take you up north, Reby," Walker said. "You could be free of all this."

Callie suddenly realized she was listening to Reby and Walker plan a crime: Helping a slave escape was a crime. Shouldn't she do something? Shouldn't she stop them?

She moved back from the wall. She shouldn't be listening to this. It wasn't her business. It wasn't a conversation meant for her ears.

Carefully she stepped onto the stairs and walked the two flights up to her floor. Now that her aunt and uncle were her guardians, she understood a little better why Reby or Walker or anyone else would want to be free at any cost. No human being had a right to enslave another human being. She didn't know why she hadn't understood this all before. But now she felt it in her bones.

She should not own a person. A person was not a piece of furniture. No one should own anyone else. A husband shouldn't own a wife. Parents shouldn't own children. Most definitely nobody should own another person in order to force them to work for them.

Now that she knew these things to be true, she wasn't quite sure what to do about it.

Maybe in the morning she'd have an answer.

Callie waited until after breakfast, after her aunt and uncle had gone into town and all the slaves were out doing the laundry or in other parts of the house. She lit a candle, popped open the door behind the wardrobe, and then walked down the first flight of stairs.

She held the candle up to the walls as she walked around the landing looking for a door. She pushed on the walls, but nothing gave.

So she continued down to the next floor. She listened for any sounds, and then she again looked around for a door. The stairs ended and then a corridor went off into the darkness one way. She pressed her hands against the wall, near where she had been listening last night.

A part of the wall popped open slightly. The kitchen was empty so she stepped out and closed the slender door behind her. The door was right next to the pantry. Now that it was closed, she could not tell it was there. She pushed against the wall to pop it open again, but it didn't move. She tried again and again.

She hurried out of the kitchen, down the corridor, into the entry hall, and then went up the stairs. By the time she got to her room again, she was out of breath and her candle was out.

She closed her door and locked it. Then she lit the candle again, breathed deeply, and went behind the wardrobe. She walked down both flights of stairs until she was at the kitchen landing again. This time she didn't open the kitchen door. Instead, she walked to the end of the corridor. Once there, she pushed gently against the wall. Nothing. She was at a dead end.

That didn't make any sense. She bent down and pushed on the wall near the floor. She heard a click and a small door—like a half door—opened. Sunlight flooded in. She blinked and looked out. A leafy bush grew in front of the door. Good. She didn't want anyone to see her. She looked around enough to get her bearings. She was a hop, skip, and jump from the stables.

She quickly moved back and shut the door.

The house had been built just before the Revolution. She vaguely remembered her father mentioning once when she was young that his ancestors had hid in the secret passages when the British came during the Revolutionary War. She hadn't known then who the British were or what the Revolutionary War was. The only thing that had interested her at the time had been the hidden passages. Her father hadn't known if the story was true, and she hadn't been able to find any secret passageways, so she had soon lost interest—and she had forgotten all about it until now.

Since the house had been in her father's family and she and her father had been the only remaining Carters, odds were that no one else knew about the secret passages.

Except, apparently, for some of the slaves.

How could she find out who knew what without letting Reby know she had spied on her last night?

That was the least of her problems, Callie thought.

While her aunt and uncle were still out, Callie decided to look for the condolence letters. Either everyone in town was lying about writing to her—including Benjamin—or else her aunt was keeping them from her. She couldn't imagine why Elizabeth would hide letters written to her, unless it was to isolate her and make her depend upon them only.

Callie went through the whole house looking for them. She opened every door, every drawer, and every cupboard searching for the letters.

She left her mother's desk in the east parlor for last. Elizabeth had moved most of her mother's things out of the way, but her inkwell was still there—and her stationery.

Callie remembered her mother sitting at this desk while Callie played at her feet when she was little. Callie would look up at her mother throughout the day, and her mother looked down at her, smiling, pen poised in her hand.

"What are you writing about?" Callie asked her mother more than once.

"I'm writing to my friends about my wonderful life here with you and your daddy," her mother answered. "I'm telling them all about the wildflowers. About how the blue iris surprises us here and there in ditches and out in the fields. How the coneflower looks like a young girl in the wind with her arms outstretched, her pink hair flowing behind her. There's such beauty all around us."

Now Callie sighed and opened her mother's desk drawers.

Sitting here made her ache.

She didn't find any letters.

She got up quickly and left the room.

Eight

That night in bed, Callie whispered into the darkness, "Mother and Father, I don't know what to do. How can I protect this land, how can I protect myself, how can I do what's right? How can I survive this?"

She could almost hear her mother say, "One question at a time, Callie love."

But she didn't hear her mother. Or her father.

"I can't let them have this place," she whispered. "But I can't take it from them. I've tried fighting them. They're stronger and more powerful than I am."

Her mother used to say wildflowers could fix anything. Uncle Charles had seen that one lone jewelweed next to the tombstone in the graveyard and he had yanked it up and thrown it away. The green leaves and the small orange flower had been like a light in the graveyard—so visible and easy to snuff out.

Her mother had told her jewelweed often went unnoticed. It didn't usually grow alone but in a tangled community of leaves and blossoms. It was a wonderful kind of masquerade: to be disguised amongst all those who looked like you.

Right now, Callie stood out. She was angry, grieving, outraged. She was like that one jewelweed in the graveyard. Someone was going to come by, yank her up, and throw her away.

Maybe if she acted like everyone else, she could do whatever she needed to do to save herself and everyone else on the plantation.

She had to go back to her original plan: to pretend to be the inconsequential teenage girl. She had to blend in. At least until she figured out what she needed to do.

"I shall become like the jewelweed," Callie said. "In fact, I will become Jewelweed, a great heroine who can outwit any fiend by pretending she is completely ignorant and aligned with them in all things."

Every time her aunt and uncle did something to outrage her, she would become Jewelweed. She would pretend to be obedient, somewhat doltish, without a care in the world.

"Thank you, Mother," Callie said. "And you, too, Father. Don't worry. I won't let Uncle Charles bankrupt Mount Joy. Not while I have breath in me. I don't know yet how I'll stop him, but I'm working on it."

Callie closed her eyes and fell to sleep quickly for the first time since her parents died.

Callie became Jewelweed, and she got quiet. She began to watch everything and everyone. She had never done that before. When she was a girl she had been at the center of everything. Even if she was pouting or angry. Now she was quiet and agreeable. If her aunt or uncle asked her a question, she answered as though she was glad to be part of the conversation.

Same with the slaves. She watched and was quiet. She realized they watched, too. They probably wondered what she was up to. But no one mentioned it. Not even Reby. Probably because Callie talked easily with her, as though nothing had changed, as though her parents had never died, Heddie had never been beaten, and Callie had never overheard Reby talking to her brother about an organized effort to take slaves up north.

Callie wondered who Momma Gospel was. Normally she would have asked Reby. But not now.

Nothing was the same. She had no friends. No safe harbor.

She couldn't talk to anyone about what was happening—or what might be happening—without possibly getting someone else in trouble.

So she watched. And listened.

She planned the "ball" with her aunt. She made suggestions about music, food, flowers, but she didn't argue with her aunt, even when she thought her choices were gaudy. Elizabeth seemed to like a lot of gold. She said she wanted people to know Mount Joy was prosperous, and seeing gold everywhere would put them in the mind-set of prosperity.

Her aunt did agree not to call it a ball since it would be taking place only six months since Callie's parents had died; instead, it would be a welcome home dinner for Callie, only they would have music, too. And beautiful gowns.

Barnaby stopped by for tea now and again. Callie usually sat quietly sewing in the parlor while he and his mother talked.

"Why is my cousin so quiet?" Barnaby asked one day. "Is she afraid you're going to tell the world she is a pickaninny?"

Aunt Elizabeth took a sip from her cup.

"She is no such thing," Elizabeth said. "I'll thank you to be civil to Callie. She is the daughter I never had. Your father had you. Now I have Callie." She flashed a smile at Callie. "Unfortunately the Ames men aren't known for producing many children. Except for Peter, and then I think that's Charlotte's doing. She's a little rabbit. Of course she drinks more than I do. Maybe that was my problem. I should have drank more. Anyway, my family, the MacDonalds, are as fertile as rabbits. But I knew going in that I might not get the large family I always wanted. Perhaps it wasn't the men. Callie's mother and father only had her. And all I got was you. You, Barnaby, who hardly ever say a word to me. It can get so tedious spending your day making certain the servants do as they should. And to only see black faces all day long, except for Callie and sometimes your father. It is better here than at our plantation, at least; we are not so far from everyone. Callie and I have been having such fun planning the ball. Er, the welcome home dinner. I've had more conversation with her over the last week or so than I've had with you for your entire life, Barnaby. It's been most pleasant, hasn't it, Callie?"

"Indeed, dear aunt," Callie said.

A daughter? Her aunt saw her as a daughter? Callie blinked slowly. The idea made her sick to her stomach.

"I do apologize, Mother," Barnaby said. "I didn't mean anything by it. And I certainly didn't mean for you to launch into a diatribe against the reproductive systems of the Ames family."

Callie didn't look at her cousin, but she knew he was not sorry about anything.

"I think I'm having a difficult time remembering that Callie's all grown now," Barnaby said. "And we cannot tease each other like we did when we were children."

Reby walked by the parlor door just then. Barnaby watched her until she was out of sight.

"You were a mean boy," Elizabeth said. "And you should work harder to distance yourself from that mean boy image. You should be courting and finding a wife. I'd like some grandchildren to spoil."

"I am working on that," he said. "In fact, I'm hoping to have news soon on that front. Now, I must find Father and get some work done. I'll leave you two to your women's work."

Callie looked up at him. He said "women's work" with such derision that he nearly snarled. She had not realized that she could hate anyone as much as she hated her cousin. For a second she wished she wasn't her mother's daughter so she wouldn't have to be related to him.

When she was in control of the plantation once again, she

would not allow him on her property.

Barnaby left the room. Callie listened to his footsteps fade away as he went.

After a moment or two, she said, "Aunt Elizabeth, I wonder if I could ask you about something. I am embarrassed to bring it up. I fear you will think less of me."

"What is it, child?" Elizabeth said. She set down her cup and looked over at Callie. "I want to help you in any way I can."

"Could it be our secret then?" Callie asked. She put down her sewing and gazed at her aunt. "Just between us two. Like mother and daughter."

"Did you have secrets with your mother?" Elizabeth asked.

"Of course," she said. "Didn't you with yours?"

Elizabeth shook her head. "No, my mother was a tired mean old woman. Even when she was young."

Callie smiled. Elizabeth smiled and then laughed. Callie laughed, too. It was almost a genuine laugh.

"I've been a little lonely," Callie said. "I know you wanted Reby down here working, but I wonder if she might sleep upstairs with me. I've never slept alone, except for these last few weeks, and sometimes I am afraid."

She was afraid Barnaby was going to catch Reby alone one of these days. Or nights.

"If Reby could come up with me," Callie said, "she could sleep in my room. Or there's a tiny maid's room near my room. I would appreciate it."

Elizabeth chewed her bottom lip.

"But I wouldn't want anyone else to know," Callie said. "I wouldn't want Barnaby or Uncle Charles to think I'm a coward."

"Of course not," Elizabeth said. "It'll be our little secret. Reby can go upstairs with you to sleep. But I want her up bright and early working."

"I promise you that," Callie said. She smiled. "Thank you so much, Aunt Elizabeth."

Elizabeth picked up her cup again. She had a faraway look in her eyes. Callie wondered if she was reconsidering her decision.

"My mother always thought you were such a wonderful addition to our family," Callie said. "She was glad when you married Uncle Charles. She told me that. I see why now."

Her mother had actually said that Charles was lucky anyone had agreed to marry him at all, and Elizabeth was not the worst of the bunch.

That was nearly the same as saying Elizabeth was a wonderful addition to the family.

"Yes, well," Elizabeth said. "The Ames brothers did not have an immaculate reputation. I made a leap of faith. So far, fate has been kind to us. Now, the seamstress is due any time. Have you decided on the style of your dress?"

Callie smiled. "I wanted to wait and see what you thought."

Elizabeth smiled and said, "Well, then."

Callie thought it interesting—and odd—that she could hide her entire true self and no one seemed to notice. It made her feel lonely, but she didn't dwell on it. She was amazed at how much the feeling in the house had changed since she had decided to pretend to be compliant. She no longer felt as though her life or the plantation was in immediate danger. And now that Reby was in the room next to hers, sleeping with the door locked, Callie felt confident she was no longer in danger from Barnaby, at least at night. So her temporary loneliness was of no matter.

People began dropping by the house, mostly Elizabeth's friends. Callie had never had many friends and the few she had were mostly married now. Some had left the county. Some hadn't. Callie had seen the guest list for the welcome home dinner, and she hadn't recognized many of the people on it.

One afternoon, Betsy Turner and her daughter Mary Jane came for tea. Mrs. Turner and Elizabeth sat on the sofa talking and drinking tea. Mary Jane and Callie sat at a table near the window. Mary Jane drank tea while Callie sewed.

"I cannot wait for your ball," Mary Jane said. "Do you think there will be many men there? Momma says nearly all your aunt's male relatives will be in attendance, from all over."

"Truly?" Callie murmured, pretending she didn't care.

"Oh yes," Mary Jane said. "To help you find your bridegroom." She laughed, then put her hand over her mouth. "Maybe I can scoop up one of your leavings."

Callie didn't look at the girl. She barely knew her, yet Mary Jane had not stopped talking since she arrived. Callie carefully pierced the white cloth with her needle and then pulled it through to the other side. She was glad Mary Jane talked so freely because now Callie understood the reason for this welcome home dinner: Her aunt and uncle wanted to make certain Callie married someone in the family. Someone they could control, no doubt.

Mary Jane started describing the dress she was going to wear to the dinner. Callie let Mary Jane's voice fade to the background as she listened to the conversation between Mrs. Turner and Elizabeth.

"You heard about the darkie they found north a ways," Mrs. Turner said. "He was helping escaped slaves find the underground road, to leave here. When do you think they had time to build an underground road? We keep them plenty busy on the farms. Have to. They're so lazy; if you don't beat them constantly, they won't work. Hard to believe they built an entire underground road on their own."

"Betsy dear," Elizabeth said. "It's not an actual road. I believe the Northerners call it an underground railroad, run by escaped blacks and other criminals to take slaves up north."

"They have a *train*?" Betsy asked.

Callie wished she could see Betsy's face. Her eyes must have been as big as saucers.

"It's not a railroad either," Elizabeth said. "I think it's some fable the Northerners came up with to entice the slaves North. I don't believe it's real."

"No, I think not! We would have noticed an entire train of blacks going up and down the countryside."

Callie wanted to laugh. Elizabeth sighed deeply.

"I don't believe this underground railroad has ever run south of the Potomac in fantasy or in reality," Elizabeth said. "We have nothing to fear."

So that was what Reby and Walker had been talking about:

the underground railroad. Callie had heard some gossip about it before she left for France. In France, a man at a dance she attended asked her about it once, and she had told him she had no idea what it was.

"It's sounds quite heroic actually," the man had said. Callie couldn't remember his name now, only that he was English and had that clipped superior way of talking. "To help take people to freedom. To help shake off the shackles of slavery."

"Most slaves don't wear shackles," Callie had said.

"That's hardly the point," the man said. "These men and women who live like dogs, only worse, somehow manage to escape detection while tramping through fields and swamps, to find their way north because a few brave souls help them on their way."

Someone had asked her to dance then, and she had gratefully escaped to the dance floor. At the time, she had not wanted to continue the conversation. Now she wished she could remember every word the man had said.

"Mary Jane, could you stop prattling on about your dress," Betsy said. "You'd think you had never been to a ball before. Why can't you do something useful like Callie?"

"I didn't think to bring my sewing," Mary Jane said. "May I help you, Callie?"

Callie picked up the other end of the tablecloth she was repairing and gently put it in Mary Jane's lap.

"It will help if you hold it," Callie said. "Thank you."

The girl smiled at her. "I heard you were in school in France. That must have been something! I couldn't make the journey. I get seasick just thinking of being in a boat. See. Right now I'm getting sick."

"Tell me what your summer plans are," Callie said.

"Well, my cousin Daniella from Georgia is coming—"

And so she was off.

Callie tried to prick her ears toward Elizabeth and Mrs. Turner again.

"Callie has certainly mellowed," Mrs. Turner said quietly. "I remember her as quite a headstrong child."

Remembered her? Callie certainly did not remember *her*.

"It's a testament to your tutelage that she is coming along so nicely," Mrs. Turner said.

"Thank you," Elizabeth said. "But I've only been with her for a month or so. Her mother is to be congratulated."

"Yes, well, if only we could."

Callie glanced up, but her aunt was not looking at her.

"You don't suppose anyone in our county would help escaped slaves?" Betsy said.

"No!" Elizabeth said. "The people here are law-abiding."

"But the Quakers," Betsy said. "I've heard rumors."

"It's all nonsense," Elizabeth said. "You shouldn't believe everything you hear."

"Dr. Sawyer's mother is a Quaker, you know," Betsy said. "And I believe she's freed all her slaves."

"Betsy! You are so gullible. I wish you would stop spreading such gossip. No one around here would help any slave escape and you should be particularly careful about saying such things around your own slaves. You wouldn't want to put ideas in their heads."

"No, certainly, no ideas. You are right as always, Elizabeth. Thank you."

The two women sipped their tea.

"Have you invited Mrs. Sawyer to the ball?" Betsy asked.

"It isn't a ball," Elizabeth said. "It is a welcome home for our Callie. But yes, of course, I've invited Mrs. Sawyer and her son. They are old family friends, and it's good for Callie to keep in touch with old friends while she makes new ones. And you wait and see, Mrs. Sawyer won't be helping any slaves escape. I promise."

Callie could feel Elizabeth's gaze on her, but she kept drawing the thread through the cloth. She wondered if everything and everyone was really far more complicated than she could have ever imagined.

Nine

The day of the welcome home dinner, the house began filling up with company by noon, mostly with people Callie did not know. Aunt Elizabeth had invited Therese Sawyer to stay overnight as a companion for Callie. Callie knew Benjamin far better than she knew his sister, who was a couple of years older than Callie. But Therese was harmless enough, and it would be nice to have a temporary companion.

Therese arrived after lunch. Elizabeth put her in a room down the hall from Callie. Some of Elizabeth's nephews bunked on the third floor, too.

The rest of Elizabeth's family stayed on the second floor. Elizabeth introduced them to Callie, but Callie couldn't tell them apart. They all looked alike in a nondescript kind of way. Pale with blond hair. Pudgy but not fat. She could tell they did not work out of doors—or anywhere else, for that matter.

Callie hadn't realized Elizabeth had so many relatives. Her many nephews each practically licked their lips when they first met Callie. They smiled at her, raised an eyebrow, and then looked around the house, as though calculating how much it was worth.

They were so vulgar that Callie could hardly stand to be in the same room with them for even a few seconds. She wanted to slap their faces or tear them down with a particularly witty and vicious comment, but she knew that would not serve her. Instead she closed her eyes for a second, and when she opened them again, she was Jewelweed.

"My, my," she said more than once. "I had no idea Aunt Elizabeth had such charming and handsome relations. Tonight will be glorious for certain. I do so look forward to making your acquaintance."

Barnaby was staying at the house, too, unfortunately. She hoped no one had mentioned where Reby was sleeping. Her aunt seemed to have forgotten about the small room near to Callie's where Reby now slept. She was looking forward to talking with her Uncle Peter who was coming to the dinner with his wife, her aunt Charlotte; maybe then she could set things right.

Callie sat in front of her mirror while Reby gently laced up her corset.

"Not too tight," Callie said. "I like it looser, like how the French women wear them. You remember, Reby."

Reby nodded.

Martha pinned Callie's dark black hair on top of her head,

except for two curls that fell down to her shoulders on either side. Callie watched herself in the mirror as Martha wove a purple ribbon through her hair.

"You look beautiful, Miss Callie," Martha said. "All grown-up now."

When she had turned sixteen, her parents had thrown her a ball—a kind of coming out party. She had been so excited. She had felt grown-up then, ready to create a new life for herself, away from her parents.

She and her mother had gotten ready for the ball down in her old room.

Callie sighed and blinked away tears. She didn't want to do this. She didn't like parties much. She got tired of the gossip. She heard the same stories over and over, true or false. All everyone seemed to be able to talk about was who had made the latest faux pas, or who had offended whom. Or if it wasn't that, the girls were talking about which boy they would or would not marry. The boys only wanted to talk about themselves and how they would take over their father's plantations once they finished school.

Hardly anyone thought about the whole wide world. Or if they did they didn't talk about it. Callie wanted to discuss poetry or music. Or the way the trees changed color in the fall. Or how beautiful the swans were when they returned to Far Pond every year. She wanted to talk about something besides the color of someone's dress or the continued outrage over some trivial slight.

When she was younger, she had tried to fit in. She knew to do otherwise would have meant she'd have a lonely life, and she wanted her parents to be proud of her. It had been their idea to send her overseas. She was good at painting and her parents thought Parisian teachers could help her get better. And they thought she would meet more worldly people than the ones she knew in St. Charles.

Reby pulled the corset tighter, and Callie closed her eyes. Strange how she had not thought much about drawing since she had gotten home. In fact, she had nearly forgotten she had ever drawn or painted.

She had been a good botanical artist. Better than most. She had taken some pride in that, until one of the Englishmen she had met in Paris clucked when she told him she was doing botanical art.

"You mean you draw flowers? How charming! But doesn't every young woman draw flowers? Why travel all the way to this hedonistic country to draw flowers? Don't you have flowers in America?"

Something about the way he said "flowers" and "America" made Callie want to slap him. Yet she guessed he was only articulating the scorn other men felt about her avocation.

She loved plants. Was there anything on creation that was more amazing than plants? They ate sunlight. They converted sunlight into food. They were, essentially, sunlight, in all its various guises, brought down to earth.

She had come to her appreciation of flora naturally. When she was a child she walked the fields, woods, and plantation gardens hand in hand with her parents. Her father knew the names of all the trees, lichen, and moss; her mother knew the flowers. Callie had never been very good at remembering the names, but she could remember their structure, their color, which way the leaves grew off the stem, their smell.

Now tears filled her closed eyes.

"Miss Callie?" Martha asked. "Are you all right?"

Reby handed Callie a handkerchief, and she wiped her eyes.

"I'm fine," she said.

Reby and Martha continued to look at her, concern on their faces. She nodded and smiled. She didn't need to burden them with her sudden flood of memories and grief.

She had been happy in France away from her parents. Now she wondered how she could have been so happy without them.

It was natural, her father would have told her. She was growing up. She was becoming an adult. She was an adult. She should take joy in pleasures away from her parents.

If she had been home, would her parents have been in that carriage?

Or would they have all been in the accident together?

Callie shook her head. No. It was useless playing out these what-if scenarios in her head.

Reby finishing tying the corset. Callie stepped into her petticoats. Next came the hoop skirt, another layer of petticoats and then finally, Reby and Martha lowered the dress carefully over Callie's head. The dress was made from fabric that was such a dark purple it looked almost black.

"There," Martha said. "You are a beauty."

Reby smiled. Callie knew they felt sorry for her. Because she had lost her parents? Because she had to go to this dinner? Because she had to pretend to be someone else? Had either one of them even noticed the change in her? Why should they? She didn't notice anything about their lives. She didn't know where Martha's family was, or even if Reby had other siblings besides Walker. She had never known.

Maybe someday she would ask, but not this day.

"Mrs. Ames wanted me to help some of the other ladies," Reby said.

Callie nodded. "Go, both of you. I'm fine."

After they were gone, Callie left her room and walked slowly down the stairs. She felt like she was going to burst out crying. She couldn't break down now. She had to be Jewelweed. She breathed deeply, shook herself, and kept walking.

The first part of the evening was a blur. Callie politely and enthusiastically greeted everyone as though she hadn't a care in the world.

While she shook hands and curtsied and asked how everyone was doing, she tried to take in all that was happening. Several new slaves were helping out. She vaguely wondered if they were Aunt Elizabeth's slaves or if they had brought in some field slaves.

Soon enough the house was filled with guests. The servants had set up sideboards in the dining room so people could eat when they wanted. On the other side of the sun parlor, in the ballroom, a small orchestra played. The scent of freshly cut flowers mingled with the smell of perfume and sweat.

Mrs. Sawyer embraced Callie when she and Benjamin came into the entrance hall. Callie held onto her tightly. She blinked away tears before she let go of her.

"It's so nice to see you," Callie said. "You've met my aunt and uncle, I'm sure."

"Of course we know Mrs. Sawyer," Elizabeth said. "How are you, Maeve? And Dr. Sawyer. So nice to see you."

"Welcome," Uncle Charles said. As though he was welcoming Mrs. Sawyer into his home. "How was the ride over?"

"Hello, Callie," Benjamin said as his mother and her aunt and uncle chatted.

Callie smiled at him, the big wide smile she had been flashing at everyone. "Why, it's so nice to see you, Dr. Sawyer."

He frowned. Callie realized her voice sounded a little high.

"Save a dance for me," Benjamin said.

"Of course," Callie said.

"Now, she knows you like a brother, Dr. Sawyer," Elizabeth said. "We want her associating herself with some of the fine young men who have come from all around the countryside to meet her. We are more interested in those who might want to court her."

Callie bit the inside of her lip. Benjamin caught her eye. She smiled and batted her eyelashes. She was going to have to get better at pretending.

Just then, Uncle Peter came down the stairs with Aunt Charlotte. Callie hurried over and embraced her aunt and uncle warmly. She had always liked them.

"None of my cousins are coming?" Callie asked her aunt.

"They are so busy with school or their new families," Charlotte said. "But they all send their love."

"And Janice would love for you to come for a visit,"

Charlotte said. "She just had her first baby, and she's feeling a bit lonely out on the plantation with her husband gone so much."

"I would love to visit," Callie said. "I shall write at once!"

Her uncle Peter kissed her on the cheek and then said, "Later on we will talk. Unfortunately your aunt and I need to leave first thing tomorrow."

"Yes, of course," Callie said.

Callie flitted from group to group. She made certain each guest had enough to eat and drink, and she encouraged everyone to go into the ballroom and dance. A few of her old schoolmates were amongst the guests, but she didn't have much to say to them. She was afraid if she talked with anyone she knew well, she might say something wrong and give her "pretend" self away.

She ate little and drank even less. Her aunt kept re-introducing her to her nephews. Callie danced with them one by one, although she could barely tell them apart. They all smelled alike—some kind of pungent metallic odor—and their palms were sweaty. She knew they couldn't help either of these physical manifestations. Maybe she could have ignored their physical anomalies if even one of them had an interesting thing to say. But none of them did. They never asked about her. Instead they talked on and on about hunting and fishing and keeping their slaves in line. They talked about profit margins and wondered what would happen if the war started. They were all secessionists and assumed she was, too.

She was relieved when it was time to dance with Benjamin.

"You look beautiful," Benjamin said before they began the dance, "as always."

"Thank you," she said brightly. She was so tired she wanted to rest her head on Benjamin's shoulder, but they were doing the Virginia reel, so she didn't have an opportunity to do anything but dance and smile.

When the dance ended, Benjamin said, "Do you want to get some air?"

Callie looked around the dance floor. One of the MacDonald cousins was making a beeline for her. She took Benjamin's arm.

"Yes, please. Let us step outside."

They walked through the crowded ballroom and sun room, then crossed the drawing room and headed for the back entrance. She saw her uncle Peter across the room and he nodded. She mouthed the words, "I'll be right back."

"Callie!"

Callie turned to see who was calling to her. She saw Judge Zebadiah walking toward her. She curtsied to him.

"Welcome," Callie said cheerfully. "I hope you have gotten something to eat."

"We have indeed," he said. "Your aunt puts on a good party." He seemed to be watching for her reaction.

She smiled and said, "Yes, she does. Everything has turned out nicely."

"And how are you these days?" he asked.

"I am grateful for the allowance," she said, "and I feel better knowing that my slaves can't be sold from under me. That has made me feel more secure. I thank you so much."

"And Mount Joy," he asked. "How is it being managed?" He squinted as he asked the question. She remembered he had warned her about spreading false accusations about her uncle or cousin.

"I am sure it is fine," she said loudly, "because you, Judge Zebadiah, and my uncle will make certain that Mount Joy will remain prosperous for me and my children"

She smiled.

"I'm pleased to hear it," he said. "Now enjoy yourself. It's good to see you as yourself again."

He turned and walked away.

Benjamin and Callie went outside. The air was cool and clear. She gulped it eagerly.

No one else was outside. Callie supposed that meant they had thrown a good party. And no one had seemed to notice it was not a year since her parents had died. Perhaps Aunt Elizabeth was correct: Customs were changing. The threat of war did that.

Callie and Benjamin went down the walk and turned onto the garden path. Callie had barely been here since she had returned home. When she was younger, she had spent so much time in these gardens, caring for the flowers and the vegetables with her mother. She was certain Aunt Elizabeth never got her hands dirty. Who cared for the gardens now? It was too dark to see if all was well. Torchlight here and there made the shadows quiver.

"Are you having a good time, Dr. Sawyer?" Callie asked. She flipped open her fan and waved it in front of her face.

"I am," Benjamin said, "but I would have a better time if I knew why you weren't acting like yourself."

"I am acting exactly like myself," Callie said.

"No." Benjamin shook his head. "Yourself is always questioning and causing trouble. Protecting what needs protecting. Where are you?"

Callie looked around. She hoped no one was hidden by the shadows, listening.

"Benjamin," she said quietly, "everyone is happier when I am quiet and compliant."

"Are you all right?"

Callie put her arm through Benjamin's. "You are kind to worry about me," she said. "You are kind to even notice. Everyone else seems quite happy with this change in me. It's been interesting to step back and watch and see how things are done. I'm learning quite a lot."

"I enjoyed the old Callie," Benjamin said.

I'm still here, she wanted to whisper.

Instead she said, "It's about high time I learned to get along. Isn't it? Easier for everyone."

"I don't think you can be blamed for Heddie," Benjamin said. "If that's what this is all about."

"I can," she said. "You warned me. But I went ahead. And other things have happened." She shook her head. She suddenly heard the music inside, and she looked at the house. The windows were golden with light.

"I miss my parents so much that I ache," she said. "But I have to figure out a way to survive this. And I will."

"Promise if you need anything, you'll let me know," Benjamin said.

"Of course," Callie said. "But I don't want to put you in danger."

"Callie," Benjamin said, "I have this sinking feeling that you are plotting something."

"I am plotting nothing," Callie said. "I am too dim for plotting. I do need some help. I think Aunt Elizabeth wants to marry me off to one of her relatives. I've danced with every boy in her family tonight. Do you have any advice on how to discourage them without angering my aunt? You've always been so diplomatic."

"You could tell her there's too many of them," he said, "and you could never pick one."

Callie laughed. "I like that."

"Or you could tell her you are already being courted," he said.

"But I'm not being courted," she said. "And I have no desire to be courted. What good is there in getting married, for a woman, I mean? So many of the women in our community spend their lives being pregnant, having nine, ten, eleven children! My mother was fortunate not to have had more children. I think most men view us as nothing more than brood mares!"

Benjamin laughed. "Now that is the Callie Carter I know and love."

Callie growled. "You bring it out in me," she said. "It is difficult to be stupid around you. The others expect it."

"So you admit you've been pretending!"

"I admit nothing," Callie said.

Benjamin patted her hand on his arm.

"If need be," Benjamin said, "you can tell them that I am courting you and that you are interested."

"That's not fair to you, Benjamin," Callie said. "Isn't there someone you'd like to court truly?"

"Not now," he said. "If someone comes along, then I'll tell you and you can send me on my way."

"I appreciate the offer," Callie said. "For now, I will tell them I am too young, and I am still mourning my parents. Perhaps that will put an end to it. If not, I'll go with your plan. But only if we told your mother the truth. I wouldn't want to lie to her. This is beginning to sound complicated. Like one of my plans."

"It must be your influence on me," he said.

"Well, good doctor," she said. "I better get back inside. May I have another dance?"

"You could have them all as far as I'm concerned," Benjamin said.

They turned back toward the house. The air was beginning to cool. Callie thought she heard a heron call out in the near distance, down near the water.

"I don't remember noticing how kind you were when you were a boy," Callie said.

"I don't remember you noticing me at all," Benjamin said.

"Of course I did!" Callie said.

She dropped her hand from Benjamin's arm and put on her fake smile before they went back inside. She looked at Benjamin. His beautiful blue eyes seemed sad.

"Be careful, Callie," he said. "I'm concerned about you."

Callie flipped open her fan again and waved it in front of her face.

"I'll be fine," she said. "It's all going to work out."

Ten

"**D**r. Sawyer," Callie's uncle Peter strode toward them with his right hand thrust out to shake Benjamin's hand. "It is good to see you."

The men shook hands.

"May I steal my niece from you?" Peter asked.

Callie waved her fan again. "Shouldn't I be asked if I'd like to be stolen?" She smiled and glanced at Benjamin. She could tell he was about to roll his eyes, so she squeezed his arm and then let go of him and reached for her uncle.

"I wouldn't mind some fresh air, too," Peter said.

Callie put her hand through Peter's arm. She and Benjamin looked at each other. He seemed worried. When had he started to worry about her? No need. She was going to figure out how to take care of herself one way or another.

Callie looked away from Benjamin and up at her uncle as they walked out of the light and into the darkness again. For an instant, Callie saw the family resemblance between Peter and her mother, and Callie's stomach lurched. When would it stop hurting so much?

The music had stopped. More people came out of the house, leaving by the front door, the ballroom door, and the library door. All of them ended up in her mother's garden.

Peter walked away from the others, toward the kitchen end of the house.

"I got your letter," Peter said. "As you can imagine, I was quite distressed by it. I've talked with Charles, Elizabeth, and the judge. I've also gone over the books, cursorily."

An owl called out in the distance. Looking for its mate? At this time of night it should already be out hunting.

"And what do you think, Uncle?" she asked.

He patted her hand. "I think the death of your parents has been a great shock to you," he said. "As it was to all of us. I think it was wrong for Charles and Elizabeth to have made you stay in Europe. If I'd known it was against your will, I would have sent you the money to come home. I'm worried that all that has happened the last six months has unsteadied you a bit."

"What do you mean?" Callie asked. She felt a little sick to her stomach.

"You accused your uncle and cousin of misdeeds in public," he said. "You refused to eat until your own cook was brought back to the kitchen. You've spent little time out of your room since you've gotten home."

"I helped Aunt Elizabeth plan this dinner," Callie said, "this dinner which I believe goes against our mourning customs. But still, I was obedient. I think I've been doing quite well."

"I know your Uncle Charles and his wife can be difficult to get along with," Peter said. "Charles has ambitions. As does Elizabeth. But I do believe they have your best interests at heart. The books look fine as far as I can tell. They've given up the idea of having Barnaby as overseer." He cleared his throat. Callie could hear the murmurs coming from several other conversations taking place in the garden. She could distinguish no words. It reminded her of the sound the swans made at night, at Far Pond, as they settled down to sleep and dream.

Peter stopped and faced his niece.

"I've talked to the judge," he said. "He's given you an allowance. That should help things."

He seemed to be trying to look at her eyes, discern something from her face.

"Callie, it's important that you try to fit in," he said, "that you get along with everyone. I know why your parents sent you to Paris. I'm afraid others might find out, and it would do nothing for your reputation."

"I'm sorry," Callie said. "I don't know what you mean. My parents wanted me to broaden my horizons and take art classes from the masters."

Peter stared at her. She could see the torch flames reflected in his eyes.

"I know about Abraham." He said these four words as if

that would explain everything.

"I'm sorry, Uncle," Callie said. "I am completely mystified. We had a stable boy here named Abraham. But Father sold him before I left for Paris."

"Callie," he said, "I don't wish to pry but your mother spoke to me about this. She asked for my advice."

Callie bit the inside of her lip. What was her uncle talking about?

Callie looked at her uncle, her eyes wide to indicate she had no idea.

He leaned toward her and whispered, "She told me you had developed an affection for this boy."

Callie shook her head. "Of course I had affection for him. I have affection for all the slaves. They are my responsibility."

"She believed you had a different kind of affection for him," he said. "The way a woman has affection for a man she marries."

Callie stepped back. What? Her mother would not have talked to her uncle about something like this. It was not possible.

It was true that she had looked forward to seeing Abraham. And maybe she had sometimes devised plans to be in his company.

Reby had once asked her if she was sweet on Abraham. At the time, she had felt her face becoming red as a beet, so she had turned away from Reby and said, "Certainly not! How could you ask such a thing?"

One day she saw Reby and Abraham kissing in the stables. She'd told her mother. Soon after, her father sold Abraham.

Reby had been teary-eyed for weeks.

Callie had always wondered why she told her mother. It had been out of character for her.

"Uncle Peter, I can assure you that my mother was absolutely mistaken!" she said. "I wish she had spoken with me about it. I would have reassured her."

"She didn't want to embarrass you," he said. "She thought it would be good for you to get out into the world and meet new people. But your aunt tells me you still have an unnatural devotion to your slaves."

Callie didn't know what to say to him.

"I don't understand," Callie said. "Are you saying I'm sweet on Henry or the stable boy Joseph?"

"No, of course not!" he said. He lowered his voice and took Callie by the arm. "I'm saying if you have any notion of freeing your slaves like Mrs. Sawyer did, you had better stifle it. Dr. Sawyer suffers to this day for his mother's decision. Notice he can barely make his living as a doctor."

In that moment, Callie understood that Uncle Peter would not be her savior. No one could save her from her circumstances.

She sighed.

"Did my mother talk to anyone else about Abraham?" she asked. "She was mistaken, of course! But I would hate for anyone else to know."

"I don't know, Callie," he said. "Your mother didn't confide with many people, but she did occasionally come to me for advice."

"As did I," Callie said.

"My advice is to go on with your life," he said. "Be young and free. Go to dances and balls. Socialize. That's what all the young people are doing. Secession may or may not come. War may or may not come. Trust that the court and your relatives are taking care of your finances. You'll have enough money and property to find yourself a good husband."

"Thank you, Uncle," Callie said. She felt sick to her stomach.

"Let's go back in," Peter said. "You should be in dancing! That's how I met your aunt, you know, at a party like this one."

In another moment, they were back inside the house. Callie felt woozy. The room seemed to tilt a bit. Her uncle kissed her cheek and then walked away. She tried to look around and find someone to lean on, to ask for help. There was no one. In disgust, she turned away from the party.

She needed to get a bicarbonate. Something. She was supposed to ring for a servant. She didn't want to talk to anyone. To ask anyone anything. Even a servant. It was too noisy here. Too much light.

She went through the dining room and into the front pantry. Darkness.

She sat on the stool there and put her head in her hands.

She breathed deeply. After a bit, she began to feel better.

She got up, walked through the hall and the office and into the kitchen.

In the semi-darkness, Callie saw Reby and Joseph crouched over someone on the floor. The someone was groaning.

"He's shot clean through," Joseph said.

"We've got to get him out of here," Reby said. "Before—"

She looked up and saw Callie standing over them. Reby gasped and stood.

Callie saw the face of the man on the floor. It was Walker.

He looked up at her. His face was ragged with pain. And anger. He gazed at her with hatred.

She looked down at his leg. She couldn't see anything amiss in the darkness.

"What happened?" Callie asked.

"He was shot in the leg," Reby said. "Slave hunters. Somehow he made it back here."

"And put you all in danger," Callie said.

Callie heard voices in the dining room. Footsteps.

"Hurry up," Callie said. "Put him in the secret passage. Take him up to my room. Lock the door and don't let anyone in but me."

Reby stared at her for only a moment. Then she reached under a cabinet. The narrow door Callie had come through the other day now popped open. Reby and Joseph helped Walker up.

"Quickly!" Callie said.

The three of them disappeared into the darkness behind the door. Callie hurried to the door and leaned against it to shut it just as Aunt Elizabeth walked into the kitchen with Barnaby.

"There you are," Elizabeth said. "Someone thought they saw you come in here."

"I was feeling sick to my stomach," Callie said. She opened a cupboard. "I was trying to remember where the sodium bicarbonate was. Oh, here."

She took the bottle down from the cupboard.

"Poor thing," Elizabeth said. "I've never seen a child so sickly."

Aunt Elizabeth got her a glass of water. Callie poured some bicarbonate in the glass and stirred it with her finger.

Barnaby looked around the kitchen.

"Did you need something, cousin?" Callie asked.

He shook his head. "No. I thought I heard you talking to someone."

"I was," Callie said. "I was talking to myself. Wondering why I was feeling unwell. I certainly didn't want to spoil Aunt Elizabeth's party."

Callie took a gulp of the bicarbonate. She made a face.

"Nonsense," Elizabeth said. "Go lie down for a bit. Come down when you feel better. The boys will anticipate your return. Next time, ring for a servant. That's what they're here for. I don't like you back here."

Callie nodded. She set the glass down on the counter.

"Thank you, Aunt Elizabeth," Callie said. She kissed her aunt's cheek. "Cousin." She bowed slightly and walked past them.

She went through the office and then stopped in the pantry and listened.

"I thought I heard someone else in here," Barnaby said to his mother.

"What does it matter?" Elizabeth said. "All is well. She's spoken to Peter. He'll be gone soon and all will be normal again."

Callie quietly grabbed a couple of clean towels and a bottle of vinegar. She then hurried through the pantry and the dining room. In the entrance hall she looked around. Should she ask for Benjamin's help? Or would that endanger him?

She hurried up the stairs before anyone noticed her.

Her heart beat in her throat as she ran up the next flight of stairs and then down the hall to her room. Fortunately, the third floor was empty of people.

She knocked on her door.

"It's Callie," she said.

She heard the key turn. Then the door opened. Callie went inside, closed the door quickly behind her, and turned the key in the lock. They had lit the lamp and drawn the curtains. Walker lay on the floor. Callie handed Reby the towels and the vinegar.

"I didn't know what else to get," Callie said. "Elizabeth and Barnaby came into the kitchen."

She grabbed a pillow from her bed. She handed it to Joseph, and he put it beneath Walker's head.

Reby pulled up Walker's pant leg. Callie could now see the wound on his calf.

"I think it went straight through," Joseph said.

Reby rolled up one of the towels.

"I'm going to put some vinegar on the wound, Walker," Reby said. "You can't scream." She handed him the towel. He opened his mouth and bit down on it. "Joseph and Callie, hold his leg still."

Joseph moved around Reby so that he could put his hands on Walker's thigh. Callie held his ankle.

Reby gently cleaned the wound with the other white towel. Then she poured vinegar on the wound.

Walker's leg shook, and the towel drowned out his scream.

A moment later his leg stopped moving, and he took the towel out of his mouth.

"Should I get Dr. Sawyer up here?" Callie asked.

Reby shook her head. "He doesn't have a fever. We can tie it up and he can leave tonight."

Callie shook her head. "He'll just get caught if he goes out tonight. He can stay here. No one would guess this was where he was."

Reby, Walker, and Joseph looked at one another.

"Joseph, you should probably get back to the stables," Callie said.

He looked at Reby. She nodded.

"Go out the secret passageway near the stables if you think you can do it without anyone seeing you," Callie said.

"I know the way," he said.

He got up and went behind the wardrobe and disappeared from Callie's sight.

"Reby, can you get Walker some fresh water and food? Say it's for me if anyone asks. See if you can find some bandages, too."

She nodded, got up, and left the room.

Callie locked the door.

Then she stood over Walker. "Looks like it's just the two of us." She grinned. "What would people say if they saw us now?" She laughed. Then she covered her mouth with her hand. What was wrong with her?

"Did I land with a crazy woman?" Walker asked.

"I think so," Callie said. "Can I get you anything to make you more comfortable?"

He shook his head. He looked around the room.

"You've been here before, haven't you?" Callie asked. "I think you've slept in my bed."

"No, Miss Callie," he said. "I wouldn't do that."

"No sense playing dumb now," Callie said. "I heard you the other night. I heard you and Reby down in the kitchen."

"That was private," he said.

"Yes, it was," Callie said. "I shouldn't have been listening. But this is my house. I wondered why a strange man was running up and down secret staircases. I figured it out, though. You're part of the underground railroad. I heard you talk about Momma Gospel."

Walker made a noise and lifted himself up onto his elbows.

"I need to get out of here," he said.

"Oh, lay on down," Callie said. She felt reckless and strangely free.

"I'd rather die standing," he said.

"You think you're going to die?" she asked. She bent over and looked at his wound.

"It isn't bleeding," she said. "At least not much. It doesn't look infected. You will mostly likely live. Unless you're discovered in here. Then you'll be dead. They'll kill you, I'm sure. Hang you, for certain, if they don't run you through."

She began pacing as she talked. She glanced over from

time to time at Walker and saw that he was watching her.

"I have had my home taken from me," Callie said, "and my parents are dead. My only other living relative who gives a damn about me is missing. I was told today that my other relatives believe I am close to going insane. They figure this because they believe I was attracted to a slave boy." She looked at Walker. His eyes widened. She suspected he really did think she was crazy.

"That's a reason to declare me crazy," she said. "That and the fact that I publicly tried to get the law to do something about my cousin Barnaby. I believe he is a thief and a gambler. Now I'm supposed to sit around while ugly, smelly, and stupid boys try to woo me. Ugh! I won't do it. I've been pretending that I'm stupid, that I agree with them about nearly everything. I can continue pretending, but only if it is in service to something or someone. So I have decided in this instant—or maybe I decided it before and couldn't say it out loud—but now I say it out loud. I have decided I want to help in the underground railroad. I don't think anyone should be enslaved to anyone else. I can't free my slaves because I have no legal rights. But I can help as many escape as possible. Or help others escape. I don't care. I want you to take me to Momma Gospel."

Walker looked up at her. "My sister never told me you were crazy."

Callie sat on the floor and leaned against her bed. Walker moved back until he was propped up against the wall near the wardrobe.

"Why is that crazy?" she asked. "Don't other white people help in this underground railroad?"

"There are some," he said. "But it's difficult to believe someone like you could suddenly have a change of heart and want to help us."

"It isn't a change of heart," she said. "It's a change of understanding. I didn't understand before. I thought things were the way they were. It didn't occur to me they could be different. Now I see they can be. Now I see that but for the grace of God, I could be you."

He frowned.

"If my skin were black," she said, "or if the world were different. I just learned how different the world is from what I believed." She rubbed her eyes. "I just learned my parents sent me to Europe because they believed I was lusting after our stable boy. Can you imagine?"

"Imagine you lusting after Joseph?" he asked.

Callie looked at him. Odd how free she felt to say anything to him. Even if the anything might seem improper to someone else.

"Not Joseph," she said. "Abraham. He was a nice boy. I painted his portrait with Sergeant."

"Abraham," Walker said. "So that's what happened. I wondered why he was sold so suddenly. Did you know Reby and Abraham had an understanding?"

Callie groaned. She had forgotten Reby had been sweet on Abraham. She had forgotten Walker was Reby's brother.

"Now I suppose you'll tell Reby and she will hate me even more," Callie said. "Go ahead. It doesn't matter. She should hate me."

"I think a little you're upset," Walker said. He grimaced as he adjusted his leg.

"You think I'm not thinking clearly?" she asked. "You're right. I'm not clear and I'm clearly selfish. You're lying there bleeding onto my floor and I'm trying to coerce you into taking me to Momma Gospel." She looked at Walker, and he looked her straight in the eyes. She didn't see hatred this time.

"Let's say I do ask Momma Gospel," he said. "You would have to be discreet. Are you capable of discretion? I haven't seen any evidence of that."

Callie felt like her head was spinning. All her thoughts kept going around and around.

"I know I'm young," Callie said. "And lately I've learned that I am also ignorant. But I can learn. I've learned to keep my mouth shut and listen. I discovered you in the secret passages and I didn't tell anyone, and I have no intention of telling anyone. Now I have a chance to do something good with my life, by helping you and others."

Walker closed his eyes. Callie leaned over and looked at his leg.

"Does it hurt?" she asked.

He shook his head. "I'm trying to figure a way out of all this," he said. "Without anyone getting hurt, including me. I was helping someone escape from a plantation up the river. You don't need to know who or where. The slave hunters caught up with us. I went one way, he the other. Heard shots and then it felt like a flame was being held to my leg. Not sure what happened to the other man. They'll still be looking for me. Their hounds might follow the blood all the way here. I didn't think of that. Not sure why I came here. It was the wrong thing to do, like you said, leading them straight here."

"If they follow the scent here, they won't come into the house," Callie said.

At least she didn't think they would.

She'd have to make certain the slave hunters didn't come into the house.

Someone knocked on the door.

"Miss Callie." Reby's voice.

Callie got up and unlocked the door. She opened it slightly until she could see that Reby was alone, standing near the door carrying a tray with a sandwich and a glass of milk on it. Callie opened the door wider and Reby came inside the room. Callie locked the door again, and Reby dropped down beside her brother. She set the tray next to him and then handed him the sandwich.

"It is all sixes and sevens down there," Reby said. "Mr. Kaiser from down the road came in and said they were huntin' some escaped slaves. I could swear I heard their dogs howling and coming this way, although Mr. Kaiser said they were a couple of miles away."

Reby pulled a roll of bandages from her pocket. She checked Walker's wound and then began wrapping it.

"If those bloodhounds get the scent of my blood," Walker said, "they'll come right here. They'll blame Reby if they find me. I should leave." He started to push himself up.

"It's a little too late to be reasonable now," Callie said. "Where did you come onto the property?"

"I came in by the stables and then through the secret door that comes out that end of the house."

"I heard hot peppers can throw dogs off the scent," Callie said. "That might be an old wives' tale, but I'll try it. Plus I'll take some of your blood to confuse the hounds." Callie leaned over and picked up the bloody towel. She folded the blood inside and made a ball out of it.

"You can't go running outside in that dress," Reby said. "You're bound to get blood or dirt on it. How would you explain that?"

"Your brother thought I was crazy," Callie said. "So I'm sure I can convince everyone else I'm insane too."

"Why not wear your cape?" Reby said. "I haven't put it away yet. It's in the back of the wardrobe." Reby quickly finished wrapping Walker's leg. Then she jumped up and hurried to the wardrobe. She opened the doors and reached inside and pulled out Callie's long black cape.

"Perfect," Callie said. She put the cape on and pulled it around her dress. She stuffed the towel into one pocket.

"If someone knocks on the door," Callie said, "Walker better go into the secret passageway."

Reby nodded. "Of course. Where will I say you are?"

"I went to see how the party was going," Callie said. "With any luck, I'll be back soon."

Callie went behind the wardrobe and popped open the door. She slipped into the passage and quickly went down the stairs toward the kitchen. She pressed her ear against the door and didn't hear anyone. She opened the door a crack and looked around. The kitchen was empty. In distant parts of the house, she could hear people talking. No music played.

She left the door open and reached up into the cupboard

for the hot peppers. Pearl liked to grind some into dust every year. Callie grabbed the jar and put it into the pocket of her cape. Then she went back into the secret passage and closed the door behind her. She hurried down the dark corridor until she came to the end of it. She listened at the door. Then she crouched down and opened it carefully.

She slipped into the night. She kicked the dirt at her feet, hoping to confuse the dogs if they got this far. Then she took out the jar of hot peppers, opened it, and sprinkled some on the ground all around the door.

She thought she heard men talking, but she wasn't certain where the voices came from. She held her breath and listened. By now her eyes had adjusted to the darkness. Several torches burned at the stables. Henry and Joseph and any of the other stable boys were probably playing cards inside while they waited for the party to be over.

Callie began walking away from the house. Crouching down, she continued to sprinkle the hot pepper dust onto the ground. When she got to the stables she stopped and looked around. Yes, there were Henry and Joseph, sitting at the other end of the stables, just outside, smoking and talking.

Callie kept walking. She noticed something in the light-colored dirt near one of the torches. She bent over. Drops of something dark. Maybe Walker's blood.

"Damn," she said. She sprinkled hot pepper over the drops and kicked at the dirt to disperse it all. Then she hurried to the bushes on the other side of the stables. She took out the towel, opened it, and rubbed it on one of the bushes furthest from the stable. She walked a little ways farther, continuing north away from the house, farther into the night and toward the river. She heard crickets and frogs chirping and burping. They stopped every now and then as she moved and then started up again once she was still. Suddenly fireflies began blinking off and on all around her.

Callie whispered a thank you for their light.

She kept walking and pressing the towel against this bush or that tree. She glanced back several times and watched the lights of the mansion getting farther and farther away. She could only hear her own harsh breathing now. It was too hot and humid to be running around in the dark in her black cape.

In the distance she heard dogs barking.

Her heartbeat sped up. She broke out in a sweat. The ground felt soggy. She was near the marsh. She thought she could hear the river flowing by not too far away. If she wasn't careful, she would end up in the river, drowned.

She heard the sound of men's voices coming from the direction of the house. Coming nearer. And the dogs were howling. They had picked up the scent. She could tell by their baying. They were coming eagerly toward her.

She faced the river and balled up the towel as tightly as she could. Then she threw it with all her might.

She put her hands behind her ears and gently pushed them out—her father used to call it making deer ears—and she listened above the men hollering at the dogs, listened above the dogs baying.

She heard the plop as cloth hit water.

She hoped the swift water quickly took it away, downstream.

She immediately started walking back toward the house. The lightning bugs continued to surround her. She could see the smaller torches the men carried bouncing up and down as they walked, the light of the torches blotting out the light from the fireflies.

The dogs were almost on her.

Did bloodhounds attack? She didn't know. She had no idea what would happen next.

Suddenly the bloodhounds surrounded her. Their howls were deafening. She put her hands over her ears and stood in one place as they encircled her. A moment later, several white men she didn't know stood a few feet from her. They looked astonished to find her.

"I demand to know what you are doing trespassing on my property!" Callie said. "Call off your dogs at once."

"Who are you?"

"Who am I? Who are *you*! I am Calantha Carter, and you are walking upon my land and your dogs are attacking me!"

One of the men stepped forward and made a noise that caused the dogs to stop barking. They sniffed the ground near her feet.

"I'm Dave Tenant," he said. "Tonight I'm working for the folks at the Whetner plantation. They've got an escaped slave. What are you doing out at night so far from home?"

The other four or five men stood quietly, watching her and holding onto their torches.

"It is none of your business," she said. "But if you must know, the party gave me a headache and I thought a short walk in the night air would do me good."

She knew she shouldn't lie because the men might check her facts. "And then my cat Snooky raced by me and I went after her. I was afraid some nefarious creature would try to eat her for dinner."

They did have a barn cat, although Callie hadn't seen her in ages. Aunt Elizabeth and Uncle Charles wouldn't know anything about a barn cat one way or another.

The dogs began baying again. They headed toward the water.

"Who gave you permission to come onto my land?"

"We don't need permission," Tenant said. "We are slave hunters."

"I don't think being slave hunters exempts you from everyday laws or common decency. You may *not* be on my land without my permission no matter who you are or what you are doing."

"You better take that up with Charles Ames," Tenant said. "He gave us permission. Now if you'll excuse us, we need to follow those dogs."

The men were still looking at her. Callie suddenly understood why her mother had warned her about running around alone at night where she might run into strange men.

They all followed the dogs. Callie hoped they didn't find the towel. She watched them file past her until she was alone in the dark again.

She took out the hot peppers and sprinkled the rest of the contents of the jar all around her, in case the dogs came back this way.

Then she picked up her cape and dress so the hem didn't drag and she practically ran back to the house.

Eleven

Callie went through the hidden half door. Then she listened at the secret kitchen door before she pushed it open and went into the kitchen. She put the hot pepper jar back in the cupboard. Then she shook off her cape. She turned up the kitchen lamp and looked down at the hem of her dress. Not too bad. Her shoes were a little muddy and wet. She grabbed a towel and quickly wiped her shoes off. She started to toss the towel onto the table, but she stopped. Someone might get in trouble. Instead she pushed it into her cape pocket. She opened the secret door, tossed the coat into the passageway, and then shut the door again.

She hurried through the pantry and the hall and back into the dining room. She heard no music coming from across the way. People milled around the buffet table and nodded to her as she passed. She barely recognized anyone. When her parents had given parties, she knew everyone. Who were these people? Parents of the boys Elizabeth was trying to push on her?

Callie smiled and nodded at everyone.

"I hope you are having a lovely time," she said several times.

She crossed the entrance hall and then wove through her guests as she went through the parlor. She saw Barnaby standing next to Therese. Barnaby looked over at Callie. Therese smiled and waved. She looked starry-eyed, as though she had imbibed a little too much punch or wine. She flicked her fan in front of her face as she grinned at Callie.

Callie saw Benjamin across the room in the sun parlor with Lucy Johnston. Her blond hair was piled up on her head. It looked as though pearls and baby's breath had been woven through her golden locks. The pale blue dress she wore made her skin look whiter than it already was. Benjamin stood next to her, his hands behind his back. His curly black hair looked tousled, as it often did. Callie smiled. He could be her brother. They had similar coloring and features.

He saw her and smiled. Callie nodded. How beautiful he and Lucy looked together. She felt a tinge of jealousy, or something. She shook her head and quickly looked away from him. Why should that matter to her? She wanted him happy. He was a man who should have a good steady wife and lots of children. He was a good man. A family man.

She glanced over at him again as she hurried through the parlor. She had thought about having him look at Walker's wound, but she was not going to bring him into her criminal enterprise, no matter how worthy it might be. She would not put his livelihood or his freedom in jeopardy.

She wished she could talk to him about what she had discovered tonight—about why her parents had sent her to France. Not because they thought she was a talented artist who should see the world. But because they thought she was about to run off with a stable boy.

How could they have never talked to her about Abraham? Had they such little faith in her judgment? She would never become involved with a slave! People didn't do that.

She picked up the skirt of her dress and hurried into the ballroom. She looked around the golden-lit room. She recognized more people in here, especially her new acquaintances: Elizabeth's nephews. The room smelled of perfume and cologne even though all the doors and windows stood open. She saw Elizabeth standing near the musical stand, wringing her hands.

Callie hurried over to her.

"What is it, dear aunt?" she asked.

"Oh, it's a disaster," she said. "First you become ill and then the slave hunters! Now all people can talk about is war, and the musicians don't want to play for fear of throwing the dogs off."

Callie laughed. Her aunt looked at her.

"I'm serious," she said.

Callie put her hand on her aunt's arm.

"I'm much better now," she said. "I got some air. And the musicians will play when we tell them to play. Don't let these minor things upset you so."

Callie stepped away from her aunt.

"Attention all guests to Mount Joy," Callie said. "Attention!"

Soon the murmuring ceased as everyone turned to look at Callie. She smiled and gazed around the room.

"It is so good to see so many old friends," Callie said, "and so many new friends. This land, this house, was created for joy. Thus the name!" She smiled. Across the sea of faces, Callie saw Benjamin come inside the room with Lucy on his arm. "I have just been outside, looking for my cat, Snooky. She wandered toward the marsh again. I swear some alligator's gonna wander up this way and snatch her, or some Yankee is gonna wander down this way and corrupt her, try to set her free!"

The audience laughed appreciatively. Benjamin smiled wanly. She hoped he remembered she was only pretending.

"In any case, I encountered the slave hunters," she said, "and their dirty smelly dogs. Yes, I appreciate dogs, but I am a cat person. They have more personality, and I more easily succumb to their charms."

She knew her audience. Everyone was laughing and smiling. She glanced at her aunt. Uncle Charles had come to stand next to Elizabeth. Even they looked like they were relaxing. They were enjoying her acting like the perfect Southern belle, too.

"The dogs got their scent," she said, "and they were headed toward the river. I don't really care what the dogs are doing now. Mount Joy is a place for happiness and joy. I want to hear music and I want to dance with every handsome man here—and that includes all you gentlemen! So maestro—" She turned to look at the conductor. "—may we have some music?"

The conductor smiled and nodded. He raised his baton.

Callie looked back at her guests. "What do you say, a clog?"

"No!" was the universal response.

"A Virginia reel then?"

Callie laughed as everyone cheered. She almost felt like herself. She looked around for her parents, to see how they felt about her performance. Like a punch to her stomach came the realization—again—that they were gone. She sucked her breath in and quickly turned to the conductor and nodded to him.

The music began.

Immediately one of Elizabeth's nephews came up to her and asked her to dance. She accepted.

The dance began.

Callie danced for a long while. She didn't hear the dogs again. She didn't see the slave hunters. She didn't see Uncle Peter leave. When the musicians took a break, Elizabeth's nephews gathered around her. She listened as the boys boasted about signing up to go off to war as soon as it started. Whenever it started.

"Tomorrow or ten years from now," one of the red-haired boys said, "I will defend our state."

The rest agreed. Callie tried to appear interested while ignoring them. She had succeeded in bringing the party back to life. But now she wished everyone would go home so that she could check on Walker and then figure out a way to get him out of the house.

Still, she hoped for one more dance with Benjamin. The nephews never seemed to leave her side, and it wasn't like Benjamin to intrude when he thought he wasn't welcome. When she saw Benjamin and his mother leaving the ballroom, Callie excused herself and went and linked arms with both of them. Benjamin motioned to Henry to get their coats.

"Mrs. Sawyer, did you have a good evening?" Callie asked.

Maeve Sawyer looked at Callie. "I did indeed," she said. "You have become quite the accomplished young woman. Your parents would be proud."

"Don't be fooled by all the Yankee stuff I said," Callie whispered.

Maeve patted her hand. "We all have to do what we have to do," she said. "You keep yourself safe and happy."

"Can you be safe and happy?" Callie asked. "It seems one would prevent the other."

"I don't know," Maeve said. "What do you think, Benjamin?"

Callie and Maeve looked at him.

"I believe one can be safe and happy," he said. "As long as one is living in a place of truth and honor."

Callie and Maeve looked at each other.

"Just like a man," Callie said. "I don't think he said a thing but he tossed in words like truth and honor—like a cook tossing crisp bacon into a salad. Once you eat it, you've forgot-

ten all about the carrots and the lettuce and cabbage and cau-
liflower and all you remember are those bits of bacon that
tasted so good. And that's all I remember about your little
pronouncement: truth and honor. Bravo, Benjamin."

Maeve laughed. Benjamin smiled. He shook his head.

"I could never fool you," he said.

Henry brought over their coats. He helped Benjamin on
with his and then Benjamin helped his mother on with hers.

Callie hugged Maeve and kissed both her cheeks.

"Come by and see me soon," Maeve said.

"I will," Callie said.

Callie held out her hand to Benjamin. He took it. Then she
leaned in, and he kissed her on both cheeks. She felt a spark of
electricity on her skin where his lips touched her cheek.

He whispered, "And you could never fool me either. Don't
go doing anything you'll be sorry about."

They looked at one another while he held onto her hand.
She wanted to tell him. She wanted to take him upstairs and
show him Walker and ask him what she was supposed to do.
It was all a great deal of responsibility, and she wasn't certain
she was up to it.

Callie smiled and squeezed Benjamin's hand. Then she let
it go.

"Good night, Dr. Sawyer," she said. "I will think seriously
about everything we discussed this evening."

Then the Sawyers were gone.

Eventually the only guests left were those who were spending the night. Callie asked her aunt's permission to go to bed,
to release her from her obligations to the nephews. Elizabeth

kissed her and told her to sleep well. Callie waited until she was on the second set of stairs, the ones leading to the third floor before she wiped the kiss off.

She hurried down the hall to her room. She tried the door, but it was locked. She knocked lightly on it.

"Reby, it's Callie," she said.

She heard the key turn. She opened the door, slipped inside her room, and locked the door again.

Reby turned the lamp up slightly. Walker was curled up on the floor, his head on one of her pillows. He appeared to be asleep.

"No fever," Reby said. "The wound seems to be healing well. He ate, and he's been drinking. He'll be able to go soon."

"Not until we know that the slave hunters are gone," Callie said, "at least from our property. He can sleep here tonight. We can all stay here together. Let's get him on my bed."

Reby shook her head. "He can't sleep on your bed!" She sounded disgusted.

"What? What did I do now? I've been running around all night pretending I'm someone I'm not so that your brother doesn't get caught and beaten or worse. Why are you angry at me?"

"Leave him where he is," Reby said. "He'd get blood on the bed and blood on the divan. He's slept on the floor all his life."

Callie made a noise. "I don't know what you want or expect from me. I didn't do any of this. It's not my fault that your stupid brother got shot!"

"Shh." Walker. "I'm trying to bleed to death here," he said softly. "Can't you argue later?"

Callie and Reby knelt next to him.

"How are you feeling?" Callie asked.

"Better," he said. "I appreciate you throwing them off my scent. Reby, you can be angry with her all you want, but she's right. I shouldn't have come here. I put you in harm's way. Miss Callie did a very brave thing. If she had been found out, it would have been very bad for her and all of us."

"She would have lied her way out of it," Reby said. "She's very good at playacting. She would have playacted the victim of her terrible slaves."

Callie rolled her eyes. "Get some rest, Walker. It'll be morning in a few hours. Then we'll figure out what to do then."

Someone knocked on the door. Reby and Callie looked at each other.

"Who is it?"

The doorknob jiggled. Someone was trying to get in.

"It's me, Therese. Let me in. Please."

"Just a minute."

Callie pointed to the wardrobe. But she realized that would take too long. She pointed to the bed. Reby helped Walker half-crawl to the bed. Reby flipped up the valance, and Walker pulled himself underneath the bed. Reby turned down the lamp so the room was almost in darkness.

Callie went to the door. She glanced at the bed once and then at Reby. Then she turned the key and opened the door slightly. Therese stood on the threshold, dressed in her nightgown.

"May I come in?" she asked. "Please."

"I'm getting undressed," Callie said. "It's been a long night. May we speak in the morning?"

"It's important," Therese said. She pushed open the door and stepped into the room before Callie could stop her. Not that Callie could have stopped her without making a fuss.

"I'm very tired," Callie said.

"I wouldn't bother you, except it's important," Therese said. "I can help you undress." She looked pointedly at Reby and then said to Callie, "I'd like to speak to you alone."

"Reby is a sphinx," Callie said.

"This is of an intimate nature," Therese said.

"Then I'm the last person you'd want to speak to!" Callie said. "I have a bit of a headache."

"But you are the one I need to tell this to," Therese insisted.

"Reby, could you get me a snack?" Callie asked. "Enough for two or three. I'm quite famished. Headaches do that to me."

Reby nodded and left the room. Callie closed the door and locked it. Therese didn't seem to notice.

"Let me help you out of your dress," Therese said.

"I'm fine," Callie said.

"Let me be your maid," Therese said. "We'll pretend we're old friends. We should be but you were always more friendly with Benjamin. You liked running around with the boys." She began unbuttoning Callie's dress. "I wanted to talk with you about your cousin."

Callie kept herself from groaning.

"I know very little about Barnaby," she said.

Therese worked quickly. Callie was already down to her corset, which Therese undid in seconds. Soon Callie was standing in the middle of the room in her chemise. She went to her wardrobe and pulled out a dressing gown and put it on.

"Maybe we should finish this conversation in your room," Callie said.

"I might lose my nerve if I wait one more second," she said. "Barnaby has been courting me. He wants to marry me, he says, but he has to get himself more financially secure."

"Do you want to marry him?" Callie asked. She tried not to sound incredulous.

"I do," she said. "I think."

For a moment, Callie almost forgot Walker was under the bed.

"Why?"

"He's handsome," Therese said. "And he finds me attractive. I haven't had a lot of beaus, Callie."

"You're beautiful," Callie said, "and intelligent. I'm sure you'll have many suitors."

Therese took Callie's hand and led her to the divan. They sat on it together. Callie was glad they couldn't see underneath the bed.

"It smells like a swamp in here," Therese said.

"I was out wandering," Callie said. "I must have brought some of the marsh back with me. Now tell me what you need to tell me so we can get some sleep."

"I do find Barnaby very attractive," she said, "but he keeps wanting to do things."

"What things?" Callie asked. "Whisper them to me if you must."

"He wants to touch me," Therese said. "And have me touch him. In a most ungentlemanly way."

"Ah, you don't need to give me the details," Callie said. "Suffice to say if he is acting improperly, then you shouldn't see him any more."

"But he says it's practice," she said, "for when we're husband and wife. To see if we're compatible."

"Oh my word!" Callie said. She leaned closer to Therese. "Are you saying he wants to have sexual intercourse?" She hoped Walker could not hear any of this.

"No," Therese said. "Why are you whispering? There's no one else here!"

"The walls sometimes have ears," Callie said.

"Haven't you ever had the urge," Therese asked, "when you're kissing a boy, an urge for more than the kiss?"

"No!" Callie said. "For one thing, I've never kissed a boy or a man."

"I sometimes forget that you are younger than I am," Therese said. "You seem to be a woman of the world!" She smiled. "I'm not certain what to do. Sometimes he seems so insistent. He said the reason white men take up with slave concubines is because their wives won't satisfy them."

"Therese," Callie said, "why would you continue to let him court you if he's saying these kinds of things to you?"

Therese shrugged. "He's a man. Men have needs. I don't fault him for that. He tells me how beautiful I am. How his desire for me is keeping him up at nights. I don't want to be the cause of him sinning."

"Have you spoken with your mother?" Callie asked. "I may be younger and inexperienced in these matters, but I can tell you he is wrong in pressuring you, in threatening to go off and force himself on some poor slave woman if you don't satisfy his carnal desires."

"When you put it that way," she said, "it does sound rather unseemly." She sighed. "I am different from my mother and my brother. They seem not to need anyone else. My brother has his career. My mother has her household and land. I need children. I need my own home. Everyone else I know is married."

"Don't let yourself be pressured into accepting someone who is not your equal," Callie said, "someone who is not good enough for you. Does your mother approve of this courtship?"

Therese shook her head. "We haven't told anyone. Barnaby wanted to keep it secret for now."

"You came here asking for my advice," Callie said. "My advice is that you don't go anywhere alone with Barnaby. You don't want him to force himself on you."

"He wouldn't," Therese said. "Would he?"

"It is better to be careful," Callie said, "and protect your reputation. There must be other boys who have come knocking on your door."

"Only Reverend Jones's son," Therese said. "Robbie. He seems so young."

"There is more to life than boys and marriage and children," Callie said.

"Maybe for you," Therese said. "But I have no other prospects. I'm not actually good at anything. I imagine I'll be good at mothering. Don't you suppose?"

"I'm certain of it," Callie said. "And how would you advise your daughter if some man were whispering the things Barnaby has been whispering into your ear?"

She nodded. "This gives me much to think about," Therese said. "Thank you. I will leave you to sleep now."

Callie walked Therese to the door. She unlocked the door and opened it. Therese left as Reby walked up carrying another tray of food. Callie let her in and then locked the door again. Reby set the tray down and then the two of them leaned over and helped Walker out from underneath the bed.

Callie turned up the lamp a bit.

"What was that all about?" Reby asked.

Walker and Callie glanced at one another. Then Callie said, "Nothing important. Let's all eat something and then get some sleep."

Reby slept on the divan, and Walker curled up near her. Interesting how one could adapt to strange circumstances so quickly, Callie thought in the moments before she fell to sleep. Maybe it was because this year had been filled with such strange and awful things.

Twelve

Callie slept without dreams.

Her aunt had given her permission to have breakfast in bed because of the party. Reby woke her up when she left to get breakfast so she could lock the door behind her.

After Reby was gone, Callie examined Walker's wound.

"It looks like it's healing," Callie said. "Much faster than I would have thought."

Walker pushed himself up and put his weight on his left leg.

"Does it hurt?" Callie asked.

"Nothing like it did yesterday," he said. "I can leave any time."

"If they're still out there looking for you, all we did last night will be for nothing if you get caught," Callie said. "Is there somewhere safe you could go? If so, I could take you there."

Walker watched her. "It seems you've always got some kind of plan. And yes, if I could get a little farther north, I could get in contact with Momma Gospel. When I see her, I'll let her know that you're willing to help."

"I'm willing to offer this house, too," Callie said. "We'd have to be careful because of my aunt and uncle, but we can use the secret passageways."

Walker shook his head. "I'm trying to think about all this. I've never worked with—"

"With a white person?" Callie asked.

"I was going to say I've never worked with a crazy person," he said.

Callie looked at him. He smiled.

"Forget all those things I told you yesterday," Callie said. "I was feeling crazy."

"Not today?"

"Today I know I'm crazy," she said, "but I want to do this. Did you hear what Therese and I were talking about last night?"

He nodded.

"You could have covered your ears," she said.

"I could have," he said, "but I didn't. That man has a reputation all through the county. I don't want him anywhere near Reby."

"That's why I moved her up here," Callie said. "I was trying to keep him away."

"He's forced himself on many women," Walker said. "And

girls. If that woman is your friend—"

"Her brother is my friend," Callie said. "I suppose I should tell him or tell her mother. I don't know why she told me. Maybe I should talk to Barnaby myself."

Walker shook his head.

"What?"

"You think you could handle him?" Walker asked. "He's a big man. I think he's a violent man. If I were you, I wouldn't let myself be anywhere alone with him, just like you told your friend."

"He wouldn't hurt me," Callie said. "Not in a million years."

"Don't be so certain," Walker said. "Certainty can get you into trouble. Look at me. I was certain I could help that man better than he could help himself. He knew the area better than I did, and now he's been caught, and I've been shot."

A few minutes later, Reby returned carrying a tray with three cups and three plates on it. The plates were heaped with food: eggs, potatoes, sausages, grits, toast. Steam rose from the coffee cups.

"Fortunately no one was in the sun parlor," Reby said, "so I scooped up what I could from the sideboard. Your aunt is asleep with a headache and your uncle has gone into town. Pearl said she heard the slave hunters have headed west, away from the river."

"That means I could take Walker north," Callie said.

Callie sat on her bed. Reby gave Callie and Walker plates and forks. Then she sat on the floor, and they all began eating.

When Callie finished eating what she could she gave the rest of the food to Walker. Then she went to her writing table and wrote a note to her aunt: "Dear Aunt, I promised Mrs. Sawyer I would stop by for a visit. If you want me home before dinner, just send Joseph to get me. Otherwise, I will see you this evening. Your niece, Calantha Carter."

She folded the paper in half and slipped it into an envelope. She turned around to face Walker and Reby. Reby was checking Walker's leg.

"This is what I'm thinking," Callie said. "Reby, you go downstairs and give this note to Henry for my aunt. Ask him to have Joseph get the big carriage ready. Dad used to call it his stagecoach. Ask Joseph to bring it out to the secret entrance nearest the kitchen. Then you and Walker can get down the secret staircases and to the door at the end of the house. Walker can go inside the coach and you can cover him with a blanket. Then I'll come out. Does that sound too complicated?"

"Yes," Reby said, "but I can't think of anything simpler."

Reby took the note and went downstairs. Walker got up and went into the secret passageway while Callie got dressed. Reby returned in time to help lace up Callie's corset.

"Tight?" Reby asked.

"No!" Callie said. "You've known me long enough to know the answer to that." She looked over her shoulder at Reby who was smiling. "If I could get away with not wearing one, I would do so in a heartbeat!"

"You could pretend you are a boy," Reby said, "like you did when you were younger."

"I wasn't pretending I was a boy," Callie said. "I liked being comfortable."

Callie looked at her reflection in the mirror. It would be easier to be a boy. Then she could do anything she wanted. If she'd been born a boy, she probably wouldn't have had to endure the guardianship of her aunt and uncle now.

But she wasn't a boy. She was a girl. A woman now. She had to dress like a woman.

Soon enough, Callie was dressed. She left her room while Reby went into the secret passageway to take Walker down to the carriage. Callie went down the hallway and knocked on Therese's door. No one answered.

Then she walked down the stairs. She was surprised at how quiet the house was, especially since there had been so many sleepover guests.

Henry stood near the parlor. The doors were closed, but Callie heard some of the nephews and their parents inside talking. She wanted to avoid them.

She motioned Henry over to her. When he came, she whispered, "Have you seen Miss Sawyer?"

"Yes, she left with Mr. Barnaby," he said. "After breakfast."

"Were they alone?" she asked.

"Yes, Miss Callie," he said.

She nodded and then quietly tiptoed across the hall, through the empty dining room, down the hall, through the pantry and into the kitchen. The kitchen teemed with slaves. They'd be cleaning up from the party all day.

Everyone stopped what they were doing and looked at her when she entered the kitchen. Callie glanced at Pearl and then looked away.

"Just going out the back door," Callie said. "Don't pay me any mind."

Callie kept walking. She could see the carriage outside. She went out the door. Joseph stood next to the carriage and opened the door as Callie approached. She put one foot on the stool and then stepped into the carriage.

Joseph closed the door behind her.

Reby sat across from her. A brown blanket covered a bundle on the floor. Callie closed the curtains.

"Did he tell you where to go?" Callie asked Reby.

She nodded.

"What did my aunt want you to do today?" Callie asked.

"Help clean up after the party," Reby said.

"Then you should stay and do that," Callie said. "We don't want her to have an excuse to be angry with either one of us."

Reby glanced down at her camouflaged brother.

"He'll be all right," Callie said. "I promise. Tell Joseph where to go on your way out."

Reby opened the carriage door and stepped out. Callie heard her give Joseph directions.

"And Joseph," Callie said, moving the curtains aside on the open window so she could see him. "If someone is coming our way, give a whistle so I know." He nodded.

Callie closed the curtains. The carriage sprang forward. She listened to the horse's clip-clop, clip-clop until they were out on the road. She closed the window and made sure all the curtains were tightly closed.

"Walker, get up. There's no reason to stay on the floor."

She pulled off the blanket. Walker unrolled himself slowly. He grimaced a bit as he pushed himself up onto the seat across from her.

"Are you all right?" Callie asked.

He nodded. "Hurt a little more than I thought it would going down two flights of stairs."

"But no one saw you?"

"No one except Joseph," he said. "As far as I could tell."

She nodded.

"Thank you for doing this," he said. "For keeping me safe."

"Of course," she said. "Tell me what you've been doing since you left Mount Joy so long ago."

"I went up north," he said, "and I've been working for a lawyer in Boston. Helping freed slaves stay freed. And other black folks who need legal help."

"Did anyone ever try to bring you home?" she asked.

"You mean to Mount Joy?" he asked. She nodded. "No. The man your father sold me to set me free."

"Why are you running then?" Callie asked. "You can walk around as free as any bird."

"Doesn't matter to the slave hunters," he said. "They'll capture any black man and bring him south. Any black woman, too. Because of the Bloodhound Law, a free slave doesn't have a right to trial."

"I didn't realize that," she said. "What about the man who set you free? Couldn't he tell law enforcement that you're a free man?"

"Why would he go out of his way for me?" Walker asked. "No, I'm on my own. Except for Momma Gospel and the others."

"Have you a family up north?" Callie asked. "Someone you can go back to?"

He shook his head. "No, my family is all down here. Mom died last year. But there's Reby. And I've got other brothers and sisters. I want to help them all get free."

"I'm sorry about your mother," she said. "I didn't know. Did she work for us?"

Walker looked at her. "You don't remember her?"

Callie shook her head. "No, I don't. Should I?"

He shook his head. "She was a house maid but she was sold a long while ago and was working in the fields. It broke her. She wasn't strong enough for field work."

They were silent for a few minutes. The carriage rocked forward and back as it went down the road. Joseph whistled a couple of times. Callie looked out the window. Another carriage passed by without stopping.

"It's all right," she told Walker. "No one is paying any heed to us. Do you do anything for fun in Boston?"

He shrugged. "I write poetry. I go and listen to other poets read poetry. I write letters. Receive letters."

"Who taught you to read?" she asked.

"My mother taught me and Reby to read the Bible," he said. "I learned more and better once I went up north."

"And you write poetry?" she said. "I wish I could write poetry. My mind is too undisciplined. Can you recite any of yours to me?"

"Let's see," Walker said. He thought for a moment and then recited, "A Primer on Dismantling Metaphor. Begin slowly. Remove your name and place it in a protected area for safekeeping. You may want it later. Now face the world as your own true self, unencumbered by the mask of the word you have been known by. Feel your flesh melt into the Earth. Taste your spirit flying through your tongue and draw the world as close as a nameless stranger asking for help."

"'Remove your name and place it in a protected place for safekeeping,'" she repeated. "I feel that I've done that. That I've hidden myself, for safety's sake, but one day I will face the world as my true self. That is an amazing poem. So unlike the ones I read in school."

"Thank you," he said.

"I haven't picked up my paints or pencils since my parents died. But now I suddenly feel as though I want to paint again. Paint that poem."

"I don't think I could ever draw," he said. "You need patience for that and I have very little. Plus you have to be satisfied with imperfection. That is difficult for me."

Callie laughed. "I have no patience. But yes, a living thing is perfection, so by definition a drawing will be imperfect. I like drawing the details on a plant, so that people can really see it. Sometimes it seems as though people only actually see the truth when they look at it drawn."

Walker nodded. "I hadn't thought of that."

"What a funny look you are giving me," Callie said.

"I was remembering you as a child," he said. "You couldn't sit still then. You were always getting into one thing or anothei. You ran around like a boy."

"I ran around like a person who happened to be free," Callie said. "You call it being a boy. I don't."

"I'll give you that," he said.

"And now, what surprises you about me?" she asked.

"You seem different," he said. "More thoughtful."

"I need to be," she said. "So much can happen if I do the wrong thing. I've learned that the hard way. Or perhaps I should say those around me have learned the hard way. I hope this turns out well, that my interference doesn't cause you harm."

Walker shrugged. "I'm still alive. That's good news to me."

They travelled out into the country. No one stopped them. Callie and Walker continued to talk about poetry and books. He told her about his meeting with Frederick Douglass.

"He looks at you when he speaks to you," Walker said. "Right into your eyes. As though you are important. He believes women should have the right to vote."

"Hah!" Callie said. "Slaves will be free long before women get the vote. White men trust white women even less than they trust black men."

"Have you read the Declaration of Sentiments from the Seneca Falls Convention?" he asked.

"I have," she said. "When I was in Europe. No one here told me about it, of course. I do admire Elizabeth Cady Stanton. She is a visionary and a great writer. 'We hold these truths to be self-evident: that all men and women are created equal.' I don't think I realized until I read the Sentiments that women are civilly dead once they marry. Knowing that, why would a woman ever marry?"

"They actually argued at the convention about whether they should ask for the right to vote, whether they should put it in the document. Stanton was for it, but Lucretia Mott was against it."

"She's the Quaker woman?"

"Yes," Walker said. "Frederick Douglass stood up and argued for women's right to vote. He said he could not accept the right to vote if women couldn't vote too. So they included it in the Sentiments. I agree with Mr. Douglass."

"Trying to speak up for your sex, eh?" Callie said. "One exceptional man does not make up for all the cruel and unexceptional men. Or two exceptional men, I suppose."

"That is an argument for another day," Walker said.

"I don't argue," Callie said. "I fight."

"I don't fight," Walker said. "I discuss."

"I don't discuss," Callie said. "I am serenely correct in all my pronouncements."

Walker laughed. "I suppose you are right about that."

An hour or so after they began, Joseph stopped the carriage. Callie opened the door and looked around. She didn't recognize where they were—the edge of some woods.

Joseph jumped down. Callie didn't see anyone else or any sign of human beings. She couldn't see a building in any direction. Just woods, the road, and rolling hills.

Walker climbed out of the carriage and stood on the road with them. He was still favoring his wounded leg. Of course, Callie reminded herself, he had been shot only yesterday. She could hardly believe it. It seemed as though weeks had gone by.

"I want to thank you, Miss Callie," Walker said. He held out his hand.

Callie took his hand. Why was Elizabeth always harping on about how brown she was? His skin looked so dark next to her pale skin.

They shook hands.

"Let me know what you all decide," Callie said.

They let go of each other's hand.

Walker went into the woods with barely a limp. He looked back once. Then the darkness swallowed him.

"If anyone happens to mention seeing us," Callie said to Joseph, "I'll say I asked you to take me for a ride in the country. Just one of my larks. It will be my responsibility."

"I'm not worried," Joseph said.

Callie looked at him. "You remember what happened to Heddie?"

He nodded. "What's done is done," he said. "Where to now?"

"Dr. Sawyer's home," she said. "I've got some bad news to deliver."

Thirteen

Callie opened the windows to the carriage and let the spring air inside. She folded up the blanket and checked for blood. She didn't find any. Good. She wouldn't have to explain blood to anyone, and the lack of blood meant Walker was healing. She watched the landscape go by. Hyacinth covered one field like a purple blanket. Pale, pale blue chicory plants grew up in the ditches next to dandelions. Farther down the road she saw blue vervain and the furry leaves of mullein. Tall stalks grew up from the center of some of the mullein. Later yellow flowers would bloom from those stalks.

Callie half-wished she had brought her paints. She smiled and stuck her hand out the window. It felt good to want to do something again. To be with the wildflowers. Perhaps learning embarrassing things about herself and saving a man's life was rejuvenating to her creativity.

Once they were at the Sawyer house and she was standing at their front door, Callie realized she had not brought any gift for Mrs. Sawyer. If she was going to continue living this clandestine life, she would have to remember to act normal at all times—or at least act like Jewelweed, the person who could pretend to be anyone, who never worried about what someone thought of her.

Benjamin answered the door.

"My, my," Callie said. "Is this your new profession, answering the door in the middle of the day?"

Benjamin smiled. "It's Sunday, Callie. Everyone has the day off. And Mother has gone to church."

"Oh yes, Sunday," Callie said. "I had completely forgotten. Is Therese here?"

"She and Barnaby took Mother to church."

"Oh." Callie wasn't sure what to do now. Maybe it was none of her business what Barnaby was doing with Therese. Or what he might be doing to Therese.

No maybe about it. It wasn't her business.

"Would you like to come in?" Benjamin asked. "I made myself a sandwich and tea. You can have half."

Callie followed Benjamin into the front parlor and sat next to him on the couch. He poured her a cup of tea. He put half of his sandwich on a saucer and handed it to her. She set the plate on the table.

"I'm sorry to just show up," Callie said. "I promised your mother I would stop by, and I was out for a ride in the country and I thought today was as good a day as any."

"You were out for a ride in the country after your big party?" he said. "I thought you'd be asleep."

"It was such a beautiful day," she said.

"I'd think you'd be out on Meager instead of cooped up in the coach."

Callie frowned and sipped her tea. Then she said, "Did you ever notice you ask me a lot of questions? I feel as though I'm being interrogated."

Benjamin laughed. "I'm so sorry! I was making conversation."

"When have we ever had to make conversation?" Callie asked.

"I can't pull your braids any more," he said, "so conversation is the next best course of action."

Callie set her cup down.

"Benjamin, I think I need to tell you something," she said. "I was hoping to talk with your mother, but I'm afraid if I don't tell you now, I will never tell anyone. I will be betraying a confidence, but I'm worried."

"You can tell me anything," Benjamin said.

"You're not going to like this," she said. "And if he finds out it came from me, he could make my life miserable."

"Him?" Benjamin looked at Callie. His eyes narrowed. "Barnaby. What has he done?"

"He's been pressuring Therese," Callie said. "To do things."

"What kind of things?"

"Things a gentleman would never ask a lady to do," Callie said.

Benjamin jumped up from the couch.

"I will kill him if he touched her," he said. He began pacing. "I thought she wasn't serious about him. How could she be? She's so bright."

"She's also twenty years old," Callie said. "All her friends are married. She's feeling old. She wants to get married and have children. If it makes you feel any better, she says she is still . . . chaste."

"We've talked to her about Barnaby," he said. "We've told her how unsuitable he is."

"That probably stoked her ardor," Callie said. "I certainly don't understand the attraction, but she says she cares for him. Apparently he is known throughout the county for pushing his attentions on women who don't want them—particularly slaves."

Benjamin stopped and looked at her.

"I'm sorry," Callie said. "I shouldn't have said that. I'm repeating rumors and I shouldn't. But the other part, about Therese, she told me. She made me promise not to tell anyone, but I thought you should know."

Benjamin sat next to her again.

"You can't kill him," Callie said. "No matter what. No duels, Benjamin. Then everyone would know, and Therese would be ruined."

"I know," he said. "I know. Thank you for telling me. I will keep your name out of it. I will speak with my mother first, and then we'll talk to Therese."

Callie nodded. "Now finish your sandwich."

Benjamin looked at her. "I don't know if the old Callie

would have told me this," Benjamin said.

"Who is the 'old Callie?'"

"You always seemed in your own world," he said, "of wildflowers, trees, animals. People weren't a big part of your world."

"Of course people were a big part of my world," Callie said. "My parents were my world. It's true I didn't have many friends. You were my friend. But then you went away. I had other friends, but I don't have much in common with them."

He nodded.

"I don't know that I want to have much in common with them," she said. "It seems like there's so much more in this world than making babies. Or making certain some man gets his meals on time."

"That's how you see marriage?"

"Don't you?"

"I see marriage as a collaboration," he said, "that benefits both parties."

"The benefit is all to the man," she said. "He gets to go out into the world while the woman stays locked up in her bird-cage called a house. My mother was so smart and talented. Yet she did very little with her life besides raise me."

"That is no small thing," he said.

"No, if that's what she wanted to do," she said. "But she didn't have an option. Neither did my father. If a man and woman could work side by side as equals that would be one thing, but I don't see examples of that anywhere."

"You could be the example," he said. "You and your husband, whoever he is."

"Right now," Callie said, "I'm trying to save my home. I'm trying to keep my head above water. And I'm trying not to take anyone with me if I go down."

"That sounds mysterious again," Benjamin said. "I wish you would tell me more of what's going on in your life."

"You've already offered to court me," Callie said. "That's quite a sacrifice. Especially since I saw you with Lucy Johnston last night. She looked quite smitten with you."

"Lucy is a very nice woman," he said. "She will make someone a wonderful wife. She is the embodiment of most men's dreams."

"Most men's?"

"I'm not looking for a wonderful wife," he said. "I am looking for a partner."

Callie looked at him. "If only there were more men like you," she said.

"Are you going to tell me what's going on at Mount Joy?" he asked.

"Nothing is going on," she said. "I am happy as a clam in high water."

Benjamin shook his head. "I hope one day you will trust me."

Callie put her hand on Benjamin's arm. "I realize now you are not in league with the devil that is Barnaby. Not that I ever really believed you were. I know you are my friend. I have few friends so I must take great care of the ones I have. Which means I won't drag you into my escapades. Not that I have any escapades."

"You're speaking in riddles," he said.

"I better get back to the old homestead," Callie said, "before my dear auntie sends out a search party."

Callie and Benjamin stood.

"This was our little secret," Callie said.

"Of course," he said.

Callie put her arm through his as they walked to the entry hall, and then out the door.

"Let's have a picnic together soon," Callie said. "Down by the tree where we first kissed."

Benjamin smiled. The smile did not spread to the rest of his face. His forehead was furrowed. She resisted the urge to reach up and smooth out the wrinkles.

"Don't worry so, old friend," Callie said. "Perhaps it isn't so bad. You'll nip it in the bud."

"I feel I have been too wrapped up with my practice," Benjamin said. "I didn't realize this had gotten so serious. I never would have suspected Barnaby could act in such a heinous manner."

Joseph brought the carriage up to where they were standing.

"Let me know how it turns out," Callie said. "You're a good man, brother Benjamin. Be well." She kissed his cheek. She stepped on the stool and took Benjamin's hand to steady herself as she got into the carriage. When she was in, she let go of Benjamin, Joseph grabbed the stool, and Benjamin shut the carriage door.

Benjamin waved. Joseph slapped the reins and the horses jumped forward. Callie leaned back. She hoped her aunt was still asleep when she got home. She didn't feel like pretending today that she liked her. She didn't feel like pretending anything today.

Fourteen

The next day, all the guests left Mount Joy. All the nephews elicited Callie's promise to write to them.

As soon as they were gone, Callie got out her canvases and paints and pencils and paper. She took them, along with an easel, outside to the gardens. The garden had been attended to only sporadically since her mother died, so Callie first pulled weeds. Many of the garden beds were filled with wildflowers and not many weeds had found their way in. Not that Callie was overly concerned with weeds. Callie and her mother agreed with Mr. Ralph Waldo Emerson who had said that a weed was just a plant whose virtues had not yet been discovered.

The vegetable beds were a bit overrun, though. Many of the crops had self-started, or else someone had been planting, because the collard greens were already coming up. Carrots, cucumbers, parsnips, spinach, and squash were growing well, alongside lush tomato and potato plants. Callie was happy to see the peas had already pushed themselves up and out into the sun.

Callie spent most of the day in the dirt, pulling and digging, digging and pulling. No one bothered her. Reby brought out lunch and lemonade. Callie ate and drank eagerly.

She thought of all the hours and days and weeks she and her mother had spent in these gardens, tending them, sitting on the ground and harvesting—sometimes eating more than they actually took back to the house. Callie lay across the grass and looked up at the clouds. It was good to remember her parents alive. For too many months she could barely think of them because she'd imagine the accident that killed them. Now at least some of the happier memories were returning.

Callie washed up for dinner and ate with her aunt and uncle. Aunt Elizabeth was happy about the success of the party. She wanted to do more socializing and suggested she and Callie go visit her sister in Richmond.

"You'd get more time with my nephews!" Elizabeth said. Her grin was so wide that Callie realized her ruse had worked: Elizabeth believed Callie would now acquiesce to her every wish.

"Dear aunt, I appreciate the invitation," Callie said, "but I wonder if you would mind if I had some time to myself. I'd like to start painting again and mourn the loss of my parents properly."

"I don't want you wallowing!" Elizabeth said. "I've lost

my parents. Your uncle has lost his. We move on."

"You are better people than I am," Callie said. "I need some time."

"You had all that time in France," Elizabeth said.

"Leave her be, Elizabeth," Charles said. "I miss your mother, too, Callie. Take all the time you need."

Callie looked at him. She realized with a start that Charles was his mother's brother. She knew that, of course, but she hadn't thought about how he might feel, having lost his only sister.

"I'm sorry, Uncle Charles," she said. "Of course you must miss her. I will be more social soon. I promise. I did well at the party, didn't I?"

Elizabeth made a noise and shook her head. "Yes, you were fine. Very well. I cannot stay cross with you for long. We can go to Richmond later on in the summer."

The next day Callie worked in the flower gardens. The tulips, hyacinths, anemones, starflowers, late daffodils, and Spanish bluebells were all in bloom. So much color: blue, orange, yellow, white, purple, and every shade in-between. Odd how Callie hadn't been able to look at the gardens until now, couldn't take in their colors. Now she put her face in the blooms and felt like she was smelling her mother again.

Finally Callie sat on the ground with her pad and paints and began painting what she saw. The luxurious black insides of the tulips. The pale blue petals of the starflower and its bright yellow interior like hidden pieces of the sun. And the bells of the bluebells and the other hyacinths, tall and color-ful, like strange soldier beings marching in line. She laughed as she painted. What a strange thing to think of. Flowers and soldiers.

Later Callie wandered away from the gardens and into the woods. She found jewelweed and sketched the little orange trumpets hiding out in a sea of green. As she walked amongst the wildflowers, she felt better than she had in months. Maybe her mother had been right: Wildflowers could fix anything. For this little while she forgot her parents were dead. Forgot her mother had sent her off to Paris to get her away from a slave named Abraham. Forgot that Walker might even now be talking about her to Momma Gospel.

For several days, Callie worked in the gardens and painted. She felt peaceful some of the time. Other times she felt as though she was waiting for something to happen. She didn't know if it was something bad or good. Just some *thing*.

Then one night she got into her bed and found a note under her pillow. She got out of bed, turned up the lamp, and held the paper to the light so she could read it.

"Tomorrow night at nine. Meet at the Old Home up Ridgeway. Come alone."

Old Home was a deserted house a few miles from Mount Joy. No one lived on the land any longer, and the house was hidden from the road, down a long drive. How was she going to get away from the house at nine at night?

She tore the note into tiny pieces and then dropped the pieces onto the lamp flame. The paper hissed as it burned up.

Callie got back into bed and made her plans.

After breakfast the next morning, Callie went out to the stables and found Joseph, alone, currying Sergeant. She asked him to have Meager saddled and ready for her around 8:30 that evening.

"But no one can know," she said. "And I'm not riding side-saddle."

He nodded.

"Will this cause you any problems?" she asked.

He shook his head.

"You wouldn't tell me if it would," she said.

"I would feel better if you'd let me come with you," he said. "I don't know how safe it'll be for you riding alone after dark."

"I think I'll be all right," she said. "But if I'm not, I'll swear I saddled the horse myself."

She spent most of the day with her aunt. She asked if she could paint Elizabeth's portrait. Elizabeth dressed in her best violet silk dress and sat in the parlor for Callie.

"You are such a patient subject," Callie told her again and again. Frequently she said, "Now take a break. Rest and eat something. We won't finish this today, of course."

After dinner, Callie asked to be excused to go to bed early.

"And you, dear aunt, should do the same. I want to work on your portrait early tomorrow. We should both be rested." She kissed her aunt on the cheek. Her aunt practically glowed from the attention

"You are so right, Callie," she said. "I will retire forthwith. Husband, come with me and read to me."

Her uncle glanced at Callie as if to say, "I blame you." Callie smiled. Her uncle chuckled.

Callie hurried up to her room. She locked her door. Then she took off her dress and got into the black breeches she had retrieved from her old room. She pulled on a black shirt. Then she pinned her hair close to her head and put a cap over it.

She looked in the mirror. She could pass for a boy—or a man—if no one got too close.

Her mother would be appalled.

When it was time, she opened the secret door and went inside the passageway and shut the door behind her. Then she quietly walked down the two flights of stairs and the long corridor until she reached the hidden half-door. When she was certain no one was around, she slowly opened it, then stepped into the night.

Fortunately the moon was up. Her aunt and uncle's room did not face the stables, so she wasn't too concerned about them seeing her. She ran to the stables and found Joseph on the other side of the building, holding Meager's reins.

"Please let me come with you," he said. He didn't even appear to be surprised to see her dressed like a man. But then he had been around during her early teenage years when her mother could not get her to wear a dress.

"No," Callie said. "This is my risk." She patted Meager's neck. Then she got on the stool, put her left foot in the stirrup, grabbed the saddle horn and pulled herself up into the saddle.

She took the reins between the fingers of her left hand. "I won't be long," she said quietly.

She clicked Meager forward. They went down the drive and then turned left and headed north. She hoped with the moon out she would easily see the drive to Old Home.

Meager trotted for a while, but Callie soon reined him in. She didn't want to wear him out. The moon lit up the country-side. She had never been out at night alone on horseback before. Actually, she'd never been out alone at night at all in this country, except on her own property, and even that was rare. She didn't know many people who went out after dark. Too much danger of running into highway robbers, people said, especially since they were so close to Yankee country.

Callie smiled. Probably just stories.

An owl called out and Callie started. Meager whinnied. Callie patted him.

"I hope this isn't another crazy thing I've gotten myself into," Callie said.

Soon enough they came to the drive leading up to Old Home. Trees and bushes had nearly overgrown the driveway, but Callie clicked when Meager hesitated and he bounded through it. Callie soon saw a light up ahead. Meager hurried toward it.

Meager stopped in front of the rundown cottage. Callie got off him, then wrapped the reins around a post. She walked up the steps and onto the porch. The floorboards creaked. She went to the door and knocked. The door moved open when she touched it. She pushed it open.

A lantern on a stool spilled a reddish glow around a small room. An old woman sat near the lantern, on a chair Callie couldn't see. She held a stick in one hand and was drawing something in the dirt. Next to her stood Walker.

"Hello," Callie said. "I'm Calantha Carter." She held out her hand to the woman.

Using the stick, the woman pointed to a chair across from her.

Callie dropped her hand and sat on the chair. It moved slightly and she was afraid she might tip over, but it steadied, and so she steadied. The woman stared at her, and Callie stared back. The woman's eyes seemed darker than the room. Her hair was curly gray, covered mostly by a scarf. Her skin was the color of the night in this room.

"We don't use our true names here," the woman said. "I am called Momma Gospel. You already know this man. But you shouldn't call him by any name you ever knew him by. We call him King Poet. What should we call you?"

"Jewelweed," Callie said without hesitation.

Momma Gospel nodded. "Jewelweed is sometimes called the impatient weed. We make tea out of it to give to those who can't sit still, for those who have no patience. Is this true for you?"

"It was true for me," Callie said. "But I am learning to wait. I am learning that I can see more by being still, by being patient."

"I understand impatience," Momma Gospel said. "It is because of my impatience that I keep doing the work I do. I can't wait for people to come to their senses. We must take action now. But we also have to be careful. We take a great risk even speaking with you about what we do."

"I understand that," Callie said.

"Do you?" Momma Gospel asked.

Callie nodded. "I understand the danger," she said, "although I know getting caught would mean something different to you and Walker than it would to me."

"We don't have many white people helping us," Momma Gospel said. "Not in the South, for sure. But you have a house in the middle of a county that has been very dangerous to those trying to escape. If people could stay for a night or two, until it was safe, and they could get some food and drink, that would be good. I understand your aunt and uncle live with you."

"It's true," Callie said, "but if the . . . travelers . . . came in through the secret passage, my aunt and uncle would never see them. They don't know anything about the passageways. I didn't even know about them."

Momma Gospel stirred the dirt with her stick.

"We need to get as many people out as possible," the woman said. "Once the election is over and war is imminent, it will be much more difficult. Whole families want to escape. That is always very difficult, especially when they have to travel hundreds of miles on foot."

"How can I help with that?" Callie asked.

"Your coach," Walker said.

Callie looked from Momma Gospel to Walker. "I don't understand."

"You could move an entire family across the county quickly in that big coach of your poppa's," Momma Gospel said.

Callie nodded.

"I know a man in Richmond who can do anything with

wood," Momma Gospel said, "and he is an expert when it comes to carriages and coaches. A Mr. Smith. He could take out the seats in your carriage and put in hollowed out seats. Several small people could hide in these seats for short periods of time."

"Of course," Callie said. "If you think this would work, I will do it."

"You'd have to take the carriage into Richmond," Walker said. "But he could take out the seats and put in new ones in less than a day, I suspect."

"I could go on the pretext of visiting my uncle," Callie said, "or shopping for cloth or paints."

Momma Gospel nodded. "Good. For this to work, you can't do anything to draw attention to yourself. Sometimes we will ask you to give shelter to travelers at your house. We'll call your house Jewelweed Station. Don't get anyone else in the household involved. Joseph and Reby know, but keep them out of it as much as possible. King Poet will be your contact. We'll let you know when to go to Richmond to fix the carriage. Later, we'll let you know if we need your help in smuggling a family out. Do you understand?"

Callie nodded. "I think so."

"Good," Momma Gospel said. "If all goes well, we will never meet again, at least not until everyone is free. Now turn around and leave and don't look back. Everything is changed now for you. You can never look back."

Callie glanced at Walker, but his face was impassive. Callie stood. She hesitated before leaving. She wanted to say "thank you" or "I'm sorry," or something. No words seemed adequate. She turned around and left. She got on Meager and rode away from the ramshackle house.

As she and Meager trotted into the darkness, Callie wondered what her parents would think of her now.

Fifteen

The ride back seemed quicker than the ride to Old Home had been. Meager hurried to the barn. Joseph slipped from the shadows as soon as Meager and Callie came up to the stables. He grabbed Meager's reins and Callie got off the horse.

"Thank you, Joseph," she said quietly.

"All is well?" he asked.

She nodded.

She hurried back into the house, via the secret passageway, and up to her room. Everything looked the same. The door was still locked.

"I did it," she whispered.

She peeled off her men's clothes. Then she put on her nightgown and got under the covers.

She stared at the ceiling in the dark for a long while and listened to her heartbeat slowly go back to normal. She was now a criminal. A revolutionary. A do-gooder.

Or almost.

She smiled. Then laughed.

It felt good to finally do something on her own. As though she had slipped from beneath the thumbs of her aunt and uncle without them even knowing it.

The next few days were quiet for Callie. At first she felt impatient. She wanted to help someone now. She wanted to be a part of this great historical event right this moment. But then she forced herself to settle into a kind of routine. Uncle Charles worked; Aunt Elizabeth wrote letters or had company. Callie almost stopped comparing her aunt to her own mother: Stopped wondering why she and Elizabeth didn't help with the laundry or why they didn't help much with the sewing like she and her mother had.

Elizabeth walked around the house sometimes rattling the household keys and ordering the servants around, but she was no longer so abusive with the servants or Callie.

Fortunately Barnaby stayed away from the house.

Benjamin stayed away, too. Callie wondered what had happened with Therese. Had Benjamin and Mrs. Sawyer talked to her? To Barnaby?

She missed Benjamin.

One day Callie took her paints and easels down to the river, under the black willow, near a mayapple not far from the tree. A solitary, white flower grew beneath a pair of large, deeply lobed leaves that arched over the mayapple flower as though they were protecting it from the sun and rain. Callie dipped her brush in dark shiny green paint, then touched the brush to her paper.

She wondered what Walker was doing. Would she see him soon? She liked him. She had been comfortable with him right away. He wrote poetry. He was articulate. He trusted her enough to recommend her to Momma Gospel. Plus he was a good-looking man.

Good thing her mother wasn't around. She'd send Callie back to France for that thought.

A hawk called out. Callie looked up and didn't see anything. The hawk called out again.

That meant someone else (or some predator) was in the woods. A hawk always called out once as a warning. If the person or predator kept coming, it called out again and then flew away.

Maybe Walker was coming to give her news about their upcoming mission together.

Probably not in broad daylight.

Callie heard footsteps.

In another moment, Benjamin came down the path toward her. He was dressed in his going-to-meeting clothes. He held his hat in his hands.

His eyes lit up when he saw her, and he smiled. Callie smiled, too, and put down her brush. She wiped her hands on her smock and then held out her hands to him.

He took her hands, leaned close, and kissed her cheek.

"Hello, stranger," she said. "Where have you been? I've

missed you."

"I doubt that," he said.

She sat on the stool at her easel. He leaned against the black willow.

"You look troubled," Callie said. "Can I help you?"

"I have some news," Benjamin said. He worried the rim of his hat between his fingers and looked at the forest floor.

Callie didn't say anything.

"There's going to be a wedding," he said.

Callie's heart sank.

"Yours?" she asked.

He looked up at her. "You sound disappointed."

She frowned. She couldn't explain the unease in her stomach.

"I would miss my childhood friend," Callie said.

"It's not me," he said. "Therese. Therese is marrying."

"Oh, no," Callie said.

Benjamin nodded.

"What can you tell me?"

"We talked to her after you left," he said. "At first she denied everything. But a few days ago, she admitted it all. Only she said it had gone much further than any of us could have imagined."

"Benjamin, you're frightening me," Callie said.

"She is with child," he said. "Mother is speaking to your aunt and uncle now. I'm on my way there. Barnaby was at our house yesterday. He has agreed to marry her. Therese seems happy about it all, even though I have reason to suspect he may have forced himself on her."

Callie groaned.

"Obviously no one can know any of this," he said.

"Why must she marry him?" Callie said. "She can't love him. He's such an idiot. She could go away to New England and have the baby there. Tell everyone she is going off to school. No one would be the wiser. I've heard of women doing that."

"Yes, someone else in the family could raise the baby," he said. "Only then we'd have to tell the family, and Therese doesn't want that. She's embarrassed."

"You and I could marry," Callie said, "and we could raise the baby. You've already offered to court me."

Benjamin smiled crookedly. "You can always make me laugh, even in the worst of times."

"I'm serious," she said. "If that would help your family I would make the sacrifice."

"The sacrifice of marrying a man you don't love?"

"Of course I love you," Callie said.

"Like a brother," he said.

"I suppose," she said, "although I've never had a brother so I don't actually know how one loves a brother."

"I appreciate the offer," he said, "and while I am truly tempted, I don't think it's wise."

Callie got off the stool and went over to Benjamin and put her arms around him. He hesitated and then returned the embrace.

"I am so sorry this has happened," she whispered. "And so sorry someone in my family did it. Please let me help somehow."

When they let each other go, Benjamin looked into her eyes and smiled grimly.

"Seems you're all grown-up now," he said. "Overnight."

She laughed and went back to her easel. "Remember, I am good at pretending. Now, shall I go back with you to the house?"

He shook his head. "I don't think it'll be very pleasant, and it'll probably anger Barnaby if you're a party to any of it. I don't trust him, Callie. Certainly not with my sister." He shook his head. "And if he feels trapped into this marriage he might get even more dangerous. May I suggest you stay out of his way?"

Callie wanted to go back to the house and see her cousin humiliated almost more than anything. But she knew Benjamin was right. And she needed to remain unnoticed. Especially now that she was part of the underground railroad.

She wanted to laugh at the thought it.

She was part of the underground railroad.

If anyone found out, her aunt and uncle would be ruined.

She hoped.

Of course, that was not why she was doing it. She was doing it because slavery was wrong. She was doing it for the greater good.

She wished she could tell Benjamin about all of it. He'd be proud of her, wouldn't he? He might also be afraid for her, and he'd want to help. She was not going to be responsible for him losing his practice or going to jail.

"I better go," he said. "I hope to see you soon."

Callie nodded.

Then he was gone.

A moment later she heard grass rustling again. She turned around in time to see Walker step out of the marsh.

She looked around quickly, instinctively. No one else was around. She smiled at him.

"It's good to see you," she said. "Is all well?"

"Hello, Miss Callie," he said. "Our person in Richmond is ready to do the work on the carriage. Is there some way you could go there in the next few days?"

"I'll figure something out," Callie said.

Walker held out a piece of paper. As Callie took it, her fingers brushed his. Her stomach felt fluttery. She looked at Walker, and he looked away.

"That's the name of the man," he said, "and his address."

"Mr. Smith, I remember," Callie said. "How will I contact you when I get back?"

"We'll know," he said. "Have a safe trip."

He started to turn around to go back into the tall grass.

"Wait," Callie said. "Can't you stay?"

He looked back at her.

"I enjoyed our talks before," she said.

He turned around to face her.

"You mean when I was bleeding to death on your bedroom floor or in your carriage?"

Callie laughed. "Yes, both times. Quite enjoyable for me."

"I'm sure it would be," he said. "You had a captive audience."

"Nearly," she said. "I—I did like your poetry. I admire that talent."

He came closer and looked at the painting on her easel.

"I admire this," he said. "You've painted the soul of that flower."

"The flower has a soul?" Callie asked.

"Everything has a soul," he said. "Even you."

Callie laughed again. "Yes, I suppose you're right."

"I better go," he said. "If someone came—"

"Of course," Callie said. She held up the piece of paper and then stuffed it into the pocket of her smock. "I will do as you ask."

Walker nodded. Then he disappeared into the grass.

Callie waited until some time had gone by, and then she packed up her easel and paints and headed back to the house. She sang softly to herself as she went, trying to figure out how she could get to Richmond.

Henry took her paints and easel when she came into the entry hall. He nodded toward the parlor, silently telling her that something was happening within. He quietly left, and Callie listened at the closed door.

No one was shouting. No raised voices.

Callie knocked on the door, then opened it.

Inside the parlor, Mrs. Sawyer, Therese, and Elizabeth sat on the sofa. Barnaby, Benjamin, and Charles stood in various places about the room.

Therese jumped up when Callie came into the room.

"Callie," she said. "I'm so glad you're here! I just arrived myself. You are in time to learn the good news. Barnaby and I are to be married. And what's even better, we're to be married right away!"

Even though Callie expected this news, she was still startled by it. She did her best to cover her surprise. She and Therese embraced.

"Best wishes, Therese," she said.

She looked over at Mrs. Sawyer, but she didn't meet Callie's gaze.

When they let go of each other, Elizabeth said, "Yes, this is most exciting news! I wanted a big wedding, of course, but the children have other ideas. A small wedding. Then a reception. We'd like to have it here, since Therese's family is closer to Mount Joy than they are to our plantation."

Callie could tell Elizabeth wanted to put her head in her hands and cry. Instead she smiled. She was a practiced pretender, too.

"Yes, I love a good party," Elizabeth said, "and this will be grand. For our son to marry into such an illustrious family!"

She could barely choke out the words. Callie knew why. Mrs. Sawyer was a Quaker so she didn't believe in slavery, and Benjamin was a doctor, not a true businessman. Therese would have no real dowry to speak of, unless Mr. Sawyer had left her one.

Callie sat in a chair near to Benjamin. She looked at her cousin Barnaby. She hated him now more than she had ever hated him. To manipulate a decent young woman like Therese into having sexual relations with him was despicable.

"No congratulations for me?" Barnaby asked. "No kisses for your cousin?"

"I think not," Callie said. "Save those for your bride."

"I must get my dress made," Therese said. "They have no modern fabrics in the mercantile here. I don't know what I'm going to do!"

Callie smiled. How quickly an opportunity had come her way.

"There's a wonderful mercantile in Richmond," Callie said. "Not far from my uncle's place. They have a dressmaker there who does amazing work, quite quickly. I would gladly go with you."

"That's a wonderful idea," Elizabeth said.

"Yes," Mrs. Sawyer said. She looked like she was going to weep.

"You can come, too, Mother," Therese said.

"I don't think I can," she said.

"But you don't even know when we're leaving," Therese said. Now it was Therese who looked like she might burst into tears. "I want my mother with me!"

"I have business in Richmond," Benjamin said. "I will accompany you both."

"We'll take my carriage," Callie said. "So it's settled then? We'll leave tomorrow?"

"That's a little soon to spring it on your uncle," Elizabeth said. "We'll send him a letter first, to let him know you're on your way. You can leave the day after next."

"When is the happy day?" Callie asked.

No one said anything for a moment. Then Elizabeth said, "Oh you mean the wedding day. Yes, well, two weeks."

Callie looked over at Benjamin. He glanced at her, but she couldn't read anything from his expression.

"I think we should open a bottle of wine and celebrate," Barnaby said.

"Yes, let's do make this a party," Elizabeth said. "It is a happy occasion."

"It is," Therese said. "It is a very happy occasion."

Sixteen

The morning after the news of the engagement, Callie noticed a large bruise on Elizabeth's right arm. It looked as though someone had grabbed her arm and twisted it.

"What happened?" Callie asked.

Elizabeth looked down at her arm and immediately pulled down her sleeve to cover it.

"I ran into the door," she said. "I am a very clumsy woman. Ask your uncle. I'm always running into things."

"Do you need to see Dr. Sawyer?"

"Whatever for?" she asked. "I'm perfectly fine! Quit fussing. Let's write that letter to your Uncle Peter and Aunt Charlotte. I'm sure they would love to have you and Therese visit."

Callie followed Elizabeth into the parlor. She hoped what

her aunt said about her bruise was true. She didn't want to believe her uncle was hitting her. Callie did not particularly like her aunt, but she did not want any harm to come to her, especially not at the hands of her own husband.

Elizabeth soon received word that Uncle Peter and Aunt Charlotte would welcome a visit from Callie, Therese, and Benjamin. Elizabeth had too many things to do to prepare for the wedding, she said, so she wouldn't be able to accompany them. The following morning, Pearl prepared a picnic basket full of food for the trip. Callie took it with her out to the carriage. A morose-looking Elizabeth stood on the threshold of the house and waved to Callie as she got into the carriage.

Callie took her seat and waved to her aunt; then she called up to Joseph. The carriage pitched forward. Callie wished she could be happy that her aunt was unhappy. But she didn't want this marriage either. She didn't want to see Therese ruin her life by marrying Barnaby. And that's what it would be: ruination.

At the Sawyer home, Callie went in for tea while Therese finished getting ready. She sat on the couch next to Mrs. Sawyer who was pale and quiet. She said nothing as she handed Callie a cup of tea. Benjamin was his usual calm self, standing near the mantle, holding his hands over a non-existent fire. Callie supposed that was Benjamin's way of expressing anxiety.

"Do you need to light a fire?" Callie asked.

Benjamin looked over at her and then put his hands behind his back.

"Habit," he said.

Callie smiled. She was sorry she had called attention to his nervous tic.

"Are you sure you don't want to come with us?" Callie asked Mrs. Sawyer. "I don't have your sense of style or taste when it comes to helping Therese with a wedding gown."

Maeve sighed. "I can't come," she said.

Callie looked at Benjamin. He shrugged.

"Perhaps it won't be as bad as we all fear," Callie said softly.

Maeve set her cup down on the low table in front of them. The china cup rattled slightly on the saucer.

"I'm afraid it is already as bad as I feared," Maeve said.

Callie saw one of the servants in the entrance hall carrying out luggage. He was followed by Therese who then came into the parlor.

"I'm all set," she said, smiling brightly. "Mother." She went to Maeve, leaned over, and kissed the top of her head. "I'm sorry you won't be there and I hope you will approve of the dress. You'll take care of the rest of the arrangements while I'm gone?"

Maeve nodded.

Benjamin came and rested his hand on his mother's shoulder. She reached up and squeezed his fingers. Callie set her cup down and got up.

"Thank you for the tea," she said. "We'll be home soon."

The three of them left the house, got into the carriage, and were soon on their way.

At first Therese talked excitedly about the wedding: what

her dress would look like, how handsome Barnaby would be, what kind of food and music they would have at the reception.

After a time, her enthusiasm waned. The three of them sat in silence looking out the carriage windows until Therese started feeling sick to her stomach. Callie had Joseph stop the carriage. Benjamin hopped out and reached up to help Therese, but it was too late. She leaned out the door and vomited.

When she was finished, Benjamin asked if she wanted to return home. Without saying a word, Therese sat down again, and Benjamin got back into the carriage. They continued down the road.

"I guess my breakfast didn't agree with me," Therese said.

Callie got crackers from the picnic basket and handed them to Therese. She took one and ate it slowly.

"Benjamin told you, didn't he?" Therese said.

Callie didn't say anything.

Therese looked out the window. "Of course he told you," she said. "He's never kept anything from you. And you told him in the first place, after you promised to keep my secret. You are the worst secret keeper in the world!"

"That's not true," Callie said. "I will keep all your secrets, unless that requires putting you in harm's way. I felt you were definitely in harm's way."

Therese made a noise. Then she wiped away a tear.

"Don't blame Callie," Benjamin said. "Maybe if we had known earlier."

"Don't blame Callie because I am a ruined woman?" Therese said. "I know you wish she was your sister. Well, she isn't! I was tired of waiting. I'm not smart like Callie or beautiful like Lucy. The pickings are slim, in case you haven't noticed. I wanted a family and my own home, and now I'm going to have it."

"I have never wished Callie was my sister," Benjamin said.

Callie looked over at him. He seemed unusually adamant about that.

"And you are smart and beautiful," he said. "We will deal with whatever comes next, Therese. We're your family. It'll be all right."

Therese nodded. "Yes, it will be. Barnaby is not the monster you all believe him to be. I don't want to talk about it any longer. Callie, please ask Joseph to pull the carriage over again."

The ride to Richmond was longer than expected, but they made the best of it. They took frequent breaks in an effort to calm Therese's stomach. During the trip, Therese often leaned against Callie while Benjamin told stories he remembered from fairy tale books. Sometimes Therese slept. Sometimes Callie slept.

Eventually, they arrived at Peter and Charlotte Ames's home in Richmond. Callie hadn't been to Richmond since she was a child, so she barely remembered the house.

Several of her young cousins ran out to greet her and her friends. They tugged on her hands and led her into the house.

They all talked at once, or so it seemed. Charlotte laughed over the din. Callie smiled. She got her cousins to let go of her long enough for her to speak to her uncle Peter.

"I'm getting some work done on the carriage," Callie said. "Would you have a spare vehicle for us to take around tomorrow?"

"Of course," he said. "How are you doing? You look much better than the last time I saw you."

Callie smiled. "I am quite myself again."

Peter patted her hand. She went outside to the carriage and told Joseph where to take the vehicle.

"Tell Mr. Smith that you're bringing it in for the specified repairs," she said. "He should know what that means. He should have a place there for you to board the horses. And you can stay there if they have a room for you."

Joseph nodded. Callie felt like she should say something else, but she didn't know what to say. Did he know he was taking the carriage to get it altered so that she could transport runaway slaves to safety? Would he be glad? Afraid?

"Be safe, Joseph," she said. "Thank you so much."

"You're welcome, Miss Callie," he said.

Soon Callie sat at a large table with her relatives, Benjamin, and Therese. She could not keep track of all her cousins. She was embarrassed she didn't know all their names or anything about them. Her mother had tried to keep her apprised of their comings and goings, but Callie hadn't always paid attention.

Now they passed plates of food around the table. Charlotte fussed over Therese, saying she was now a part of the family.

"And you, too, Dr. Sawyer," Charlotte said. "You are now a cousin to all these children. Beware. I am going to ship them off to you as a group for a long vacation."

The children squealed. Callie looked around the table. Mostly boys. Yes, except one girl, and she was more talkative and aggressive than any of the boys. Good. It would serve her.

Or it would cripple her.

Callie sighed.

The life of a woman was not easy in this world.

What was the girl's name? Alexandria? She looked up and saw Callie staring at her. She grinned.

"Yes, Alex is a tomboy like you were when you were a girl," Charlotte said. "It frustrated your mother to no end."

Charlotte passed a bowl of potatoes to the son at her right hand.

"Alex, don't hog those sweet potatoes," Charlotte said to her daughter. "Our guests have been on the road all day. And Therese looks a little green. You all right, darlin'?"

"Just something I ate," Therese said. "I'm feeling much better. In fact, those chicken legs look mighty appetizing!"

Uncle Peter laughed. "We need more women with appetites."

After dinner, Therese and Callie rested in the room they shared. Therese fell instantly to sleep. After a while Callie quietly left the room to look for Benjamin. Or Alexandria. She felt suddenly social in a house full of her cousins. She heard a raised voice and followed the sound without thinking. Before she knew it, she was standing outside the front parlor.

She heard a hand strike skin. Someone had just slapped someone else's bare skin.

Then she heard weeping.

"Eloise, you can't cry every time I discipline you," Charlotte said. "It's for your own good! If another mistress saw what shoddy work you'd done on this tablecloth they would beat you senseless. I'm only looking after you, in case you ever get sent to another home, where the people are not quite so generous."

"Please, Mrs. Ames, don't send me away. My momma is here. My sister! I will do better now. I will."

"I know you will," Charlotte said.

Callie hurried away and went outside. She breathed deeply and looked at the pink magnolia and purple lilac flowers. They smelled sweet and a little citrusy at the same time. Beyond them, dogwoods were in bloom, too.

Callie wanted to think about the flowers, not what had just happened in the house. She wanted to smell flowers. See flowers. Callie couldn't remember a single time her mother or father had laid a hand on any of the servants. On any of the *slaves*. They were slaves. Callie didn't want to forget that by calling them servants.

Had her parents hit their slaves when she wasn't around? Maybe they had beaten them, and she never knew about it. She couldn't imagine it. She had always held Aunt Charlotte in such high esteem. She wouldn't have imagined her hitting her slaves before tonight. She could imagine her striking her children. Most parents disciplined their children. How was it any different?

Because slaves were not children.

Besides, how did doing violence to a child help that

child?

Everything was changing. Including nearly every thought Callie had ever had.

She began walking toward the dogwoods. These gardens were overgrown in such a way that Callie felt as though she was in the wild—or in some kind of organized chaos.

She smelled tobacco smoke. A moment later, she saw her uncle standing next to a bench amidst the foliage, puffing on a pipe.

"Hello, Uncle," Callie said. "Thank you so much for your hospitality tonight."

"Of course, Callie," he said. "We're glad to see you. And we're happy to participate in this happy occasion. We were all beginning to wonder if Barnaby would ever settle down. Therese Sawyer seems like a fine choice. I've heard nothing but good things about the Sawyers, if you disregard the fact that Mrs. Sawyer is a Quaker. But you can't hold someone's religion against them, can you?"

"No, of course not," Callie said. "By the way, have you seen Dr. Sawyer?"

"He just left," Peter said. "He borrowed one of my horses to go visit a young lady friend of his who is staying in town. Lucy Johnston."

"Oh," Callie said. She had thought Benjamin agreed to this trip to assist his sister and share Callie's company. Apparently she had been wrong.

"This is quite a garden," Callie said. "I've never seen any-thing like it."

"After one of the little ones was born," Peter said, "Charlotte went through an unusual bout of melancholy. I remembered what your mother always said: Wildflowers can cure anything. So I planted whatever I could—with your mother's help. Charlotte seemed to find solace coming out here, and it's been growing like this ever since."

Callie gently touched the upturned orange petals of several tiger lilies leaning over the path. Tiger lily petals always reminded her of a ballerina's costume, and the stamens were the ballerina's legs, ending in shoes now covered in pollen. Gold pollen fell like dust onto the tips of Callie's fingers. Without thinking, she put her fingers in her mouth.

She felt like she was going to cry.

Her uncle put his arm across her shoulders.

"I miss her, too," he whispered.

Callie rested her head on her uncle's shoulder.

A few moments later, Callie heard her aunt Charlotte say, "There you are! I've been looking all over for you. Therese has rallied and the mercantile has stayed open for us. Shall we go?"

Peter let go of Callie. She smiled at him and then looked at her aunt.

"Yes, let us go!"

The ride into town didn't take long. Soon the three women were walking into the mercantile. Callie couldn't see but she could feel the James River to the south of them. It was as though the water in her blood recognized the water of the James River that ran so closely to Mount Joy and to Richmond. It connected the two places in her heart.

She didn't mention this fanciful connection to her aunt or

Therese who chattered non-stop about fabrics and designs and lace. Callie laughed at the appropriate times—she hoped—but it was difficult to muster any kind of interest in a dress. Especially a dress that would be worn in a wedding to Barnaby Ames.

No wonder Therese felt sick.

The owner of the mercantile, Mr. O'Shaughnessy, led the women to the wedding fabric. Therese and Charlotte excitedly ran their fingers over various bolts of cloth. They pointed to which ones they wanted Mr. O'Shaughnessy to show them. They had forgotten all about Callie.

She was glad.

She mumbled something about getting some air. Then she stepped outside. She looked around. Richmond was a big city. Noisy. Smoky. Not big like London or Paris. But something about it always confused Callie when she visited. It felt haunted. Or unfinished. Or about to be finished.

She wasn't sure what.

Maybe it was because this was where the slave trade had bloomed for so many years.

No, that was the wrong word. Flowers bloomed. Love bloomed. The slave trade had nothing in common with flowers. It was more like a sore festering.

How could her parents have continued to own slaves?

She shook her head.

If she wandered around long enough, would she find the place where they were refitting her carriage?

Or would she find where Benjamin and Lucy were rendezvousing? How could he have left his sister like that?

How could he have left her? Men were so easily swayed by a pretty face.

Callie started walking. She had no idea where she was going. Maybe she could get a cab to take her to the stables. What would she do there? Watch them rebuild her carriage? Hope that Walker was around? Why would he be here? He wouldn't. And then by the time she got back to the mercantile, Therese and Charlotte would probably be gone.

Callie sighed. She turned around and walked back to the store. No, she had to stay here. She had to play her part. She couldn't draw any attention to herself.

It was for the greater good.

She felt inexplicably sad. It was difficult to pretend she was someone she wasn't. It was difficult not to shout the truth from the rooftops. Slavery was wrong. It wasn't for the good of the blacks or the good of the South. Or for the good of anything except the pocketbooks of the slave owners. Free labor.

Did everything in life revolve around money and profit? That was the world of Uncle Charles and Barnaby. She supposed it was everyone's world. Everyone needed to eat and take care of their families—but not at the expense of others.

It was not a dog eat dog world. She had never believed that. If that were true, there'd be one dog left at the end of it all and he'd have indigestion. That was not a society with much durability.

"Callie, there you are," Charlotte said. "You keep wandering away! Come, see what you think of this pattern."

"Oh dear," Callie said, "I hope I haven't missed anything."

Seventeen

The next day, Therese spent more time with the seamstress who had two slaves and a couple of white women to help her with the wedding dress. Callie went with Aunt Charlotte and Therese to the mercantile and feigned interest. She even pretended she was upset that she had not been asked to be a bridesmaid.

"It's such a small wedding," Therese said. She stood on a stool as the seamstress hemmed the cream-colored material.

The dress already looked halfway finished. Callie and Charlotte sat on a sofa together sipping tea and eating scones. Not very fresh scones. Callie picked out the currants and ate them first.

"A small wedding is as it should be," Therese said. "Modesty is my watchword."

Callie guessed Mrs. Sawyer had refused to give her much in the way of a dowry or wedding expenses.

"I will only have a maid of honor," she said. "June and I had promised each other when we were children. So I can't go back on my word."

"I perfectly understand," Callie said. "And who will be Barnaby's best man?"

Therese laughed. "Why Benjamin, of course. They've been best friends since childhood."

"Really?" Callie said. "Speaking of your dear brother, where is he?"

"He left early this morning," Charlotte said. "He'll be back for dinner. He had some kind of business."

"What kind?" Callie said. "He's a doctor. Does he have patients here?"

"He probably wanted to visit with Miss Johnston again," Charlotte said. "I think he's smitten. And I think you are a little jealous."

Callie looked at her aunt. "Are you talking to me?"

Aunt Charlotte laughed. "I'm not speaking to his sister."

"I couldn't care less who Benjamin Sawyer is smitten with." She said the word "smitten" with a little too much emphasis. If she didn't care she wouldn't sound so annoyed.

"We always thought the two of you would marry," Therese said.

"What?" Callie said. "Why?"

Therese nodded. "I think Mother secretly wanted it. But you didn't see much of each other while he was getting his medical training, and then you went away."

"Benjamin and I have always been friends," Callie said. "I wish him well, but I have no intention of marrying him and I doubt he has ever had such a notion."

He had said they could pretend to be courting so that Aunt Elizabeth wouldn't keep sicking her nephews on her. But that wasn't because of any kind of romantic affection between them.

"I do wonder where he is," Callie said, "since he came on this trip to accompany us. And now he's run off."

Charlotte laughed again. "For someone who claims not to care, you seem very interested in his whereabouts."

"Quite frankly, I would prefer Lucy as a sister-in-law," Therese said. "She and I can talk for hours about all kinds of things. You and I don't have much to say to one another, Callie. You care about the world and what happens beyond our county. Mother and Benjamin are that way, too. I am not. I am not embarrassed to admit it."

Callie glanced at her aunt, who shrugged. Clearly she was embarrassed or she wouldn't have mentioned it.

"You talk complete nonsense," Callie said. "I care about the same things you do: dresses, parties, boys, finding a husband. We're all alike."

"Then Paris changed you," Charlotte said, "because you were always the oddest little girl I had ever met. So unlike anyone else. You preferred boy's clothes. Your mother had some made for you because you kept running off with any of the slave clothes they were repairing. It mortified her. Elizabeth always told your mother you were some kind of changeling child who wanted to be a boy and a slave."

Callie felt her face flush. She said, "My lord, Aunt Charlotte, no one would ever want to be a slave. And as for being a boy, I think I liked their clothes better. They didn't have to wear quite as much as we did and it was certainly more comfortable. You should try it."

"Yes, well, speaking of Elizabeth," Charlotte said. "How has it been living with her and Charles?"

Callie looked at her aunt. She wished she could tell her the truth.

"I am grateful for Uncle Charles and Aunt Elizabeth," she said. "They are taking good care of me."

Callie looked out the window. The streets were filled with people and buggies and wagons today. The sun was shining, but clouds from the north were moving in.

"You'll turn eighteen soon," Charlotte said, "and maybe you can convince the judge you can be on your own." She looked back at her niece. "By the way, it's too bad you and Benjamin aren't courting. Elizabeth sent a note to one of her nephews who is sweet on you. Matthew, I think his name is. He's coming to dinner tonight."

Callie groaned before she could help herself.

Therese and Charlotte laughed.

Callie stood. "All right, I better go track your brother down and beg him to marry me."

Therese stepped off the stool and went into the dressing room.

"Charlotte," Therese called, "I wonder if we might go home. I'm feeling a little tired. I'd like to beg off lunch."

"Certainly," Charlotte said. "I have some things to do at

home."

"I'd like to explore Richmond a little," Callie said.

"By yourself?" Charlotte asked.

"I won't be long," she said. "I'll rent a cab. It'll be perfectly safe."

"Do you have any money?"

Callie nodded. "Yes, Uncle Peter got me an allowance!" She smiled and hurried to the door of the mercantile.

"Be back by dinner," Charlotte said. "Matthew is your beau, not ours."

"He most definitely is not my beau!" Callie said. "But I will be back in time. Goodbye, Therese!"

Callie was glad to get away from the store and the fitting. She didn't know how people could stay still for so long. Mr. O'Shaughnessy stepped out of the store behind Callie and flagged down a cab for her. He apparently didn't like the look of the first one, so he waved the man away. The second cab he accepted. O'Shaughnessy held Callie's hand while she got into the buggy. She told the cabby to drive to Smith's Stables and Carriages.

Once there, Callie told the cabbie to wait. She got out of the cab, picked up her skirts, and made her way through the mud to the stables. Joseph came running out before she made it all the way to the horses.

"Miss Callie," he said when he reached her.

"Hello, Joseph," she said. "Is all well?"

"All is as it should be," he said. He glanced back at the stables. Callie squinted. She could see another man standing in the shadows. He shifted position, and she saw it was Walker. She started to smile and wave, then quickly realized that would be inappropriate. She was just a dull white Southern woman checking on her carriage.

"You didn't need to come here," Joseph said.

She frowned. "Why? Wouldn't it be normal for me to see if work is going according to plan?"

She heard a door open and looked to her right where a white man was coming out of his workshop. He wiped his hands on his smock and walked over to her.

"Miss Callie Carter," he said. "I am Damon Smith. I am glad to meet you. Can you come into my office for some tea?"

"Of course," she said.

She followed him through the work area where her carriage rested with doors open, insides scattered here and there. It reminded her of a gutted pig. At the back of the shop, Mr. Smith opened a door and Callie went into his office. He came in behind her and shut the door. The small room was remarkably uncluttered, except for piles of books tottering here and there.

Callie heard a knock.

"Come," Smith said.

The back door opened.

Walker came inside.

Callie smiled. She was uncommonly glad to see him.

"We've got a situation," Smith said. "A young boy ran away. His master whipped him good, and he found his way here. If he goes back, I'm afraid they'll kill him."

"What can I do?" Callie asked.

"The carriage is almost finished," Smith said. "We were wondering if you could go for a ride tonight for a little bit. Just outside of town where there's a safe house. They're lookin' all over for him in this city. No one would search this carriage with you in it."

"I'd be the driver," Walker said. "Not Joseph. We don't want to put him in the middle of this. I'm not sure we want to put you in the middle of this."

"I already am," Callie said. "I want to help. Besides, if I have to listen to any more talk of weddings or dresses, I believe I'll go crazy. Do we have to wait until tonight? My aunt and uncle think I'm out sightseeing. Why not go now?"

Smith glanced at Walker. He nodded.

"I need a couple of hours to put the carriage back together," Smith said.

"I will go for lunch and return later," she said. She felt her heart beating in her chest. Was she really going to do this? "What about the boy's wounds? Have they been attended to?"

"Why? You want to fix them?" Walker asked. To Smith he said, "She is a halfway decent nurse."

Callie smiled. "Your sister did all the work. I talked so much your body healed quickly so you could get away from me."

"Not at all," Walker said. "Not at all."

Callie smiled at him. He seemed so gentle and in charge all at the same time. She wondered how he did that.

"There's a decent restaurant about a block from here," Smith said. "Cramer's Spot. Have a long lunch and then come on back."

Smith came around his desk and opened the door for Callie. She glanced back at Walker, nodded, and then left, trying to be gentle and sure of herself all at the same time.

She picked up her skirts again and walked around the mud and dirt back to the cabbie.

She had him drop her off at Cramer's Spot.

The restaurant was packed, but a man led her to a large common table where several other diners were already eating. She nodded hello to them. They did the same, then went back to their conversations with one another.

Callie ordered the chicken special from a tall sweaty man who spoke enthusiastically about all the menu items. A short plump woman brought her tea. Callie asked her if she had any paper. The woman frowned, didn't say a word, and turned around and left. A few minutes later the woman returned with Callie's lunch of chicken, grits, and carrots. After she set the plate down in front of Callie, she dug around the pocket of her apron, then pulled out a pencil and square piece of paper.

"Thank you," Callie said. She smiled. The woman nodded and disappeared. Callie looked around for a face in the crowd that looked interesting to draw. The din was a bit overwhelming. She breathed deeply and began to sketch a man hunched over the bar; the noise faded and became like wind through trees.

"Miss Callie Carter? Is that you?"

Callie looked up. A young man stood over her, so close she could smell the mint on his breath. He must have detected her alarm because he stepped back slightly. Callie squinted. He had red hair and looked vaguely familiar.

"Miss Callie, it's me, Matthew MacDonald, Elizabeth's nephew. Don't tell me you've forgotten me already? May I sit?"

He pulled out a chair before she could say no. He turned to face her and grinned. She wanted to tell him that his kind of charm was completely wasted on her.

"Hello, Matthew," Callie said. "It's nice to see you. Aren't you coming for dinner this evening?"

"I am," he said. "But how fortunate it is to see you here now. I'll have the pleasure of your company for two meals."

"Yes, how nice for me," Callie said. "I was dreading eating alone."

The waitress came and looked at him glumly. "I'll have what she's having," he told the waitress. "Please, eat, Callie Carter. I will sit here and watch you in utter joy."

"I would be obliged if you did not watch me while I eat!" Callie said. "Tell me what you've been up to."

Matthew went on to talk about his various business endeavors. Callie nodded and ate and could not get a single thing he was talking about to stick in her mind. She kept wondering how she was going to steal away from him when it was time to go back to the carriage shop and stables.

The waitress brought his meal.

"And you're here to help Miss Therese Sawyer get her dress, I understand," he said. He ate too quickly. Gravy dribbled off his lower lip. Callie looked away.

"I am," Callie said. "We came up with Dr. Sawyer." She thought if she mentioned Benjamin, perhaps he would think she and Benjamin were courting.

"But why this part of town?" The gravy fell back to the plate, and Matthew wiped his mouth with his napkin.

Callie wondered if she should tell him part of the truth. Lies were always better if they were partially true.

"I am having work done on the carriage at the stables nearby," she said. "When it's finished, I'll pick it up."

"I'm surprised your aunt let you do this on your own," Matthew said. "It is unwise for young women to wander around this city alone. Allow me to accompany you back to the stables."

"The work won't be done yet," Callie said. "I'd like to sit and relax."

Callie couldn't tell him to leave. She was certain he would report back to Aunt Elizabeth. Then Elizabeth would interrogate her about why she was in this particular part of town by herself. So Callie sat next to Matthew long after the waiter took away their empty plates. One by one, people at their common table got up to leave.

Callie kept glancing at the clock in the far corner of the restaurant. She needed to leave soon. How could she get away from him without acting suspicious? Aunt Elizabeth would think anything she did to get away from the nephews was suspicious.

"I am glad to have seen you here," Matthew said. "I never got a chance to speak with you about a private matter. I was hoping to speak with you tonight. But here we are together amongst strangers!" He grinned again.

Callie wondered if these attempts at charm worked with

other women.

"Yes, here we are," Callie said.

He leaned closer to her.

"I was immediately smitten by your charms," he said. "The moment I saw you. Even before I saw you. Aunt Elizabeth described you well. What I'm trying to say is that I would like to ask Uncle Charles if I could—"

"Hello, Callie, my dear! I'm sorry I've kept you waiting."

Callie looked up and over her shoulder. Benjamin stood a couple of feet from her, his hat in hand.

"I'm afraid my horse threw a shoe," he said. "Oh, you have company. I'm so glad." Benjamin held out his hand to Matthew. "I believe we've met before. I'm Dr. Benjamin Sawyer."

Matthew looked startled. He stood and shook hands with Benjamin.

"Are you ready?" Benjamin held out his arm to Callie. "I've paid your bill. I'm sorry I didn't see you or I would have paid yours, too."

"It's no matter," Matthew said. "I—I was glad for the company."

He watched Callie stand and slip her arm through Benjamin's.

"I don't know where my head is," Callie said. "I was so fascinated with Matthew's stories that I forgot to watch for you."

"Are you two engaged?" Matthew asked. It wasn't polite to ask, so Callie feigned shock.

"Really, sir," she said.

"Not yet," Benjamin said. He smiled at Callie and winked. All in full view of Matthew.

"Thank you again, Matthew," Callie said.

When Callie and Benjamin got outside, Callie let her arm drop from his.

"You are going to ruin me for certain!" she said.

Benjamin grinned, and Callie laughed.

"You looked like a calf being led to slaughter," he said. "I had to save you. Shall I walk you to the stables?" He held out his arm to her.

She frowned. "How did you know that's where I was going?"

"I overheard you talking to Matthew. Is that his name? I was there for some time. I'm surprised you didn't see me."

She took his arm again, and they began walking in the direction of the stables.

"So you sat eavesdropping the whole time?" she asked.

"Not the entire time," he said. "I was trying not to listen. I suppose I could have moved away, but I found it amusing to listen to you try to pretend you were interested."

"I wasn't pretending," she said. "I was truly fascinated."

"Hah!" he said. He laughed. "I told you that you might be able to fool the others, but not me. I know you too well."

Callie made a noise. "I hope I can fool the others," she said.

"Why?" he said. "Why is it important that you can't be your own true self?"

Callie stopped and faced him. "Because my own true self is angry. I am furious by what has happened. I am sad and angry that my parents are dead. I feel so much rage toward Aunt Elizabeth and Uncle Charles and what's happening on the plantation. I don't even know what's happening! After I tried to tell the judge what was going on, my aunt and uncle threatened to tell the world that I was the child of a slave, and then I would have no right to any property because I was property."

She said it all in a rush. Almost without taking a breath.

"This is the family my sister is marrying into," Benjamin said. He shook his head.

"See, I shouldn't have told you that," she said. "Now you'll worry even more. You can't know, Benjamin. I have no power. If I try to challenge them, they threaten me. So for now, I must appear weak. You can't understand because you're a man."

"Someday we can have a conversation about that," he said. "I have had to make uncomfortable choices, too."

"At least you had choices to make," she said. They stood at the end of the alley.

"You don't need to go any farther," Callie said. "Unless you need a ride?"

He shook his head. "No, you go and have fun. I'll see you later for dinner."

"You're not off to see your Lucy Johnston?" Callie asked.

Benjamin turned and walked away. "Go with care, Calantha," he called over his shoulder.

Eighteen

Callie hurried down the street toward her carriage. Mr. Smith came toward her as she neared.

"We were getting worried," he said.

"I got waylaid," she said.

Walker stood next to the carriage door. He was dressed differently than he had been this morning, like a cabbie. Or maybe he held himself differently. He was pretending, too, pretending to be a slave. He wore a hat with a brim that covered most of his face.

"Hello, Mr. Walker," she said. "That is you, isn't it?"

"It is," he said. He opened the carriage door. Mr. Smith took Callie's hand and helped her inside.

A young boy sat on one of the seats. He seemed too young and too frail to be out in the world on his own. He wore frayed blue pants and a frayed blue shirt that barely covered him. He looked down and moved away from Callie as she got in.

"Hello," Callie said. "I'm—

"No," Walker said. "He doesn't need to know your name and you don't need to know his. You go on and get inside there now, son. We left a jug of water."

"Does he need to go in?" Callie asked. "No one is going to look inside the carriage. If we get stopped he can get in."

Walker shook his head. "At least until you get out of the city, he needs to be hidden. He's got water and there's air holes."

The boy looked terrified.

"He's probably right," she said to the boy. "It won't be long. Can you think of it as a temporary safe place?"

The boy stood, then lifted the seat. Callie looked inside. It was dark, but inside was a blanket, a jug, and a box of food. The boy stepped into the seat box. Callie held the seat lid until the boy was settled. He looked up at her. He tried to smile.

"I'm fine," he said. "Jus' fine."

Callie slowly lowered the lid.

"Can you breathe all right?" she asked.

"Yes," he said.

"We tried it out before you came," Walker said.

"You don't have to do anything but be a passenger," Mr. Smith told her. "Keep the curtains open so people can see you and know it's not empty."

Callie nodded. She sat on the other seat. Walker closed the door. She felt the carriage shift as Walker climbed up to the coach box. She looked out at Mr. Smith, who nodded and waved. Then the carriage rolled forward.

Callie glanced at the closed seat. It seemed like she should prop it open or something. It must feel like he was lying in his own coffin. She would not bring that up in case he hadn't thought of it.

"You'll be all right," Callie said. "It won't take too long and then you'll be on your way to . . . freedom."

They hadn't gone a block when suddenly the carriage stopped and the door swung open. In the next moment Matthew MacDonald was inside the carriage and sitting next to Callie. He put his arm across her shoulders. She pushed him away.

"Sir! You forget yourself!" Callie said. She pointed to the other seat and he sat across from her.

"Go on, boy!" Matthew shouted into the horn.

"You must leave at once, Mr. MacDonald," she said.

"I won't until I get your promise," he said. He shouted again, "I said go on!"

"He won't go until I tell him to," Callie said. "He doesn't take orders from you."

"Then I'll go out and beat him until he does!" He was still smiling, as though this was all a game.

Callie said firmly into the horn, "Go ahead, Walk—ah—Joseph. But stop at the next block where Mr. MacDonald will be getting out."

"I had to speak with you," he said. "I don't believe you and Dr. Sawyer are serious. I think you were teasing me. Telling me 'no' to encourage my solicitations. So here I am!"

He sat next to her again and tried to put both arms around

her. She pushed him away and kicked his shins. She moved to the other side of the carriage and shouted into the horn for Walker to stop the carriage.

"You presume too much, Mr. MacDonald!" she said. "Dr. Sawyer is a dear friend. And he is a true Southern gentleman who does not push his attentions on anyone. You sat with me at lunch uninvited and now you are here in this carriage—alone with me—without my permission. Your reputation might not matter to you but mine does to me! I must ask you to leave."

"Only if you'll agree to see me again," he said. "I won't let you out of this carriage until you do. You'll be stuck with me all afternoon."

Callie heard a sneeze or a cough, coming from the seat. She quickly sneezed to distract Matthew in case he heard it, too.

"I will not see you again," she said. "And I will tell my aunt all about this little encounter. I will tell her you behaved in a way that would bring shame upon your family."

The smile left his face. He looked frightened. "I had no idea you felt this way."

"That can only be because you haven't been listening!" she said. "Now get out!"

"Please don't tell Aunt Elizabeth," he said. "She'll tell my father and he will not be kind to me."

Callie didn't say anything for a moment. The carriage moved slightly as Walker climbed down from the box.

"I will do you this favor," she said. "I will not tell my aunt and uncle anything about our encounters while I was in Richmond. We will keep all this a secret. It will be as if it never happened. In return, you will cancel your dinner at my uncle's house tonight. You will tell your brothers and cousins to leave me be, and you will never ever accost and molest another woman like this again. If I hear even a whisper of something like this again, I will tell my aunt everything!"

The door to the carriage opened just then. Matthew turned toward the light and squinted.

"Yes, of course," he said. "This is our little secret."

"Sir, did you need help disembarking?" Walker asked.

Matthew didn't say anything. He sprang out of the carriage and practically ran down the road away from them.

"Are you all right?" Walker asked.

Callie's heart was racing. She felt angry, invigorated, and a little scared. She looked at Walker. She suddenly wished he would put his arms around her to comfort her. She wished they could run away and he could read poetry to her and she could paint flowers for him. She wanted to feel safe and comfortable again.

She rubbed her face.

What nonsense.

"I'm fine," Callie said. "Let's get going."

"Lock the door this time," Walker said.

Callie nodded.

Walker closed the door, and Callie locked it. She felt the carriage shift as he got back into the driver's box. Then the carriage moved forward again. She leaned over, knocked on the seat cover, and then opened it. The boy looked up at her.

"You doing well?" she asked.

He nodded.

"Miss, what makes white men so crazy?"

Callie shook her head. "I have no idea," she said. "I suppose it's because they feel entitled to have everything and everyone." The boy looked at her, uncomprehending. She didn't blame him. She didn't understand either. "Maybe it's something they eat." The boy smiled. Callie nodded. "Try to get some rest. It won't be long."

They travelled for a while without incident. When the houses and buildings began to thin out and they were traveling through something that looked more like country, Callie lifted the lid and told the boy he could come out if he liked.

He pulled himself up and out, stretched a little, then closed the seat and sat on it.

"How's your back?" Callie asked.

"It's good," he said. "They fixed it up good."

Callie wondered who "they" were, but she didn't ask. How old was he? Thirteen? Fourteen? How could he do this on his own? She had a million questions for him, but she didn't ask any of them. The answers would satisfy her curiosity; that was all.

"Company," she heard Walker call down to her. The boy quickly got back into the seat box.

Callie opened the curtain and looked outside. A group of men on horseback were passing by, going in the opposite direction. She recognized at least one of them: Dave Tenant, the slave hunter. He saw her at the same time she saw him. He squinted as if trying to remember her. Then he held up his arm to tell his men to stop. He shouted to Walker to stop.

Walker reined in the horses. The carriage rocked to a halt.

Callie slid the window open.

"My, we do meet in the strangest places," Callie said. "How do you do, Mr. Tenant?"

"You are far from home, Miss Carter," he said. "What brings you up here?"

"Every time I see you, you ask a lot of questions," Callie said. "My mother taught me it wasn't polite for a gentlemen to ask a lady anything at all. Should I take your questioning as a sign of disrespect toward me or a lacking in your own upbringing?" She smiled broadly, innocently.

His eyes narrowed. "I'm looking for escaped slaves," he said. "I want to make certain you are not being held hostage."

"Goodness no," she said. "As you can see I'm quite alone."

"For a young lady, you sure do seem to be on your own a great deal," Tenant said. "Is that safe?"

The horses moved restlessly, stirring up dust with their hooves as their riders tried to calm them. The breeze shifted, and Callie could smell the men's sweat.

"I appreciate your interest in my safety," Callie said, "but there you are with the questions again."

Tenant clicked his horse forward, closer to the carriage.

"As I said, I am looking for escaped slaves," he said. "How do I know this darkie isn't running off somewhere with you as his hostage."

"Really? Escaped slaves have been doing that?" she asked. "That's a shame. You'll have to teach them all a lesson when you catch them. But I can assure you that I am not being held hostage."

"Do you have his papers?" Tenant asked.

"I most certainly do not," Callie said.

"Maybe I better take him back to town and check him out," Tenant said.

Callie could feel Walker shift in the driver's box. She wanted to scream at Tenant to mind his own business. She took a breath: What would Jewelweed do?

"You cannot take him from me," Callie said. "He is my property and that would be theft. I believe they still hang people for theft here in the South. Or maybe it's death by firing squad. I can't quite recall. But you should know the law. Or are you from the North? You can't take people's property down here. Now I need to continue on to my friend's home. If I don't get there on time, I will have to tell my guardian and friend Judge Zebadiah about the dangers of coming to Richmond and he will have to tell the city fathers. We can't have travelers coming to Richmond only to be accosted on the roads."

Tenant glanced up at Walker and then back at Callie.

"Go on your way then," he said. "Your parents should not let you travel these roads alone. They are dangerous."

"My parents were killed in a carriage accident not six months ago," Callie said. "I am quite aware of the dangers of traveling these or any roads."

Tenant looked momentarily off-balance. He should have known about her parents. Why didn't he? Maybe he was from the North after all.

Tenant held up his hand again. He nodded to her; then they

galloped off, all at once, responding to a cue Callie didn't notice.

Callie leaned back against her seat. Was this what adulthood was going to be like? In order to get men to leave her alone she would have to constantly threaten them?

A moment later, her horses sprang forward, taking the carriage with them.

Not long after, Walker pulled the horses and carriage into a birch forest. Walker got down and opened the door. Callie opened the lid and the boy pulled himself out of the seat box. Walker took Callie's hand to help her down out of the coach. She didn't feel the spark of electricity she had felt every time she and Benjamin touched lately, but she liked feeling Walker's skin next to her own. Once her feet touched the ground he let her go. The boy followed her out of the carriage.

"Thank you, Miss," the boy said.

"You are welcome," she said. "I am sorry for your troubles."

"I am sorry for yours," he said.

"I won't be long," Walker said. "If anyone comes, get into the carriage."

Then the boy and Walker disappeared into the woods. Was a safe house nearby? Or the path to one? Was someone meeting them?

Callie walked around. She felt an almost overwhelming urge to run through the woods, run as fast as she could, to get as far away as she could. She was excited and alarmed all at once.

Mostly she felt giddy. Who and what had she become?

An outlaw.

Walker came back almost immediately. Callie grinned.

"Is he safe?" she asked.

"He's on his way," Walker said. "This is only one stop along the way for him. We should get going in case the slave hunter comes back. You handled yourself very well."

Callie curtsied. "Thank you."

"What was going on with the red-haired man?" Walker asked.

"The nephew of my aunt?" she said. "I don't think he'll be bothering me again."

"I'm not sure about you doing this," he said.

Callie smiled. "So you're worried about me? That's sweet."

Walker frowned, but he didn't say anything.

"I'm ready to do it again," Callie said. "I feel as though I'm doing some good. I'm ready to go any time again."

"Right now we should get back," he said. "Before you're missed."

Callie nodded. "All right, sir."

"Don't call me that," he said. "It ain't right, and I don't like it."

Callie felt her face redden. "I'm sorry," Callie said. "I was trying to be respectful." That wasn't exactly true. It had been her attempt at being coquettish.

"You can be respectful by calling me by my given name," he said. "And by getting in the coach so we can get out of here."

Callie hoped Walker didn't notice she was blushing. He

opened the door to the coach. She ignored his hand and pulled herself into the carriage. It wasn't exactly ladylike, but she wanted to get out of his sight. She should ask Mr. Smith to put a step on the carriage. One had been there once upon a time.

Walker shut the door and went up into the driver's box. Then he somehow got the carriage turned around and headed back to town.

Sometime later, they arrived at the stables. Mr. Smith and Joseph hurried out to greet them.

"If you could get me a cab," Callie said as she took Mr. Smith's hand and stepped out of the coach, "I will return to my uncle's home. The horses are best left here so they don't take up room at my uncle's stables. Joseph, are you all right here?"

Walker came down from the driver's box and the four of them stood together. Callie didn't look at Walker.

"I'm doing fine here," Joseph said.

"I'll send you a message when we're ready to leave," she said. "Mr. Smith, I wonder if you could put the step back on this coach. It used to have one, and I don't like to rely on other people to get me in and out of the carriage."

"Um, certainly," he said. "How did everything go?"

"Fine," Callie said. "Everything went according to plan."

Walker nodded. "She did great. She threw one man out of the coach and scared away a whole posse. She was like one of those Amazon queens or warriors of old."

"You can regale them with my great feats later," Callie said. "I should be getting back."

Joseph got her a cab, and Callie left behind the carriage

house and stables. She didn't feel quite as embarrassed now; after all, Walker had just compared her to an Amazon queen. She could live with that.

Nineteen

When Callie returned to her uncle's house, she learned that Matthew MacDonald had cancelled his dinner with them. He had come down with something he feared would be quite contagious.

After dinner, Callie and Benjamin went outside and walked in the overgrown gardens. Callie told him what had happened with Matthew.

"He jumped into the coach and put his arms around you?" Benjamin asked. "That is outrageous!"

"You should be outraged," she said, "especially since he thought we were engaged." She laughed.

"I'm glad you find it funny," he said. "He could have hurt you."

"Please don't be one of those men who warns me off going

anywhere alone," she said. "Besides, I wasn't alone. Walker would have stepped in."

"Walker? Reby's brother?"

Had she said Walker? She had to get better at lying, or covering up, or something.

Callie shook her head. "No, I meant Joseph. I mixed it up because of Matthew MacDonald and Walker. The names sound alike."

Benjamin raised an eyebrow.

"Well, I don't know why I said his name," she said. "I meant Joseph. Joseph would have helped."

"People like Matthew MacDonald should not be allowed in polite company," Benjamin said.

"But they should be allowed in impolite company?"

"That's not what I meant," he said. "I'm trying to express my outrage."

"You don't have to be my knight in shining armor," Callie said. "I took care of him. I don't think he'll be bothering me or anyone else. You don't need to challenge him to a duel or anything."

"Good thing," he said, "since I left my dueling pistols at home."

Callie laughed. "You told me we should have a conversation about freedom one day, men versus women. Don't you feel as though you've gotten to make choices in your life based on what you wanted?"

Callie sat on the wooden bench beneath a large magnolia bush. The shiny green leaves hung over the bench so that her face was right next to one of the white flowers. Something about white magnolia blossoms always took her breath away, for a moment, as she marveled at the creamy whiteness. The petals were beautiful, yet tough, not thin and fragile like a rose blossom or even a trillium. Callie resisted the urge to touch the flower. Instead she inhaled its scent.

"May I?" he asked, indicating the space next to her on the bench.

"Of course," she said. "Didn't you want to be a doctor?"

He pressed his lips together and sighed. She knew he was trying to decide if he should tell her the truth or not. He used to do the same thing when they were children. He was older than she was, so he was sometimes careful about what he said to her. Like the time she asked how mares made foals. Did they eat too much clover? He had finally suggested she ask her mother to explain that particular process.

"I did not want to be a doctor," he said. "That was my father's idea. He didn't want me to work the plantation, particularly since Mother wanted to free all her slaves. He believed being a doctor would make me a living. I thought I would get used to it, after working with Dr. Kelly for many many years. I have gotten used to it, I suppose, but I wish I wasn't on my own so soon. Doctoring is not my first love."

"I had no idea," she said. "What is your first love? Besides me, of course."

"Of course," he said. He looked at her. The flower came between them. He pushed it gently and held it away from her and against his hand. "What do you think my first love is?"

"Hmm," she said. "This is a test of our friendship, isn't it? To see how well I know you. You always liked the country.

The plants. Botany. You were the only other person who knew as much about plants as my mother. And you always liked telling everyone about what you knew. Not like a braggart. Just because you were excited about it. Only you got quieter as you got older. Ah, now I know why. It was because you felt like you couldn't be yourself. You wanted to be running through the forest like a madman. A mountain man! Reclaiming the wilderness."

Benjamin laughed.

"I think you wanted to be a teacher," she said. "And a scientist, an explorer."

"You are exactly right!" he said.

"Don't sound so surprised," she said. "That's why you and I are such good friends. We are kindred spirits." She sighed. "That's why it will be difficult when you marry. I won't be allowed to be such good friends with you."

"Oh, that's silly," he said. "Of course we'll be friends, always."

"Why didn't you become a teacher?" she asked. "Because of your father?"

He shrugged. "A doctor can distinguish himself as a gentleman," he said. "I could have rich patients who bequeath me their fortunes."

"That's important to you? Now that surprises me."

"It's not important to me," he said. "Of course, I can be sanguine about money because my parents had money. My father saw the future. He knew the South would fall one day, and he didn't want me to fall with it. Being a doctor would give me some prominence in the community; being a teacher would not."

"You think the South will fall?" she asked. "You believe there will be a war, too?"

"I have no idea," he said. "But my father didn't believe the institution of slavery was a durable economic system, because it relied on the continual cruelty exerted by one group onto another group. It is a soulless economy, a spiritually bankrupt existence."

"And yet he had slaves," Callie said, "at least for a time."

"Until he couldn't bear it any longer," Benjamin said. "But before he could free them, he died. After his death, my mother set all the slaves free. Fortunately she found a good manager, at least as far as I can tell."

"There's still time for you to be a teacher," Callie said. "There's still time for you to explore."

"Why don't we do it together?" Benjamin said. "As soon as you are of age, we'll set off together."

"We can go to South America and look for Uncle James," she said. "I have a thing or two to tell him. Or up in Canada or out West, where they still have some virgin forests. Think of all the plants we'd find."

"We'd have to marry," he said. "Otherwise it would be too scandalous."

"I like scandal," she said. "Besides, we could say we are sister and brother."

"No, we could not," he said.

"I can't marry you," she said. "What would Lucy Johnston do? It would break her heart."

He laughed.

"I wish I could help Therese," Callie said softly. "Your family does not deserve Barnaby."

"I wish you could help, too," he said. He sighed. "But it's out of our hands now."

Therese's stomach seemed to have calmed down by the time the three of them left Richmond. The carriage ride back was much quicker and smoother. At the Sawyer residence, Therese thanked Callie, and Benjamin kissed her gloved hand. Callie and Joseph returned to Mount Joy. She was glad to see her home. For a moment, she forgot that her parents no longer lived there. Or anywhere.

Elizabeth peppered her with questions about her journey. Callie told her in detail everything about the trip to the mercantile, picking out the fabric, and the fitting. She left out any mention of Therese's morning sickness or Matthew's bad behavior.

Uncle Charles mentioned he had some legal papers he wanted her to look over.

"Oh, Uncle Charles," she said. "You know I don't have the head for such things. Anything you want me to sign, just take it to my lawyer, John Bowen, and he'll tell me what to do." She smiled sweetly at her uncle and batted her eyelashes. Charles glanced at his wife. She looked a little frightened. She shrugged slightly.

"After the wedding we'll need to deal with this," he said. "We've put it off long enough."

"Of course," Callie said.

The week passed uneventfully. Callie spent time in the garden or in the woods, drawing. She helped Therese and Aunt Elizabeth with wedding plans, although most of the reception details had been decided while they were in Richmond. It would be a small affair, just family at the church. Later they would have the reception at Mount Joy.

Callie listened and watched for Walker, for any news from him or Momma Gospel. She went to sleep every night wearing a shift instead of a nightgown. No message came.

Then one night, Reby shook her awake. Callie opened her eyes and saw Reby standing over her, holding a lantern.

"You've got company," she whispered.

Callie sat up quickly. Reby went to the dresser and lit a candle for her.

"You go back to bed," Callie said. "I don't want you getting into trouble. Where are they?"

"They're already in the passageway," she said. "They could use water and food."

Callie nodded. She took the candle from Reby. Reby left the room. Callie locked the door and then went behind the wardrobe, opened that door, and slipped through it, candle still in hand.

She hurried down the narrow stairs, in bare feet.

When she reached the bottom of the last stairs, she walked down the corridor until she saw Walker standing with a woman and man wearing ragged wet clothes, looking as though they had just come from the river.

Walker nodded to her. She smiled at the new travelers and then whispered, "Welcome. What can I get for you?"

"Some blankets so they can get these clothes off and get

dry," Walker said. "Food and water."

"Of course."

She left them and went to the secret opening by the kitchen. She listened and heard nothing. No light came from beneath the door, so she slowly opened it.

She quickly stepped into the kitchen and shut the door. She set the candle down, then hurried to the linen closet down the hall and retrieved towels and two blankets.

She listened carefully again and heard only her heart in her ears. She opened the secret door, went inside, closed it behind her, and hurried down the corridor—in total darkness—until she nearly tripped over Walker and the man and woman. Walker took the proffered linens from her. She hurried back to the kitchen door.

She opened it, stepped into the kitchen, and closed it. She picked up the candle and started toward the pantry.

"Where did you come from?"

Callie jumped. Standing before her was Barnaby. In the dark, without a candle or lantern.

"What are you doing here?" Callie asked. "You frightened me half to death."

"I was hungry," he said.

She knew that was a lie. If he had wanted something to eat, he would have awakened every slave in the house so they could serve him.

He was looking for Reby.

"And you?" he asked.

"I was hungry, too," she said. "Let me make you something. When did you get in?"

"Only a couple of hours ago," he said. He glanced around the room.

"What are you looking for?" Callie asked.

"Me?" He shrugged. "Nothing. I thought I saw something when I rode up. Three slaves. A woman and two men. Only for a second, and then they were gone. Maybe one of your field slaves out for a romp."

"What would you like to eat?" she asked.

"Come to think of it," he said, "I'm not really that hungry. I think I'll try to sleep again."

"Good night then," Callie said. She followed him through the pantry. He kept going. She stayed and got smoked sausage, bread, and cheese. She went back to the kitchen and pumped some water into a jug.

She couldn't go back into the secret passageway. Not with Barnaby hanging around. She couldn't go back to her room because her door was locked and she didn't have a key. She wasn't certain what to do.

She should warn Reby. Just in case Barnaby kept wandering.

Callie hurried up the stairs. When she got on the third floor, she went to Reby's door and knocked.

"Reby, it's me," she said. She turned the knob and hurried into Reby's tiny room. She set the food and water on the bed. Reby sat up.

"Reby, I thought I told you to lock the door," Callie said.

"Your aunt won't let me have a key," Reby said.

Callie groaned.

"Barnaby is here," she said. "I caught him sneaking around

downstairs. I think he was looking for you. I need to go find a key. If you hear anyone coming, hide under the bed."

Reby grabbed her arm.

"Don't leave me here," she said.

"I don't know what else to do," she said. "If you go with me and he finds you—"

"Please," she said. "I feel safer with you."

"All right," Callie said.

She opened the door slowly and listened. No one was coming. They hurried out, shut the door, ran down the corridor, then down the stairs. At the second floor landing, they stopped and listened. Silence. They hurried down the stairs.

They went into the parlor. Callie gave Reby the candle and she went to her mother's desk—the desk her aunt used now. Callie's mother had always kept an extra set of keys in the bottom drawer. Callie pulled the drawer open. Reby held the candle closer. Callie moved papers around.

No keys.

She tried the other drawers.

Just a rat's nest of paper.

Her mother had always kept her things in order.

Callie heard a creak on the stairs. She looked at Reby. Then she blew out the candle and pulled Reby down next to her. They scooted under the desk.

Callie heard footsteps in the hallway.

Going into the dining room?

Callie and Reby clung tightly to each other. Callie held her breath.

The footsteps stopped.

Whoever it was must be looking around. Deciding what to do next.

The footsteps retreated. Walking through the dining room. To the pantry and kitchen. Again.

Must be Barnaby.

"We've got to go," Callie said. She started to get up and her sleeve caught on a nail. She went to pull it off and felt something else on the nail: a key ring.

Callie grabbed it. Then she and Reby ran out of the room and up the stairs. They didn't stop on the second floor. They kept running.

Once inside Reby's room, Callie felt around on the ring until she found a skeleton key, and then she locked Reby's door. The two of them sat up against it, their breathing ragged at first. After a couple of minutes, Callie pressed her ear against the door and listened.

Someone was on their floor.

Someone was trying the doors.

She heard a door open, then close again.

Reby grabbed her arm.

"He can't get in here," Callie said.

"What if he has a key?" Reby asked.

Callie had forgotten to leave the key in the keyhole to prevent anyone else from using their key. Too late now.

"He wouldn't do anything with me here," Callie whispered. "He's not crazy."

"He is crazy," she said. "I've heard stories of him going all over the county, looking for girls."

"That has to be against the law," Callie said. "He can't go

around raping girls who don't belong to him."

"But he can rape girls who do belong to him?" Reby asked.

"I'm saying I don't know what the law is," Callie said.

"Who would testify against him if it was against the law?" Reby said.

"Shh," Callie said.

Footsteps came down the hall. Another door opened and closed.

Then the door handle to Reby's room rattled. Someone leaned against the door from the other side and pushed.

The door didn't move.

Callie thought she heard someone breathing on the other side of the door.

Then the person walked away and tried a couple of other doors. Hers?

And then the sound of footsteps was gone.

Callie and Reby waited in silence for a long while. Then Callie unlocked the door and slowly opened it. She looked up and down the corridor.

It was empty.

"Grab the food and water," Callie said. "You're staying in my room for the rest of the night."

They hurried down the corridor to Callie's room. Callie unlocked it. They went inside and locked the door again.

"I need to get this food to our guests," Callie said. "Don't open the door for anyone but me."

Reby nodded.

"Don't look so scared," Callie said. "You're safe now."

"I'm never safe," Reby said.

Callie took the food and water from Reby and went into the secret passage. She walked down the stairs in the dark. She handed the man and woman the food and water.

"Walker, can I talk to you?" she asked.

He nodded and they moved away from the family.

"What took you so long coming back?" Walker asked.

"My cousin Barnaby is here," she said. "He found me in the kitchen."

"Does he suspect anything?" he asked.

"I don't think so," she said. "But I'm not sure Reby is safe with him around. I'll try to keep her with me until he leaves."

"It may be too dangerous to use Jewelweed Station as a safe house," he said. "With most of the houses we use, everyone there knows what is going on, and they're protective of their visitors. Here we've got to worry about one of the most notorious men in the county finding us."

"Please don't let him ruin this for me," Callie said.

"For you?"

"I didn't mean it that way," Callie said. "I mean that I'm finally doing something worthwhile. I'm not the enemy. I'm trying to help."

She went back to the kitchen entrance. She listened a long time before she slowly and carefully opened the door and stepped into the kitchen. Then she went to the parlor and slipped the key ring back on the nail underneath the desk.

She hurried up two flights of stairs again until she stood in front of her door. She knocked.

"It's me, Reby," she said.

Reby opened the door and let her in.

Callie and Reby slept in bed together, just as they had done when they were younger. Callie dreamed she and Walker were on a trail in the woods. Up ahead, she saw a bear. Suddenly the bear turned and charged them. Walker grabbed her hand and pulled her off the trail. They ran and ran. Callie laughed as she ran. She loved the feel of his hand in hers.

When she woke up, she felt as though everything would work out.

In the morning when Reby helped her dress, Callie told her about the dream.

"You can't be dreaming about my brother like that," Reby said.

"Why not?" Callie asked. "It was a perfectly innocent dream."

Reby shook her head. "You've got to stop this. This is Abraham all over again."

"Don't be ridiculous," Callie said.

"No, I think you want to do all this to be closer to Walker," she said. "And it's wrong. It's dead wrong."

"I wish you would settle down, Reby," Callie said. "It was a harmless dream. I felt safe in it. Nothing untoward about that. It's not as though we're running off and getting married."

"Don't say things like that," Reby said. "You can't say things like that."

"I don't know what's wrong with you," Callie said. "We used to be friends and since we've gotten back, you've treated me like a stranger. And now this. Am I not good enough for your precious brother. What is it, Reby?"

"You can't think of him that way because he is your brother, too," Reby said.

Reby stepped away from Callie. Callie looked at her. She blinked twice.

"I'm sorry. What?"

Reby sighed and sat on the bed.

"He is your brother," she said.

"What do you mean?"

Reby cleared her throat. "Don't make me do this. I was never supposed to tell you. You weren't supposed to know."

"Know what?" Callie said. Her heart was pounding in her ears.

"Your father is Walker's father," she said.

The room seemed to tilt a bit. Callie felt sick to her stomach.

"This can't be true," she said.

"It is," Reby said. "My mother was your father's slave. It was before he married your mother."

"Were they lovers?" Callie asked.

Reby looked at her. "My mother was married to my father at the time. Your father took a shine to her."

Callie moved away from Reby. This couldn't be true. She turned around and fumbled with the key until she unlocked the door and opened it. She ran out of the room, down the stairs, and out the front door. She ran all the way to the gardens, not noticing that she was still barefoot. She fell on the ground near a bed of cornflowers. She could smell the dirt and grass.

She began to weep.

How could this be true?

How could her dearest father be a rapist like Barnaby?

Had Reby's mother tried to lock herself in a room like Reby had last night to escape from her father?

Her dear sweet father.

Who had forced himself on a woman. Had fathered a child. A child he never acknowledged.

By rights this entire plantation should belong to Walker as the eldest. As the son.

Callie felt like she was going to throw up.

This was worse than when she found out her parents had died.

What could be worse than finding out her father was a monster?

She lay on the grass for some time.

Then she heard Henry's voice. "Are you all right, Miss Callie?"

Callie turned her head so that she could see him.

"Your aunt was concerned about you. She asked me to check on you."

Callie laughed. "I can't imagine she was concerned about me." Callie pushed herself up to a sitting position. She wiped the grass and dirt off her cheek. "Tell me, Henry. Did you know my father had a son?"

Henry blinked.

"Is that it?" she asked. "Just one son? Any other mixed babies running around that I should know about?"

"Not that I know about, Miss Callie," he said.

"Do my aunt and uncle know anything about this?" she asked.

"I don't believe so," he said.

She held her hand out. He reached down a gloved hand to her. She took it, and he pulled her up.

"I want to apologize again for what happened to your daughter Heddie," Callie said. "And I apologize if I or my parents were ever cruel or unfeeling. I swear to you that if I have anything to say about it, every one of you will be free soon. All of you."

"You must be careful," Henry said quietly. "Everything is not always as it seems."

"I am learning that," Callie said. "Tell my aunt I am ill, and please have some food brought up to my room. I'm so hungry I could eat for three. Oh, and please let my aunt know that I took the cheese, bread, and sausage from the pantry last night. I wouldn't want anyone else to get in trouble for it."

"Yes, Miss Callie," he said.

Twenty

Callie managed to get upstairs without her aunt seeing her. Reby brought her breakfast. Callie took the tray and then closed the door, leaving Reby on the other side of it.

She went into the secret passageway, carrying the tray, and walked down to the first floor and then into the corridor leading to the secret entrance to the outside.

No one was there.

The blankets and towels were neatly folded beside the door. On top was a jewelweed blossom.

Callie sighed. She sat on the pile of blankets and linens.

"Thanks, brother. I wish someone had told me you were leaving. What am I going to do with all this food now?"

She picked up a slice of bacon and bit off a piece.

Callie stayed in her room for as long as she could. Elizabeth sent word up twice that she hoped she was feeling better. Callie knew Elizabeth was nervous about the wedding because Therese was pregnant. Callie had assured her again and again that no one knew and even if they did, no one would care. Therese was not the first bride to come to the church carrying more than a bouquet of flowers.

Callie went downstairs for dinner.

"My cousin looks a little pale," Barnaby said as he held a chair out for her. "Everything all right?"

"I had a bad night," she said. "Someone was going around opening and closing doors on the third floor. It was quite disconcerting."

"It was probably Barnaby," Elizabeth said. "He used to sleepwalk when he was younger. Perhaps the stress of his upcoming nuptials has reactivated it."

"I have no stress about my upcoming nuptials," he said. "I can hardly wait. In two days hence, I shall be a married man."

"Indeed," Charles said. "With all the responsibilities therein."

"I'm well aware of my responsibilities, Father," Barnaby said. "You have taught me well."

Callie wanted to hiss at him. Or growl. Something to show her absolute and utter disgust for him and everyone like him.

Including her father.

Had her mother known? How had she coped?

Maybe that was why so many of the married women Callie knew drank or took opiates or were completely wrapped up in the lives of their children: They knew what their husbands did, and they could do nothing to stop it.

Callie had heard of such things before, of course. But she had never imagined that her father was one of the culprits. She couldn't look at Reby. Wasn't sure she could ever speak to Walker again.

Did every woman know what her man was doing behind her back? And if they did, why didn't they do something?

Callie shook her head. *She* had to do something. Walker and Reby had told her Barnaby was known throughout the county for accosting slave women. Barnaby was a criminal. Immoral. Her father too. How could she stop Barnaby? Or any of them?

After dinner, Barnaby said he was going for a ride.

Callie knew that probably meant he was going out to find some slave woman he could molest.

She wasn't sure what she was going to do, but she was going to do something.

She told her aunt she was still feeling ill. She went upstairs and locked her door. Then she took off her clothes and put on the men's black clothes she had worn the other night when she met Momma Gospel. She went into the secret passage and left the house via the entrance near the stables.

She hurried into the stables—undetected she hoped— and ducked into an empty stall. Keeping herself hidden, she looked around. Barnaby's piebald was still there, but he was saddled and ready to go.

"Miss Callie?" Joseph was suddenly behind her. So much for staying hidden.

"Miss Callie, you're not going on another night ride?"

"Yes," she said. "I need you to saddle up Meager, before Barnaby comes out."

He nodded. She waited impatiently, looking from the house back to Joseph and back to the house again.

"Come on, come on," she whispered.

Finally Joseph returned to her with Meager. She got up into the saddle quickly, thanked Joseph, and then took Meager out the back way. She went into a copse of trees where she could see the stables. And she waited.

Soon enough, Barnaby emerged, riding his piebald. He trotted past Callie and Meager, hidden by the trees and the near night. Callie waited until he was a ways ahead of her, and then she followed. She thought he might go to her own slave cabins, but he didn't. He turned at Foster Road. Callie held Meager back for a bit before she let him follow Barnaby's horse.

Barnaby must be going to the Tyler Plantation. Did he have friends there?

He went right by the road to the Tyler mansion and headed for the cabins down by the fields.

Callie pulled Meager to a stop. She watched the piebald go down to the end of the row of cabins, to a shack a bit away from the others. Callie glanced down and realized Meager was standing next to a huge wall of jewelweed. She reached over and gently pulled off several blossoms and put them in her pocket.

She felt suddenly calm and focused.

She trotted Meager down the slave road. She rode right

up to Barnaby's piebald tied to a post. She leaned over and reached into one of the saddlebags. Found two kerchiefs with the initials BA on them. She took them. She dropped a jewelweed blossom into the bag.

She leaned down, untied the piebald, and slipped the bridle off his head. Then she took out her crop and hit the horse on his rear while simultaneously screaming at the top of her lungs. It was not a girl's scream. Not even a woman's scream. It was the scream of a banshee. It chilled her to the bone.

The pie raced away. Callie kicked Meager, and they raced away, too.

She ran Meager all the way up to the Tyler plantation. A slave came running out to take her horse. In the dark. She put a jewelweed blossom in one of Barnaby's kerchiefs and she handed it to the slave.

"Tell your master someone is down in the slave quarters stealing one of his slaves," she said. "This man." She pointed to the kerchief.

"Yes, sir," he said.

Then Callie and Meager raced away. Darkness enfolded them, protected them.

On the road again Callie realized they weren't far from where Tenant, the slave hunter, lived. She took out Barnaby's kerchief and began leaning over and rubbing it on trees and bushes as they continued on.

She had never been this far afield at night before.

It didn't matter. No one knew her; and anyone who saw her would think she was a man.

She saw the Tenant homestead. Saw the kennels in the

back. She kept rubbing Barnaby's kerchief here and there. She rode around to the back. She was surprised the dogs didn't bark.

Did they recognize her scent from the last time?

She got off Meager and loosely tied him up under the tree line. Then she crept to the kennels.

She whispered, "Hey babies, not here to hurt you. Yes, good dogs."

Callie took out a jewelweed blossom and put it on top of the first kennel. Then she unlatched the door and opened it a crack.

One dog howled a bit, then stopped.

She did the same thing to the next kennel.

"Hey babies. Hey doggies. How you doing tonight?"

And then the next.

"Hey darlin' doggies. Come to me."

Soon all the dogs surrounded her.

"I've got something for you," she said. She pulled out a kerchief and let each dog smell it, pushed it up to their noses. Soon they were all baying.

"Go on!" she cried. "Find him!"

She had no idea if that was the right or wrong thing to say. But the dogs leapt forward and soon disappeared into the night, just like that, baying, barking.

She thought she heard a door slam.

She ran toward Meager. She could see him. Was almost there.

She tripped and fell. Twisted her ankle. She bit her lip so she wouldn't scream.

"Meager," she called. "Come."

A moment later, the horse was next to her. She leaned against him as she got up. Fortunately it was her right leg that was injured. She grabbed the saddle horn as she put her left foot in the stirrup; then she swung her right leg up and over.

"Let's go!" she called.

They ran into the night.

Her ankle throbbed, but she was ecstatic. She had felt a rush of pleasure when she loosed the piebald and when she let the dogs out.

"Do you see me, Father?" she called out. "Do you see what I'm doing? What I'm doing is right. What you did was wrong. Wrong! Wrong!"

Callie and Meager finally made it back to Mount Joy. Joseph came running out to get her.

"Is Mr. Barnaby back yet?" she asked.

Joseph shook his head.

"Can you help me down?" she asked. "I've hurt my ankle."

"I knew something would happen," he said.

"Yes, yes," she said. "You were right."

Joseph brought a stool and then between the two of them, they got her off the horse.

"Joseph, I need someone to go get Dr. Sawyer," she said. "Tell him I fell and hurt my ankle."

"Yes, Miss Callie," he said.

"But first get Reby and ask her to meet me upstairs," she said. "Without letting anyone else know."

She grabbed a walking stick resting against the half-open

stable door and used it to lean on as she hobbled to the secret door as Joseph ran toward the house. She felt around in the dark for a little while before she found the door and opened it. She walked down the corridor and then stopped at the bottom of the stairs.

She had not thought this through. How was she going to get up two flights of stairs?

She tried to put her weight on her right foot.

Still hurt.

She leaned on the banister and slowly made her way up the stairs.

It seemed to take forever.

When she unlocked her bedroom door, Reby stood waiting for her in the hallway.

"Oh my," Reby said as she went inside the room. "What did you do?"

"Please help me get out of these clothes and into a bed shirt," she said. "And then run downstairs and tell Elizabeth I've fallen and hurt my ankle, and I need Joseph to get Dr. Sawyer. Ask to go tell him yourself, since he's already gone. You can pretend."

Reby nodded. "Do you want to tell me what happened?"

Callie shook her head.

Reby helped take off Callie's clothes. She put on her bed shirt by herself. Then she lay on the bed and propped up her foot on a pillow.

"Does it hurt?" Reby asked. "It's swollen."

"Yes, it hurts," she said. "Could you chip off some ice and bring it up? That might help the swelling."

Reby hurried away. A few minutes later, Elizabeth knocked on the door and came inside. She was limping slightly.

"What have you done to yourself this time?" Elizabeth asked. "I swear you are the sickliest, most accident prone child I know!"

"I'm not a child, Aunt Elizabeth," she said. "And I'm so sorry. I stepped wrong and twisted my ankle. I'm sure it'll be fine."

Elizabeth leaned over to look at her ankle. She frowned. "It does not look fine. Now I'm glad you aren't a bridesmaid. You could have spoiled everything."

"Yes, I'm glad, too."

"Well, Reby's gone to send Joseph to Dr. Sawyer," she said. "He always seems to know what to do for you. Do you want me to sit with you until he comes?"

"That is very kind, Auntie," she said, "but I'm fine. Reby's bringing me some ice."

"I'll have the kitchen brew you some willow bark tea," she said. "That will help the pain."

"Thank you."

"Aunt Elizabeth, why are you limping?"

"Am I?" she asked. She looked down at her covered legs. "I fell earlier."

"Perhaps Benjamin can look at it for you?" Callie said.

"Dr. Sawyer," Elizabeth emphasized. "And I said I'm fine."

Had Uncle Charles hurt her somehow?

"Should I have Reby bring you something to eat?" Elizabeth asked. "That might help. Although Lord knows you've been eating like a horse for the last couple of days. I can't imagine you're hungry. You better watch your eating or you'll turn out like Mrs. Wilson after she had children. Now that's a sight."

Callie looked at her aunt. Just when she started to feel sorry for her she said something like that.

Elizabeth sat on Callie's bed and absentmindedly rubbed her own hip. "It would help me if you could sign those papers."

"Aunt Elizabeth," Callie said, "I told you I'd have the lawyer look over the papers. Why are they so important?"

"Your uncle needs to move things around," she said. "Sell some things so he can buy other things to make the plantation more profitable."

"That sounds reasonable." It actually sounded vague, but she wanted to reassure her aunt. "I promise by the reception I will have an answer. Will you be all right until then?"

Elizabeth got off the bed and stood up straight.

"Will I be all right? I don't know what you mean. I will be fine. I am fine. This is between your uncle and you."

She left the room without another word.

After a while Reby returned with willow bark tea and a sandwich to help it go down. She smiled at Reby as she took the tea and sandwich.

"You are good to me," Callie said. "You remembered the willow bark sometimes upsets my stomach."

"You are good to me, too," Reby said.

She sat at Callie's dressing table.

"Truly?" Callie asked. "I thought you hated me."

"I thought you hated me," she said. "Especially since I told you about Walker."

"Oh, that," Callie said. "I don't want to think about that right now. I just want the pain to go away."

Reby nodded. "I understand."

Callie was able to fall to sleep. She awakened when she felt a spark of electricity as Benjamin touched her hand. She smiled at him and pushed herself into a sitting position.

"Are you all right?" He squeezed her hand.

She felt as though she was going to cry.

She wanted to talk to someone. Tell someone everything she had been experiencing.

Who could she trust?

She looked into Benjamin's eyes. He seemed concerned. She thought she could trust him, but then she thought she could trust her father. She rubbed her face.

"Would you like Reby to step out?"

"She can't leave," Callie said. "She's in danger."

Benjamin glanced at Reby and then looked back at Callie. "What do you mean?"

"It's all right, Miss Callie," Reby said. "He hasn't returned yet."

"Then step outside the door and come back in if anything happens."

Reby did as she was told. When the door closed, Callie began to cry.

"Callie, tell me what's happened," Benjamin said.

"I'm sorry," she said. "I don't mean to cry. It just hurts."

Benjamin turned up the lamp and then examined her ankle. She cringed as he moved her foot around.

He pulled up a chair and sat in it, close to the bed.

"It's not broken," he said. "When the swelling goes down, I'll wrap it. In the meantime, ice and willow bark tea. You're already doing both. You don't really need me. But if you're in trouble, Callie, I want you to confide in me." He took her hand in his and kissed it.

Her stomach fluttered.

"Benjamin, there's so much," she said. "I just found out that Reby's brother Walker is my brother."

Benjamin sat up straight. "The man we saw in the woods that day?"

"Yes," she said. She took her hand from Benjamin and began wiping tears away as fast as they fell.

"My father molested Reby's mother," she said. "Walker is his son. My father. My beautiful gentle father. How could he have done such a thing? And Barnaby. He's even worse than my father. He molests your sister and he continues to go all over the countryside, as far as I can tell, raping and pillaging."

"How do you know all this?"

"You mean about Walker?" she asked. "Reby told me. About Barnaby? I have my sources. I have ways of knowing. Therese can't marry him. She can take herbs to end the pregnancy. No one need know. Or your mother can take her away."

"She wants this child more than anything," he said. "I've tried to stop her from marrying him. I can't forbid her. She has a right to make her own decisions."

"Barnaby is a bad, bad man," she said. "And I think Uncle Charles is beating Aunt Elizabeth. He wants me to sign some papers and because I won't, he's hitting her."

Benjamin leaned forward. "And how did you hurt your ankle?" he asked.

Callie used the palms of both hands to wipe her tears.

She had to stop crying.

She could not tell Benjamin about the underground railroad. Or about what she had done tonight—because she hoped to do it, or something like it, again and again.

"I fell," she said. "I stepped wrong and turned my ankle."

Benjamin sat back in his chair and looked away from her.

"I'm sorry about your ankle," he said. "But it will be fine. And I'm sorry about your father. Try not to judge him too harshly."

"Judge him too harshly!" Callie said. "How can you say that?"

Benjamin shook his head. "I only know that he was a good man when I knew him and when you knew him. Maybe he changed. Maybe he realized what he had done was wrong and he stopped."

"But he never acknowledged Walker as his son."

"How could he?" Benjamin asked. "There's no precedent for that here. Maybe in New Orleans. Maybe in France. But not here."

"You sound like you're justifying what he did."

"I'm not," he said. "I think you're in shock and I'd hate to see you throw away all the good memories you have of your father."

"Perhaps I should throw all men away," she said. "Maybe all men treat women thus."

"That is a ridiculous statement," Benjamin said.

"You do not sound very sympathetic," Callie said. "I have had a difficult time!"

"And how can I help you when you won't tell me the truth!"

"I can't tell you everything," Callie said. "I need to protect you. I need to keep you safe. Benjamin, you're all I have left. You're the only one who knows me, the real me."

"I don't need protection," he said. "And I'm not the only one who loves you, Calantha Carter."

"But you are," Callie said. "I can't jeopardize that or you."

Benjamin sighed. "What can I do?"

"You can examine my aunt," she said, "and make certain Uncle Charles knows you're doing it. You can contact John Bowen and make certain he's at the reception. I don't want to sign any papers without him looking them over."

Benjamin nodded. He said, "I had hoped you would ask me to run away with you."

"Someday I just might ask you to do that."

Twenty-one

In the morning, Reby came back upstairs with crutches and hot water for the basin.

"Dr. Sawyer brought these for you," she said. "He's downstairs dressin' up Mr. Barnaby."

Callie sat at the edge of the bed and tested her weight on her foot. It was much better, and the swelling was almost gone.

She limped over to the basin, washed her face, and then got dressed, with Reby's help. She leaned on the banister and Reby's arm to get downstairs. At the bottom, she put the crutches under her armpits and hobbled into the parlor.

Benjamin was bandaging Barnaby's arm. Elizabeth hovered nearby. Uncle Charles stood by the mantle with his arms crossed.

"What's happened?" Callie asked.

"While you and my mother were tripping around this house," Barnaby said, "I was out riding. My horse stumbled and I fell off. Then these dogs came out of nowhere. One of them got a hold of me. It was a nightmare."

"I still don't understand about the dogs," Elizabeth said. She leaned on a walking cane. "They're slave hounds. Did they think you were a slave?"

"They will hunt anyone," Charles said. "They must have gotten his scent somehow and off they went."

Benjamin glanced at Callie. She hoped she wasn't smiling.

"It's lucky you have no broken bones," Benjamin said, "since you say you fell from a horse."

"What do you mean by that?" Barnaby said. "I did fall from my horse. And he ran off. I sent one of our men to look for him and he found him. Someone stole my handkerchiefs and put a weed in my bag."

"You sent someone from your plantation to get your horse?" Callie asked. "My, that's far away."

"I sent Joseph," Barnaby said. "From here. One of your *slaves,* Callie. Must you constantly correct me? We all understand that this is *your* plantation and that it is much more successful than *our* plantation where we can barely feed our slaves let alone produce any cotton or rice worth anything."

"Barnaby, we have guests," Charles said. "Now, would you like to postpone the wedding until your injuries are healed?"

"Yes, that might be a good idea," Callie said.

Benjamin stood. "The black eye will heal soon, and the cut should be fine, as long as it doesn't get infected."

"We're not postponing anything," Barnaby said. "Not even dinner tonight. Now I'm going to get some sleep. It was a long night trying to get back here." Barnaby got up from the couch and walked to the open door.

"What kind of weed was it?" Benjamin asked.

"What do you mean?"

"In your bag."

"I don't know. An orange flower. Jewelweed I think they call it." He stomped away.

"This family seems to be getting hurt a lot lately," Benjamin said. "I wish you'd all be more careful. Charles, it looks like you could be next."

"I will take care," he said, "and I'll make certain my family takes better care."

"I need to wrap Callie's foot," Benjamin said.

"We have so much to do today to prepare for tomorrow's reception," Elizabeth said. "And now Callie and Barnaby can't help us. I don't know how I will cope!"

"I will help, dear," Charles said. "All is not lost."

Elizabeth and Charles left. Charles looked at Callie for a moment before he shut the door behind them. She shuddered.

"The entire county is in an uproar," Benjamin said. "Sit here. Put your leg up on the table."

Callie chuckled. "Oh, Elizabeth would be horrified. This is where she has her tea. I hadn't seen my ankle truly before now. That's a pretty color of blue and black. So tell me what's going on?"

"Someone let Tenant's dogs loose and set them on Barnaby's trail," Benjamin said. He began wrapping a bandage around Callie's ankle. "They left behind a jewelweed, like they did in Barnaby's saddle. They even stopped at the plantation house and told the owners that Barnaby was stealing one of their slaves. So not only did he get hunted down by dogs, Tyler and his men came running down to the slave cabins and found Barnaby on the road not far from there. I don't think he fell from his horse."

Callie chuckled.

"Callie," Benjamin said quietly, "did you have anything to do with what happened to him?"

"Now how could little ol' me have done any of this?" she said. "I was here in this house tripping over my own feet."

Benjamin shook his head. "By the way, your brother asked me to give you this." He took out a folded note from his vest pocket and gave it to her.

"He should not have involved you in this," she said as she took the note from him.

"Involved me in what?"

"Nothing." She opened the note. "Go toward Old Home as soon as you can. Come alone."

She folded the note.

"There," Benjamin said. "Stay off it as much as you can for the next day or so and then start trying to walk on it."

"Yes, sir," she said.

"Callie—" he started.

"Benjamin," she said. "I promise one day I will tell you everything. I promise that I will be careful. I will try not to endanger myself or any innocents. I will not make myself sick by eating peppermint."

"I knew it."

"I will not run around in the dark and trip and fall and hurt my ankle again."

"I suspected."

"And now I must go," she said. She moved her leg off of the table.

"Without breakfast?" he asked. "You need your strength."

"Don't baby me," Callie said. Benjamin stood and reached a hand out. Callie took his hand and he pulled her up. "I am perfectly capable of taking care of myself." She looked down at her leg. "Even if I do it imperfectly."

"I bow to your superior nature," he said. "And I will see you tonight."

"Could you send Henry in when you leave?" she asked.

He nodded. "I sent a message into Bowen," Benjamin said, "and I'll talk with him later in the day."

"Thanks, Benjamin."

After he left, Callie asked Henry to have Joseph prepare the buggy for her and pull it up front when it was ready. Reby brought biscuits, honey, and willow bark tea into the parlor.

Callie eagerly ate.

"I have to help get ready for the reception," Reby said. "Your aunt has said so."

Callie nodded. "Just stay around her. Don't leave her side. Barnaby can't do anything with her around. Let us hope he sleeps through the day."

With a little help from Henry and Joseph, Callie got into the buggy. She was grateful Elizabeth didn't seem to notice her as slaves went to and fro, out to the garden for flowers, out to the smoke house for food, and into the house with all sorts of goodies. Callie did not like the idea that she was essentially paying for this horrible wedding and reception, but she couldn't do much about it yet.

She slapped the reins on the back of the horse, and the buggy jerked forward. It was a beautiful clear day and her ankle throbbed only a little bit.

Soon enough, she was at Old Home. She turned the horse and buggy down the drive. Then suddenly Walker stepped out of the woods. Callie stopped the buggy and put on the brake.

"Hello, brother," she said. "So we meet at last."

"I'm sorry I didn't tell you," he said. "It never seemed like the right time."

"I'm sorry my father didn't acknowledge you," she said.

"He did set me free," he said. "I lied to you about him selling me."

"It seems everyone has been lying to me," she said.

Callie looked at Walker. She could see a bit of family resemblance. Maybe that was why she had liked him so much all along.

"Why did you need to see me right away?" Callie asked.

"There's a family escaping tonight," he said. "I think I can get them to Jewelweed Station during the dinner party. But we'll need to get them to the next stop the following day. I'm sure the slave hunters will be out by then, so it would be difficult to move that many people without getting noticed."

"You want me to take them in the carriage?" Callie asked. "How many are there?"

"A man and woman and their two children," he said.

"They're married. The woman has been accosted by the owner in the past, and now he's beginning to take notice of the daughter."

"How will I manage to transport them during the day?" Callie asked.

"We thought with all the comings and goings for the reception that you could get away. You pick when. The man can act as your coachman. He knows where the next station is. The woman can be your maid, and the children can hide in the seats. It's risky. You could get caught."

"I'll figure it out."

"By the way, Momma Gospel heard about last night," he said.

"What do you mean?"

Walker looked down at her ankle and then up again. "We heard about the jewelweed left behind. It had to be you."

"I wish the dogs had eaten him," Callie said.

"You didn't do any good, and you could have caused great harm," he said. "If you'd been caught, you couldn't help this family tonight. Please be more careful."

Callie nodded. "It was such fun letting Barnaby's horse loose and setting the dogs on him. I felt powerful. To be able to stop him from doing what my father did to your mother. I accomplished something!"

"I understand that urge," he said. "But you only saved the woman for one night."

"Sometimes one night is enough," Callie said. "You must know that."

Walker didn't say anything.

Callie sighed. "It's all so complicated."

"Take one step at a time," he said. "And try not to trip and fall."

Callie went back to the house. Since she could not easily go up and down stairs, she asked Reby to take blankets and water into the secret passageway and leave them by the entrance, in preparation for their new guests.

Callie sat in the parlor. It felt peculiar not being able to help. Some of Elizabeth's slaves arrived, including Heddie, to help with the reception.

Eventually Charles left for town, and Elizabeth went upstairs for a nap. The house got momentarily quiet. Callie remembered the keys she had found on the nail beneath her mother's desk. Because her uncle kept her father's study locked, it was one of the few places in the house she hadn't searched for the missing condolence letters and other correspondence. Her mother had always kept a key to the office on her key ring, and now Callie knew where the key ring was.

Callie got up and hobbled over to the desk. Her ankle felt much better, and she was able to put some of her weight on it. She lifted the keys from the hook, then went into the entry hall. She looked around, saw no one except Henry, so she limped to the office beneath the stairs. She quickly flipped through the keys on the ring until she found the one she thought was for her father's office door. She put it in the lock and turned it.

The door opened easily.

She glanced around. Henry watched her. She put a finger up to her lips. Then she hurried into the room and closed the door behind her.

Her stomach sank as she looked around. The room was a mess. Papers, books, and boxes were piled here and there, in no order she could discern. Her father, like her mother, had always been organized and neat. Apparently Uncle Charles was not.

"All right," she said. "Focus. What looks out of place here? Where might the letters be?"

She opened the drawers to her father's desk and quickly fanned through the papers in each drawer. She saw no letters.

She didn't have time to look through all these boxes now. Her aunt was bound to come down soon.

Callie closed her eyes for a moment, then opened them and slowly looked around the room.

Nothing.

She kicked one of the boxes. It skidded across the floor.

Behind it, under the bottom shelf of the bookcase, was a hatbox.

Callie knew her father wouldn't have had a hatbox, and she couldn't imagine why Uncle Charles would.

She retrieved the box, set it on the cluttered desk, and then opened the lid.

Inside were dozens of unopened letters.

They were all addressed to her.

"Finally!"

She pulled the letters out—too many for her to carry with one hand; she'd need the other hand to lean on the banister to get upstairs. She dropped the letters back in the box. She opened the door, leaned out, and called to Henry.

She picked up the letters again. When Henry came into the room, she said, "Henry, can you take these upstairs and put them in my room, on my bed. And don't let anyone see you?"

"Yes, Miss Callie," he said. He took all the letters in one of his hands, tucked them up under his arm, and left the office.

Callie closed the lid and put the hatbox back where she had found it. Then she pushed the box she had kicked back where it had been. Perhaps her uncle wouldn't notice the letters were missing for some time.

She left her father's office and locked the door again. After she returned the key ring to the nail hook, she limped up the stairs to her room. She passed Henry coming down the stairs, empty-handed.

"Is all well?" Callie asked.

"It is," he said.

Callie went into her room, locked the door, and sat on the bed. She stretched out her legs in front of her and rested her injured foot on a pillow. Then she put the letters in her lap.

She flipped through them. There must have been fifty of them, from nearly everyone she knew in the area. She began opening the letters. Mr. Emerick talked about how kind her parents had been and how much he would miss them. Maeve Sawyer mentioned all the summer days they had spent together and how much she enjoyed playing whist with Callie's father.

Judge Zebadiah and his wife expressed their condolences and encouraged her to continue her studies. The man and woman who owned the mercantile wrote. Reverend Jones and his family, too. Uncle Peter and Aunt Charlotte sent her several letters.

Callie began crying as she read one letter after another. She had not been alone. Everyone she had ever known had been thinking of her, had grieved the loss of her parents with her.

If only she had known.

How might her life be different if she had gotten all these letters when they were sent to her?

And Benjamin. He had written a dozen letters, at least.

She opened one and read it. The paper was blue.

"Dearest Callie," he wrote. "I chose this color in the hopes it would remind you of the great blue lobelia. It is not blooming now but next summer you will be home and we can walk—or run—through a field of it together. I remember a patch over by Far Pond. We went there before I left town. You told me I should remember that lobelia could cure almost anything, especially homesickness. When I was away it was one of the flowers you drew for me. I hung the drawing, along with all your other drawings, on the walls of my little room. Every time I looked at them, I thought of you and my homesickness ebbed.

"I've drawn one for you so that you may feel as though home is not so far away."

He had penciled in what vaguely looked like a lobelia plant, or some tall woody plant. Callie laughed.

"It is not as good as yours, but I bet it made you laugh.

"Yours affectionately, Benjamin Sawyer."

Callie wiped her arm across her eyes and opened another letter from Benjamin. A willow leaf fell out of the envelope.

It was pale green, long and tapered, making Callie think of a druid's finger, had the druid been green. Surprisingly, the leaf was not brittle.

"Dearest Callie," Benjamin wrote. "I am so sorry for your loss and that you are so far from those who love you. When my father died, nothing could assuage the grief. Eventually with time and the support of family and friends, I began to feel alive again. I hope this willow leaf—from our black willow down by the river—will help remind you that life and love await you back home. I look forward to sitting under the black willow tree with you again soon. You told me once that the Irish thought the willow trees were full of magic and enchantment. You said many goddesses loved the willow tree. I know many ancient people believed the willow could help with the grieving process. You are your own sweet powerful goddess, Callie. I hope this willow leaf helps you remember that.

"Affectionately yours, Benjamin."

Callie quickly opened the next letter.

"Dear Callie," Benjamin wrote. "I hope this letter finds you well and that these letters are giving you some comfort, the way yours gave me so much comfort when I was at school. I apologize for not writing more back then. I was feeling somewhat lost and tongue-tied. Much has changed since then.

"Today I wanted to remind you about the iris. How it is wild and tame all at the same time, cultured and chaotic, just like a certain young woman I know."

He had drawn an iris for her at the end of the letter. This time he captured the curves of the flower—the elegance of it—almost perfectly.

Callie read letter after letter from Benjamin. Each one encouraged her. Each one reminded her that she was loved, that she had qualities he missed when she was away.

The last one was about the jewelweed. First he told her they were all concerned because no one had heard from her. Then he wrote, "The jewelweed will be out soon enough. I know you love those little bursts of color amongst the green, just as your mother did. Most people call the jewelweed a weed. They want to pull it up and stamp it out. That is one of the many things I cherish about you. Nothing is a weed to you, nothing and no one. You see beauty all around you. And when something is not right, you cannot keep silent about it. I know you have relied on your parents for everything. They were your world. You've always had trouble making friends with outsiders. Not because of arrogance, but because of a kind of shyness, I believe. When you get home, we will walk together through the wildflowers and find a patch of jewelweed and we will sing their praises to the whole natural world around us.

"Today I was remembering my old Scottish grandmother. Whenever she saw us or whenever we left her presence, she gave us a blessing. 'May the strength of the oak trees be thine,' she would say. Or 'excellence of travel be on you.' So today I would like to say to you: Joy of night and day be yours. Joy of sun and moon be yours. Joy of all the wildflowers be yours. And may the love and affection of the entire world be yours as all my love and affection is already yours.

"Always, Ben."

Callie wept and pushed the letters away from her.

Benjamin Sawyer loved her.

He had never deserted her, had never forgotten her.

She loved him, too.

Her stomach fluttered.

Yes.

She supposed she had loved him all her life.

She should wait and read the rest later. She picked the pile up to carry them all over to the wardrobe, and she noticed an opened letter at the bottom of the pile. She hadn't opened it. She looked at the return address.

It was from her uncle James.

Her aunt and uncle must have opened it.

She quickly pulled out the sheet of paper and read, "January 5. Dear Calantha, This is your uncle James. How are you? How are your parents? I have not heard from either of them for some time. I'm guessing you never got my new addresses, or you never got my letters. The mail service here is not very reliable. Here are the various addresses where you can reach me. I will be home before the end of the summer."

"Oh my!" Callie said.

She jumped out of bed, hardly noticed her injured ankle, and went to her desk. She wrote a note to John Bowen. "My uncle is alive. See this letter for his address. Can you wire him?" She didn't know if they had wire service anywhere near where her uncle James was in the Amazon, but Bowen could find out. She then wrote three letters to her uncle James, all of them saying the same thing: "My parents have died in a terrible accident and Charles and Elizabeth have been appointed my guardians. Come home at once."

She made out envelopes for the three different addresses

her uncle had given her.

She rang for Henry. When he came to her door, she said, "This must get to John Bowen in St. Charles today. And these letters must get posted today, too, without delay."

Henry took the letters. He glanced at the ones to her uncle.

"You've found him?" he asked.

"I may have," Callie said. "We may be saved after all."

Henry almost smiled. Then he turned to go.

"Don't let anyone stop you, Henry," she said.

He nodded and left. Callie went back into her room. She picked up the letters and hid them in the back of her wardrobe. She started to leave the room, but she changed her mind. She went back to the wardrobe and retrieved Benjamin's letters and read them again. And again.

Then she went downstairs and waited. She knew her life was about to change again.

This time she hoped she was ready for it.

Twenty-two

Callie nearly jumped up from the sofa and threw her arms around Benjamin when he, Mrs. Sawyer, and Therese arrived for dinner and came into the parlor, but she restrained herself. Benjamin smiled when he saw her. She grinned. He looked at her quizzically.

While Uncle Charles and Aunt Elizabeth talked about the weather with Mrs. Sawyer, Callie tried to sit quietly and be still. Therese sat next to Barnaby, who all but ignored her. His black eye was a little less swollen than it had been earlier in the day.

When it was time for dinner, Benjamin came over to Callie and offered his arm.

"What's going on?" he asked quietly.

"I have so much to tell you," she said. "Later."

Callie had a difficult time concentrating on the dinner conversation or the food. She needed to find time to tell Benjamin that she had found the letters—his letters in particular. And Uncle James's letter. She kept wondering if her "travelers" had arrived at Jewelweed Station yet. She hoped they were safe and well.

The welfare of the travelers was the most important thing right now. That was where her focus had to be.

She could talk to Benjamin about the letters another time.

She excused herself from the dinner party early, claiming her ankle was bothering her. She glanced at Benjamin before she left, but he was watching his sister. Reby went with Callie to her room. Once inside, they locked the door.

"Henry told me you got a letter from your uncle James," Reby said. "What does this mean?"

"It means he was alive in January," she said. "I've written to him so I hope he'll be home soon. We'll have to wait and see."

When Callie awakened in the middle of the night, she could put most of her weight on her right foot. She quietly lit a candle and then went into the secret passageway without disturbing Reby.

She found the family and Walker down by the door to the outside. The man and woman nodded to her. The girl couldn't have been more than twelve years old. The boy looked to be about three, and he was crying softly. His mother was trying to get him to stop.

"He stepped on something," the woman said, "and it's

mighty painful."

"I tried to take it out," Walker said. "It's some kind of sliver or thorn."

"I'm so sorry you're hurting," Callie said to the boy. She handed Walker the candle. They both leaned over to look more closely at his foot.

"Maybe in the morning we can take him up to my room and try to take it out in the light," Callie said.

"We found the blankets," Walker said. "Can you get them some food? I have to leave and won't be back. I have another group to take."

"All right," Callie said. "I'll do the best I can."

Then Walker was gone, and Callie was left standing alone with four strangers.

She wanted to introduce herself, but she didn't. No names. They couldn't know her, and she couldn't know them.

"I'll get you food and water," she said.

She listened at the kitchen door. When she was sure it was safe, she opened the door and went into the kitchen and the pantry. She scavenged what she thought wouldn't be missed—since they were having the reception tomorrow, the larder and pantry overflowed with food. With her arms full, Callie returned to the secret passageway and gave the food to the family. Then she went back for water and brought that to them. The boy had stopped crying. She put her hand on his forehead. He seemed a little warm.

"I'll come and check on you when I can," Callie said.

She handed the candle to the father. The little boy looked up at her with sad eyes. The girl averted her eyes.

"Try to get some sleep," Callie said. "You're safe here."

She slowly went back up the steps to her room.

In the morning, Callie tried to persuade her aunt that her ankle hurt too much to attend the wedding. It didn't work. Her aunt made her get dressed. She didn't have time to go downstairs and check on the family either. She had hoped to spirit them away while the others were at the wedding. Instead she rode with Barnaby, Charles, and Elizabeth in her father's big carriage to the chapel.

The ceremony didn't last long. Therese's eyes were red, as though she had been crying, but she looked beautiful in her silk wedding dress. Barnaby's black eye looked worse than it had yesterday, and it matched his suit. Uncle Charles kept looking at Callie. She hoped he didn't know that she had found her letters. Benjamin hardly looked at her at all. He patted his mother's hand as she wept.

Callie left the chapel with her aunt and uncle. They rode together in her father's carriage. She wondered what her aunt and uncle would think if they knew this same carriage had been used to smuggle slaves to freedom.

"Callie, I'd like you to sign those papers today," her uncle said.

"John Bowen is coming to the reception," Callie said. "We'll let him look them over first. What's so important about them?"

"I'd like to make you an offer," he said. "I want to buy Mount Joy from you. I will run it, maintain it, and I'll make certain you have a living for the rest of your life."

"But I don't want to sell," Callie said. "It's my home."

"You'll be leaving someday to get married," Elizabeth said. "It's no different from when your parents were alive."

Callie wanted to tell them that she had found the letters and she was going to tell the judge that her uncle James was alive.

She didn't.

"How much are you offering?" Callie asked.

"I don't have much cash flow at the moment," he said, "so I was hoping you would take one dollar, in exchange for a living for the rest of your life."

Callie laughed. She couldn't help it.

"I know I'm ignorant about the ways of the business world, Uncle Charles," she said, "but that doesn't sound like much of a deal. I don't think John Bowen or the judge would let me sign that."

"That's why I was hoping we could handle this in the family," he said. "We don't want to make public your father's indiscretions. We know how proud and fond you were of him."

"What indiscretions?" Callie asked. She heard the edge to her voice, and she knew she had to smooth it out. She had to bide her time until she talked to John Bowen, maybe even until her uncle James returned.

"We talked about this before, Callie," he said. "About you being the daughter of a slave woman. This may come as a shock to you, but your father strayed before. He has the bastard child, Blackie, the boy he set free some years ago. There's bound to be others. Maybe they chose to raise you because you were so much lighter-skinned than that boy was."

Callie shook her head. "Uncle, I thought we had healed our relationship. You know I am my mother's daughter. I look just like her. No one will believe these accusations, even if you get some poor slave woman to swear to it. Your reputations will be ruined."

She glanced at her aunt. Elizabeth looked away.

"I have other ways to persuade you," Charles said. He looked at Elizabeth. She put her hand over her arm, instinctively covering the bruised place, even though Callie couldn't see it under her sleeve.

Uncle Charles wouldn't actually ever lay a hand on his own niece, would he?

Why not? He beat his wife.

"I am hoping that filial affection will rule the day," he said, "and you will agree to this offer. I would be assuming your father's debt. I'd be managing the place so you wouldn't have to think about it. Plus you would get a living from my labor."

"I will think about this," Callie said.

"I want your decision by the end of the day," he said.

"And you shall have it," she said.

She looked out the window. She wished she could jump out of the carriage and run far away.

But she had responsibilities at home. She had to see to them first.

When they arrived back at Mount Joy, the overnight guests had already started to arrive: Uncle Peter and Aunt Charlotte with their children and Elizabeth's brothers and sisters and their children. The nephews did not accost Callie this time. Apparently Matthew had spread the word. She was grateful for that.

Callie and Reby went up to Callie's room while Elizabeth directed her family to their rooms. Callie locked the door and left the key in the lock.

"Stay here," Callie told Reby as she lit a candle. "If anyone comes, just be quiet. They won't be able to get in."

Callie went into the secret passage. Her ankle hurt slightly, but she went as quickly as she could. She heard the boy whimpering before she reached the family.

The candle had burned out, and the family sat on the floor in darkness.

"He's got a fever," the mother said. "I don't know what to do. We ran out of water for him."

Callie held the candle close to his foot. The area around the wound was swollen and filled with pus.

"Damn," she said. "We need to get help. Follow me."

The man picked up the boy. The woman took the girl's hand. They followed Callie up the stairs. She cringed as she went up the steps, but she hurried as fast as she could.

Soon they were all squeezing past the wardrobe and into Callie's room.

"Put him on the bed," Callie said.

Callie threw open the curtains and let the light in. She and the mother looked more closely at the boy's foot.

It did not look any better in the light.

"Lock the door behind me and don't open it for anyone," Callie said.

She turned the lock and opened the door. She looked up and down the corridor. It was empty. She slipped out of the room and closed the door. She heard Reby inside the room turning the key to lock the door.

Callie went down the stairs. She could hear laughter and chattering coming from the second floor where Elizabeth's family was staying.

She hurried down to the first floor. Therese and Barnaby had changed out of their wedding clothes and now stood in the receiving line greeting guests with Mrs. Sawyer and Elizabeth and Charles.

That meant Benjamin had to be there somewhere, too.

She went into the parlor and looked around. No Benjamin.

She limped into the sun parlor and saw him across the room with Lucy Johnston. When he looked her way, she motioned him to come to her. She saw him excuse himself to Lucy. Then he walked over to Callie.

"Benjamin," she said softly, "you wanted me to trust you. I do. By showing you what I'm about to show you, I'm putting you at great risk."

"I'll do whatever you need," he said.

She put her arm through his. "You need to come up to my room. Without anyone noticing. And you need to bring your black bag."

As they walked past the parlor, Benjamin picked up his bag from the floor next to the chair.

They waited until everyone in the reception line was looking away. Then they went up the stairs. Callie leaned on Benjamin so that she was hardly limping at all.

When they reached the landing to the second floor, they

met Aunt Charlotte and Uncle Peter.

"Where are you two headed?" Uncle Peter asked. "Should we follow you to someplace fun?"

"Oh, no," Callie said. "He needs to look at my ankle."

Peter frowned.

"I twisted it."

"Ah yes," he said. "We'll see you soon. It's going to be a great day."

Callie and Benjamin continued up to the third floor and down the corridor. She knocked on her door. "Reby, it's me," she said.

The door opened. Callie and Benjamin went inside. Reby closed and locked the door. Benjamin hurried over to the boy.

"He's got a sliver or something," Callie said. "I think it might be infected."

Benjamin knelt next to the bed and opened his bag.

"What's your name?" Benjamin asked the boy.

"Benny," he said. He wiped his arm across his eyes. "My foot really hurts, sir."

"Well Benny," Benjamin said as he examined the boy's foot. "This is your lucky day because my name is Ben, too. And anyone with my name automatically gets better when I treat them."

"Really?" he asked. "Cuz I'm thinking you'll have to cut my foot off."

"I don't really need an extra foot," Benjamin said. "I've got two. Everyone in this room has two feet. So it looks like you're gonna have to keep your two feet for yourself."

Callie pulled Reby aside and whispered to her.

"I need you to go out to the stables and ask Joseph to get the big carriage ready for us," Callie said. "Have him wait for us right by the secret door."

Reby agreed, then left the room.

Benjamin pulled out the sliver—which was more like a small stick—from the boy's foot. He drained the pus and washed it with alcohol. Then he tied up the boy's foot.

"Does he have any shoes?" Benjamin asked. "He should try and keep this clean."

The woman shook her head. "Neither one of them has got much of anything."

"Well, do the best you can to keep it clean."

Benjamin poured the boy a glass of water from the pitcher on Callie's nightstand. The boy drank part of it quickly. Then he handed the glass to his sister, and she drank the rest.

Callie remembered that one of Uncle Peter's children was about Benny's size. ·

"I'll be right back," she said. "Lock the door behind me."

Callie left and went to the second floor. It was quiet now. Everyone must have gone downstairs. She knocked on one of the doors. When no one answered, she went inside. She searched a suitcase and the wardrobe for any shoes that would fit Benny. When she didn't find any, she went to the next room, and then to the next.

Finally she found the room the boys were staying in—and a pair of shoes. The shoes looked far too shiny and new to put on Benny's feet. They were bound to be noticed. She took them anyway, along with a pair of socks.

It was much easier being a thief than she would have imagined.

She hurried back upstairs to her room.

The mother put the shoes on the boy's feet. The girl watched in awe. Callie realized she had missed an opportunity: She should have stolen shoes for the girl, too.

Callie pulled Benjamin aside.

"Thank you," Callie said. "I'm sorry I involved you."

"I'm already involved," he said. "You helped get the boy in Richmond to safety, didn't you? The one who had been whipped?"

Callie put her hand on his arm. "I did! How did you know that?"

"I suspected," he said. "I saw the carriage there when I came to tend to the boy's wounds. And then when I heard about the jewelweed flowers left behind last night, I figured it had to be you. I had heard the name Jewelweed Station recently, from King Poet—my contact. I didn't know Jewelweed Station was *here*. Our house was used for years—all of us were involved. But after my father died, we decided it was too dangerous. Too many people already suspected we were helping."

Callie threw her arms around Benjamin's neck. He put his arms around her waist. They held each other, laughing.

When they let go of each other, Benjamin said, "So it was you who did all those things? To Barnaby. You let the dogs out?"

"What a relief it is to tell you," she said. "Or to have you guess. You don't think anyone else would guess, do you?"

"I don't think so," he said.

"That's why you acted so strangely that first time we saw Walker in the woods," Callie said. "You thought he had come there to talk with you."

"Yes, it was startling," he said. "And then to find out he's your brother."

"And here all this time I didn't tell you anything because I wanted to protect you," she said.

"I'm not as staid and safe as you think I am."

"I never thought that," she said. "I only believed you to be cautious, which makes good sense."

"What now?"

"Now I need to get this family to the county line," she said. She took his hand. "Will you come with us? That way if Aunt Elizabeth notices, I'll say you forgot something at home. Or that we wanted to go for a ride before we ate. Something."

"Absolutely," Benjamin said. "I would be honored. What is the plan?"

"Why don't you go back downstairs," she said. "Mingle a bit so people see you. Then sneak out to the stables, or near to it. You'll see the big carriage. Just get into it. Meanwhile I'll take our visitors through the secret passageway."

"There's a secret passageway?" he asked.

"I'll tell you about it later," she said. "I may even show it to you."

"Sounds intriguing," he said. He took her hand and squeezed it. Then he left.

Callie locked the door behind him and then pocketed the key.

"Are you ready?" Callie asked the family. "Once we get outside, you're going to have to move very quickly and get into the carriage without anyone seeing you."

The family followed Callie down the stairs. The stairs were too narrow, the steps too wobbly. The boy whimpered softly in his father's arm. Callie hoped the family didn't get caught. If they did, they'd probably be sold separately, and they'd never see each other again. She glanced back at them. The girl clutched her mother's hand. The mother smiled at Callie, a half-smile, a hopeful smile. They could survive this.

Callie walked to the end of the secret passageway. She listened at the half door. Then she opened it slowly. The carriage was right there, not two feet away.

Yes! She would have to thank Joseph later.

Reby was in the carriage. She opened the door and moved out of the way. First the man and the boy and then the woman and the girl went through the bushes and into the carriage.

Callie got into the carriage last. She pulled out the key and handed it to Reby.

"If you feel unsafe or like he's looking for you," Callie said, "go up to my room and put this in the keyhole."

Reby took the key. Then she put her arms around Callie and embraced her. Callie returned the embrace. Both women started to cry.

Callie let go of Reby.

"We don't have time for this," she said. "We've got to go."

Benjamin was suddenly there. Reby jumped out of the carriage. Benjamin jumped in.

He shut the door. Callie called up to Joseph. The carriage lurched forward and traveled past the stables and down by the woods.

When they were clear of the view of the stables, the carriage stopped. Joseph got down from the driver's box. He opened the carriage door. The man got out. Without a word, Joseph handed the man his cap. Then he peeled off his good jacket and gave it to the man.

"Your name is Joseph," Joseph said.

The man climbed up to the driver's box. Joseph nodded to Callie and started walking back to the stables. Callie opened the lids to the seats. Benny got into one seat; his sister got into another.

Callie looked down at Benny.

"It's going to be dark in there," she said. "Can you be brave in the dark? Can you be quiet as a mouse?"

"I like the dark," he said. "White people are afraid of the dark. I won't be crying no more. My foot feels all better."

"All right," Callie said. "I'm closing the lid now." She slowly let the lid fall.

The mother was talking to her daughter.

"She's not like her brother," the woman said. "She does not like the dark. That's when the master would come around and take me. And then he came looking for her."

Callie looked down at the girl in the seat box. "What's your name, darlin'?"

She knew she was not supposed to ask.

"Grace," she answered.

"Grace. What a beautiful glorious name. I am so glad that

you are on this journey with us. I promise you that I will make it safe for you. I will make it all right. Let me close this lid and you'll be on your way to safety."

"Are you sure?" she whispered.

"I'm sure," Callie said. "Your daddy is going to drive you straight up to safety."

Grace nodded. "I can do it. I can stand the dark then."

Callie closed the lid.

Then the three adults sat on the seats.

"Go ahead, Joseph," Callie called up. She looked at the woman. "You're my maid Rebecca, in case anyone stops us. Everyone calls you Reby."

The maid looked down at her raggedy clothes.

"Well, we're hoping no one stops us," Callie said.

The carriage lurched forward.

Once or twice, they opened the lids to give the children the water and bread Reby had left for them. The rest of the time, Callie stared out the window. Once Benjamin clasped her hand in his. Callie wondered if the woman felt alone and afraid sitting with these strangers, running for her life.

They were almost out of the county when the horses stopped. Callie leaned out the window and couldn't believe what she saw: the slave hunter Tenant with his dogs and men.

Callie leaned back and looked at Benjamin and then at the woman.

"It's the slave hunter," she said. "I've dealt with him before. Everyone keep calm."

Tenant trotted up to the window on his horse.

When he saw Callie, he grinned. It was not a friendly grin.

"Why is it that every time I'm lookin' for an escaped slave these days, I run into you?" he asked.

"Why is it every time I go out for a ride or walk in the country, I run into you?" she said.

"At least you took my advice," he said. "You're not out here by yourself."

"That's true," she said. "I've brought my maid and my fiancé. Neither one is much company so I'm glad for this little interruption." She smiled widely. "Dr. Benjamin Sawyer, have you met Mr. Tenant, our intrepid slave-hunter?"

"I don't believe I've had the pleasure," Benjamin said.

Tenant spit some of the cud he was chewing on into the dirt. Callie glanced over at the woman. She looked terrified.

Callie whispered, "He can't hurt us. Stay calm."

At the same time, Tenant said, "You're the son of that Quaker woman, aren't you? She freed all her slaves. Is she giving succor to escaped slaves? Are you?" He looked up at "Joseph."

"Does your man have papers this time?"

Benjamin jerked open the door and stepped out of the carriage before Callie could stop him.

"I will not allow you to speak about my mother in this manner," he said. "My mother may be a Quaker, but I am not." Benjamin reached for the whip on Tenant's saddle and pulled it out before Tenant could stop him.

Benjamin flexed the whip and then snapped it. Callie and the woman jumped at the sound.

What was he doing?

"What right do you have to touch my property?" Tenant asked.

"What right do you have to stop us and interrogate us?" Benjamin asked. "We live in the United States of America and we have the right to travel this road without being accosted." He snapped the whip again. Tenant's horse jumped to the side.

"My godfather is Judge Zebadiah," Benjamin said. The other men on horseback had closed in on the carriage and Benjamin. "He grants you the right to work in this county. He can rescind that right."

"The law gives us the right," Tenant said. He reached for the whip. Benjamin snapped it again.

"The judge is the law," Benjamin said. "Miss Carter has told me how you have harassed her. She was good enough not to report you. I, on the other hand, have no qualms about reporting you." Benjamin tossed the whip up into the air. Tenant leaned over to catch it. He nearly fell from the saddle.

The whip dropped onto the dusty road.

Benjamin turned his back on Tenant and got back into the carriage. "Good day, sir," Benjamin said. A moment later, the coach jerked forward.

Callie turned around and looked behind them. Tenant was getting off his horse to retrieve the whip.

"You didn't make a friend there," Callie said.

"I don't want him as a friend," Benjamin said.

"You could have made it worse," she said.

"I could have," he said, "but if I'm supposed to trust your

judgment, shouldn't you trust mine?"

Callie laughed. "I never said you should trust my judgment!"

Sometime later, the carriage left the county; not long after that, the horses stopped. Callie saw Walker step out of the woods. The coach move as he got up into the driver's box. Soon after, the horses turned down a drive and then stopped.

Callie, Benjamin, and the woman stood and let the children out of the seat boxes. The woman and children got out of the carriage and joined the man. Then they all walked into the woods with Walker.

Benjamin and Callie were alone in the carriage.

"It always happens so quickly," he said. "They're here and then they're gone."

"I was not nearly as nervous with you here," Callie said.

"I appreciate that you've wanted to protect me," Benjamin said. "But you must know I can take care of myself."

Callie smiled. "Of course, I know that. But after what happened with Heddie, I didn't want to take any chances."

"Callie," he said, "I have to tell you now that I love you. Not as a sister or as an old friend. I love you body and soul. If I had a choice I would never leave your side."

"I know," Callie said. "I found the letters today. I found your beautiful letters. Only a man in love could have written them."

"And only a girl in love could have written the letters you sent me."

"That's true," she said. "But I was a girl and didn't understand that. Now I'm a woman, and I love you, Benjamin

Sawyer."

She kissed his hand. "But don't expect me to marry you. I may, but don't expect it. Don't expect me to give up my life for yours because I won't do that. Don't expect anything from me except my undying love. For always."

"I won't pretend to be your brother if we get to gallivanting around the world."

"No," she said. "I don't think brothers and sisters are supposed to kiss like this."

She kissed him, and he kissed her.

Walker cleared his throat. They looked over at him standing near the open window.

"Since you don't have a driver, I'll take you home," he said.

"Is that safe?" Callie asked.

"Sure," he said. "Tenant can't tell one slave from another."

Callie told Benjamin that Uncle James was alive.

"At least he was in January," she said. "On the way home from the wedding Uncle Charles offered to buy the plantation for one dollar. If I didn't agree to it, he said he would tell the world that I was the daughter of one of my father's slaves. And he would use Walker's existence as proof."

"He can't be serious," Benjamin said.

"I'm not worried," Callie said. "The day is not over yet."

The ride back to Mount Joy seemed too short. Suddenly they were at the edge of the woods before the stables. Walker stopped the horses and the three of them got out.

Walker shook Benjamin's hand. Callie embraced her brother.

"Thank you, thank you," she said.

She finally let him go.

"I'll see you soon," he said, and then he disappeared into the woods.

Benjamin and Callie walked back toward the stables to get Joseph to fetch the carriage.

"You go on in," Callie said to Benjamin. "So we can make separate entrances. I'll find Joseph."

Benjamin kissed her hand, then hurried ahead of her. Callie walked slowly. Her ankle had started to throb. She went up to the hay barn and leaned against the back of it to rest for a bit.

After a moment, she began hearing strange noises coming from inside the barn.

Someone was arguing.

Someone else was weeping.

Callie walked around to the front of the barn just as Therese was walking into the building.

Then everything happened quickly.

In a flash Callie saw Barnaby trying to push a half-naked Heddie onto the ground as she struggled to cover herself and get away.

Therese gasped.

"After all you made me do," Therese said. In one motion she picked up a piece of wood with nails sticking out of it and swung it at Barnaby, narrowly missing his head. Instead the wood smashed into his arm.

He screamed and fell to his knees.

Heddie scrambled to get up.

Callie reached for her.

Barnaby kept screaming. Blood soaked his arm.

"Run," Callie said to Heddie.

Then Benjamin was there. And Elizabeth. Uncle Charles. The judge. Even John Bowen.

Then someone closed the barn door, or told the others to go back to the house.

Barnaby moaned.

Benjamin stopped the bleeding and set Barnaby's broken arm with John Bowen crouched next to him, helping.

Callie put her arms across Therese's shoulders as she watched.

"You wouldn't believe the things he asked me to do," she said. "And I did them. Otherwise he said he would find someone else. He found someone else anyway. I should have said no."

Mrs. Sawyer came and got her daughter. Callie and Benjamin went and found Heddie. Benjamin examined her to make certain she was unhurt.

The judge asked Callie what had happened.

Callie told him everything. Told him how Barnaby had been prowling the countryside looking for slave women. Therese had found him attacking Heddie and she tried to stop him. Callie told the judge how her aunt and uncle had threatened to expose her as a "pickaninny" child if Callie didn't sell Mount Joy to them for one dollar. She told the judge that her uncle James was alive, and Elizabeth and Charles had known all along.

John Bowen showed the judge the letter from Uncle James. The judge stood quietly for a moment, shaking his head. Then he said he was rescinding the custody order on the spot.

"Will you tell my aunt and uncle," Callie asked, "and make them leave?"

"Gladly," he said. "And as far as I can tell, Barnaby Ames broke his own arm. He has nobody to blame or accuse except himself."

Someone took Barnaby away from Mount Joy.

Therese and her mother sat down with the judge who instructed Therese on what to do to get an annulment.

Benjamin promised Callie he would return, and then he took his sister and mother home.

The wedding guests left, and then the relatives packed up to go.

Callie sat in the parlor as Uncle Peter, Aunt Charlotte, and Elizabeth's family left. Then Aunt Elizabeth came down the stairs. Henry and one of Elizabeth's slaves carried her suitcases.

"You are an ungrateful child," Elizabeth said.

"And your son is a monster," Callie said.

Elizabeth made a noise and left the house.

Uncle Charles stopped at the entrance to the parlor.

Callie pulled herself up so she was standing when she spoke to her uncle.

"Uncle Charles," she said, "if I find one dime missing, I will tell the world what Barnaby did. Everything. And then I will tell them you stole from me. I will sing it from mountaintops. I will tell it to every newspaper from here to there. And if you ever hit Aunt Elizabeth again, I will tell everyone about your low life son and what he did."

He stared at her. Henry came back into the house.

"One more thing," she said. "I want Heddie. I want you to sell her to me. For one dollar." She held out a coin to him. He reluctantly took it. "I'll expect the papers in the morning."

Charles left the house.

Henry strode across the hall and hurried down the corridor, no doubt on his way to tell his daughter she was safe once again.

Callie was now alone in her house—except for all her slaves. She walked to the entrance and stepped outside.

Reby came and stood next to her.

"What now?" Reby asked

"I want to paint this entrance hall," she said, "and put it back the way my mother had it before. And I will have an accountant go through the books. Then I want to figure out how to free all my slaves."

"Maybe you can free us secretly," Reby said, "so only we—the former slaves and you—will know. Then we could still be a stop on the underground railroad."

Callie nodded. "I like that idea. After everyone is free, I want to see the world. Find every weed there is and draw it."

"By yourself?"

Callie looked in the direction of the gardens. Benjamin was striding through the wildflowers, his fingers gently touching the blooms as he walked. He looked up and saw them. He smiled and waved.

"No, not by myself," Callie said. "I'll take him with me."

Callie raised her hand and waved. Benjamin hurried toward her.

About the Author

Kim Antieau has written many novels, short stories, poems, and essays. Her work has appeared in numerous publications, both in print and online, including *The Magazine of Fantasy and Science Fiction, Asimov's SF, The Clinton Street Quarterly, The Journal of Mythic Arts, EarthFirst!, Alternet, Sage Woman,* and *Alfred Hitchcock's Mystery Magazine.* She was the founder, editor, and publisher of *Daughters of Nyx: A Magazine of Goddess Stories, Mythmaking, and Fairy Tales.* Her work has twice been short-listed for the Tiptree Award, and has appeared in many Best of the Year anthologies. Critics have admired her "literary fearlessness" and her vivid language and imagination. Her first novel, *The Jigsaw Woman,* is a modern classic of feminist literature. She has also written *The Gaia Websters, The Fish Wife, Church of the Old Mermaids, Her Frozen Wild,* and other novels. Kim lives in the Pacific Northwest with her husband, writer Mario Milosevic. Learn more about Kim and her writing at www.kimantieau.com.

Made in the USA
Charleston, SC
30 June 2012